The Witch-Fiddler

Deborah Bradford

To my mother, Yvonne Palmer, *lesh graih.*

Author's Note

THIS IS A work of fiction. Any resemblance to real persons, living or dead, or to real events is purely coincidental. While my writing is informed by my love of all things Celtic, the regions in this book (the Lowland and the North Country) are my own inventions and are not meant to correspond to any real places or cultural entities.

The language that my Northern characters speak is Manx, with a little bit of Irish. I have not studied these languages in any depth. I couldn't say, for instance, whether words like *caillagh* and *ashlins,* in regular usage, really do carry all the meanings I've ascribed to them here. Additionally, the name Gwehara, which sort of resembles the Irish word for "wind," is a word I made up.

Fans of Celtic lore will recognize where I took other liberties, including with the concepts of *geasa* and *immrama.* The definitions I've given them are specific to the story and do not fully reflect the various ways they function in Celtic mythology.

That being said, it's always been my goal to write a story that can be enjoyed on more than one level. Whatever you get out of it, I hope you enjoy it a fraction as much as I've enjoyed writing it.

Deborah Bradford

Prologue

How Nemain had come to Briarvale Castle was well known. Her mother was an Outlander, a vagrant who had died giving birth at the castle gatehouse. But why Nemain was allowed to *stay* at Briarvale—and, for that matter, how she had come by the name Nemain—was a mystery to most people, including herself.

From early childhood she was large-boned and awkward, and she grew so rapidly that her clothes hardly ever fit. She had a round face, a long rope of dark hair, and no beauty except for her smile and her eyes. But her smile was a rare, fleeting thing; and her eyes, large and golden-brown under black brows, were usually downcast.

She also had a strange and terrible deformity: her hands. They were like a corpse's, withered and misshapen, the veins and sinews showing through the brittle skin. For this reason she was made to wear gloves all the time, and if she got caught without them she was punished with a birch switch.

Not surprisingly, young Nemain was rather shy. She knew that most people at Briarvale—the servants in particular—viewed her as an interloper, an unlucky thing, and she kept out of their way as much as possible. She haunted the castle like a shadow, barely visible from the corner of your eye, disappearing when you looked at her directly.

But if you gave her a fiddle and asked her to play … ah, there was magic for you! Of course she must take off her gloves, the better to feel it; but once she began, you would forget about her hands and everything else. From this untrained child—from her first clumsy scrapings of the bow, at age five, on a fiddle she could barely heft—flowed music of astonishing vigor and beauty, music that could draw the heart and soul right out of you. Some who heard it were moved to weep; others, to dance. A few (the most superstitious) held it in dread, believing that her uncanny gift, like the unnatural appearance of her hands, was the result of some faery mischief or evil enchantment.

So Nemain, even as a child, was surrounded by a sense of fear and ill omen, of things that were never spoken of and things that must not be seen. But in spite of this, she was content with her lot. Hers was a better existence than an unwanted orphan could hope for, and she took for granted, along with everyone else, that an unwanted orphan was all she would ever be.

Chapter 1

BRIARVALE WAS SITUATED on a hill overlooking a little valley of thistles and wild roses, from which it derived its name. With its neighboring village of snug timber-framed houses, it made a pretty picture against the rolling hills of the Lowland.

It was good land, the best in the region, where the winters were mild and the summer rains fell gently. And Lord Winworth was a good landlord, albeit a somewhat reclusive one since his wife had died. The days of merriment at Briarvale, the balls and feasts and tournaments, were long over; Lord Winworth no longer cared for such things. Nor, oddly, did he seem anxious to remarry and get himself an heir. He managed his estate dutifully enough, but the only thing in life that seemed to give him any joy was his young daughter.

Little Monessa Winworth was a miniature of her mother, a sweet, laughing, elfin thing with ash-gold hair and the promise of beauty in her face. Her eyes were wide and arrestingly blue—the eyes her mother had been famous for—and her skin was as delicately fair as a white rose petal. No one who met her could help loving her, and fortunately, she had one of those rare dispositions that all the love and indulgence in the world couldn't spoil.

She was a year older than Nemain, and the two were best friends. They made an odd pair—the exquisite little lady and the ungainly Outlander—but were perfectly happy in each other's company. Nemain thought Monessa the kindest, sweetest, fairest being in the world. She brushed her hair for her, made up little songs for her, followed at her heels like an adoring puppy. As different as they were, their natures dovetailed: Monessa was naturally affectionate, Nemain starved for affection; and Nemain was quick-witted while Monessa was quick to laughter. So there was plenty of laughter between them, and whenever it rang through the corridors, Lord Winworth would pause whatever he was doing and listen, and sometimes almost smile.

But if Lord Winworth approved of the girls' friendship, his sister, Lady Bronwyn, did not. "Remember your station!" was her motto and her constant admonition to her niece. She despised Outlanders in general and Nemain in particular; but since her brother insisted, for whatever reason, on keeping the brat, she relieved her outraged sense of propriety by bringing up Nemain with a strict hand.

As much as Nemain loved Monessa, she feared Lady Bronwyn, the wielder of the birch switch. Lady Bronwyn was a tower of menacing disapproval, a harsh voice raised in castigation, a pair of narrow gray eyes that missed nothing. Her presence in the room was enough to make Nemain tremble, and the threat from a servant, "Lady Bronwyn shall hear of this!" filled her with a dread that was worse than the whipping itself.

But not all of the adults at Briarvale disliked Nemain or treated her harshly. There was Master Ives, for instance, the resident tutor Lord Winworth had engaged for Monessa. He gave Nemain lessons as well—a full-time job in itself, for she was a quick and voracious learner. In the schoolroom, as in Monessa's company, her habitual shyness fell away from her. She monopolized Master Ives's attention, prattling and questioning ceaselessly, delving into his books to see for herself what they contained.

Such a child would have tried any man's patience, but Master Ives never seemed to mind. He lent her his books freely, though many of them were old and valuable. He heard her out and explained things to her with good humor, smiling when she was clever, laughing outright when she was impudent (as she all too often was).

"In this passage there are seven errors," he'd say, copying some text onto a tablet. "Point them out."

Nemain counted. "There are nine."

"Now miss, I counted them myself. There are most certainly seven."

"Well, you counted wrong."

And she would proceed to mark them. Somehow, she was always right. "There! You see, I'm better at this than you are."

The only subject Master Ives did not instruct her in was music. He taught Monessa to sing and play the lute, and Nemain would have liked to be included in those lessons as well. But having once heard her play the fiddle, Master Ives flatly refused. "As well teach a fish to swim," was how he put it.

In fact, only one person had ever given Nemain a music lesson: Tynan, the man who looked after Lord Winworth's horses. He had a battered old fiddle that he had brought with him from the North Country, and he had taught her how to hold it and tune it—not much more than that. But she had picked up a great deal just from watching and listening to him play. And though he had little to say to her or anyone else, he never seemed to mind her watching or listening.

Tynan was a broad-shouldered, taciturn giant of a man, somewhat harsh and grim in appearance, but capable of great tenderness when caring for an ailing horse or handling a skittish one. He spoke, when he spoke at all, with a North Country burr, and his words and manners suggested he had been well educated. His presence at Briarvale, like Nemain's, was something of a mystery.

Nemain liked him, and not just because he let her play his fiddle and even gave her a canter on Lord Winworth's prize jennet now and then. She liked him for himself, for what little she knew of him. His accent, his love of music and horses, his solitary nature ... all these things she found very agreeable for some reason. She felt somehow that she could learn as much from Tynan's silences as from Master Ives's lectures.

When she was about nine years old, an incident occurred that taught her a great deal more about Tynan—and, eventually, about herself as well. It was only in later years that its full significance became clear to her, with implications for her future as well as her past.

Chapter 2

ONE SULTRY SUMMER afternoon, she was sent out to the village on an errand. The air was heavy with a gathering storm, but the sun was still high and hot when she set out.

If she had hurried back, as she had been told to, probably nothing would have happened. But she was spinning out a melody in her head, and she dawdled along until thunder began to murmur in the distance.

She quickened her pace, but soon became aware that she was being followed. Turning, she saw a group of boys about her age or a little older, watching her with curious, unfriendly eyes.

"That's her," one of them said. "The Outland freak. She's wearing gloves."

Nemain immediately turned her back on them and continued walking. They followed, not troubling now to move stealthily or to lower their voices.

"My mam says she's Lord Winworth's bastard, and that's why he keeps her at the castle."

"*My* mam says her hands are all rotten like a dead person's, and that's why she wears gloves."

"Ugh! Is that true? Hey, you, girl! Show us your hands!"

She ignored them.

"Are you deaf? Can't you talk?"

"Come on, let's have a look at 'em!"

She began to run, but they quickly surrounded her and pinned her to the ground. Frantic, she clenched her fists tight and tried to twist out of the boys' grip, but they eventually pried her fingers open and her gloves off.

A sudden silence fell. They backed away a step or two, and one of them uttered a low curse. Nemain scrambled to her feet, trembling with shame and rage. Never in her life had she been spoken to or handled in that way—as if she were less than human! Even Lady Bronwyn had never treated her like that.

She tried to cry out, "Give them back!" but her voice was only a hoarse rasp, and none of the boys moved. Something in their faces—some of them leering with horrified delight, others simply aghast—hurt her deeply, struck at her inmost being. Before she knew what she was doing, she sprang upon the nearest boy and knocked him to the ground.

What happened next, she never fully remembered. There was a mêlée of fists and claws and feet, a painful blow to her stomach and another to her jaw. At some point she lost consciousness, and when she came to, the boys were gone and her gloves were nowhere to be seen.

She struggled to get up. It was raining, and the drops were cold and stinging on her skin. Her head and stomach ached horribly. She felt an odd graininess in her mouth and spat out a few tiny pieces of tooth.

Where could she go? She could not return to the castle without her gloves— she quailed to think of how Lady Bronwyn would react—and she dared not seek shelter at any of the houses in the village. Then she thought of Tynan. His living quarters were behind the stables, and he wouldn't mind if she waited out the storm there. What she would do after that, she did not consider.

Fortunately Tynan was at home, and responded promptly to her desperate beating on the door. He took one look at the shivering, white-faced apparition on his threshold and drew her inside.

"What are you doing out, *inneen?*" That was what he always called her, the Northern word for "little girl."

"I'm sorry to bother you"—even distraught and weeping from pain, she did not forget her manners—"but I've lost my gloves. Can I stay here for a bit?"

"What happened?"

Nemain sobbed out the story through chattering teeth. She was embarrassed at her own lack of composure—she was not *that* hurt, surely—and didn't know why her feelings were still so harrowed up. But evidently it was no small matter to Tynan. His face darkened with fury, and he swore in two languages while he prepared a poultice for her.

"*Mollaght mynney!* Plague take them all," he muttered. "Lie down, *inneen*, and put this against your head. Do you know who any of those boys were?"

"No."

"When I find out, I'll kill them."

She managed a faint smile. "Thanks."

"Feel sick?"

"No, just sore."

"Good. Rest now—there's a basin over there if you need it. I'll be right back."

He went out into the storm, and after a while Nemain sat up and gazed curiously at her surroundings. She had known that Tynan was poor, but she had had little idea of what that meant. Now, inside his quarters for the first time, she realized that this room was all there was. He had a wash basin, a table, a chair, shelves filled with medicinal herbs and cracked dishes, and the pallet on which she lay. His fiddle was in its leather bag in a corner. On the table, next to the lamp, was a stack of books. Nemain could never leave books alone, and she examined these with interest. The covers were of tooled leather, the pages illuminated with Northern designs. The artwork was unintelligible—to her eyes, Northern art was just a lot of whorls and squiggles—but strangely appealing; and so was the text, which was in a script she could not read.

She was still looking at the books when Tynan returned, carrying a cloth-wrapped parcel. "I've told Winworth what happened," he said. "You're to stay here tonight so I can keep an eye on you."

"Was he very angry?" Nemain had a dread of Lord Winworth, whom she rarely saw, that rivaled her dread of Lady Bronwyn. Not that he had ever been unkind to her, or even taken any notice of her; he was just the distant, stern figure on whose charity her life depended. It was funny to hear Tynan refer to him simply as "Winworth," like an equal.

"With you? No. Sensible man, Winworth. He's sent you some supper, if you feel up to eating."

Tynan unwrapped the food—some bread, cheese, and cold meat—and while she ate, he busied himself mending a shirt by the lamplight. He didn't seem disposed to talk any more, but that didn't stop her.

"What's in those books?"

"The top one is poetry." He snipped a length of thread with his teeth. "The others are history."

"Are they in the Northern tongue?"

"Aye."

"What does it sound like?"

He turned to the book of poetry and read a few lines aloud. The soft, lilting sounds brought a warmth to his voice Nemain had never heard before, and it affected her like music. She felt sorry when he abruptly stopped and went back to his mending.

It seemed strange that anyone who lived like this would have such beautiful, obviously valuable books on hand. They must be precious to him indeed—worth more than all the food and furnishings he could have gotten for their price.

"Where did you get these?"

"From my home."

"Along with your fiddle?"

"Aye."

With a tentative fingertip, she traced the stippled design on the cover of the poetry book. He must have come from a wealthy home in the North Country. She tried to picture Tynan as a wealthy man—a nobleman perhaps, like Lord Winworth—and couldn't do it.

"Why did you leave home?"

"It was not by choice."

"Oh."

Silence. Nemain wished she had not asked. Tynan set down a few more stitches before he spoke again, and his voice was calm though bitter.

"I made a mistake when I was young," he said, "and my family cast me off."

"What was your mistake?"

"Never you mind."

Nemain bit her lip and looked again at the wretched surroundings. He didn't seem to want pity, but she felt she had to say something. "I'm sorry."

"So am I." Tynan folded the shirt and laid it aside. "Most of the time."

"Not all the time?"

He looked at her for a moment. In the lamplight, she noticed for the first time that his eyes were much like her own: large, deep set, and amber in color. This pleased her, though she couldn't have told why.

"I've seen good come of it," he said. "Much sorrow and evil, too—but enough good to make me think the world a better and brighter place, even if there's no joy in it for me. No ... as much as I wish I had been wiser, I cannot wish it undone."

Nemain could not make much sense of his words, but there was no mistaking the sadness in his eyes. She wondered what he could have done that was so dreadful, that he was sorry for and yet not sorry for.

"If you've finished eating, get some sleep." He took up the book of poetry. "And rest tomorrow. No more running about for a day or two."

"All right. Thank you."

He merely grunted in response.

Nemain fell readily into sleep but drifted in and out of it for most of the night. At one point, stirred by some slight noise, she half opened her eyes and saw Tynan still sitting there, his head in his hands, weeping quietly.

Chapter 3

THE YEAR NEMAIN was eleven, Lady Bronwyn spent the summer in the Northern resort town of Senuna, visiting friends and taking the waters there. It was a splendid time for Nemain, who suddenly had all the freedom she wanted. There was no one fussing over her comings and goings, no one scolding her for taking too much food at dinner, no one everlastingly reminding her to sit up straight, look pleasant, etc. After her daily lessons with Master Ives, she could do whatever she liked without hindrance: play with Monessa in the garden, go for a solitary ramble over the hills, or just sit and read in a pool of sunshine all the afternoon.

Many things happened that summer, not the least of which was that Monessa became officially betrothed. Her intended was Gavin mac Airleas, the son of a North Country lord, and the marriage would take place nine years hence. Lord Winworth and Lord Airleas had settled the whole matter by correspondence.

"His estate is called Northwaite," Monessa reported to Nemain with delight, "and it's the biggest in all the North. Right by the sea!"

"I know where it is." Nemain smiled. Master Ives had taught her the geography of the North Country, and Northwaite was prominent on the map. "It's dreadfully far away."

"Oh, I know. And they speak two languages there. I can't imagine how that is—I'm afraid I won't understand what's going on half the time. But it's a great match, Father says. You know he's always wanted me to marry a Northman; they have a very strong sense of honor and set great store by their families, he says. I'm sure I'll be very happy. And I'll come back for visits if I can."

Nemain tried to share her excitement, but she did not at all relish the idea of Monessa getting married and moving to the North Country. Of course it was still nine years away—almost a lifetime—but she couldn't picture life at Briarvale without her best friend. Undoubtedly it *would* be grand to be mistress of Northwaite ... and likely Monessa, in her castle by the sea, would forget all about her.

"Come, I'll show you his portrait," said Monessa. "It arrived yesterday. It's in the presence chamber."

"Oh, yes? Is he handsome?"

"We-ell ... come and see."

The portrait showed a gangly, red-headed boy in his late teens and a black-haired, rosy-cheeked, very pretty girl of about twelve—"His sister Nairne," explained Monessa. Their facial features were similar, but their expressions were quite different. Nairne was smiling, her black eyes sparkling with roguery even on canvas, but Gavin looked rather aloof and uncomfortable.

"Hmm. I see what you mean," said Nemain, and the two of them giggled. "I like the looks of his sister better."

"Yes, she looks jolly. And she's my age, which is good. Gavin is almost twenty already."

Nemain's eyes widened. "That old?"

"I know." Monessa grimaced. "But Lord Airleas is willing to wait until I'm grown up, and also to accept what Father can offer for my dowry. So really, I'm very lucky. It could be worse."

"Why hasn't he been betrothed until now?"

"Something to do with his horoscope, I think. It's been difficult to find him a match. They're very particular about such things up North."

Nemain gave the portrait another critical look but said nothing more. After all, Monessa was right; as arranged marriages went, she *was* lucky. And Gavin mac Airleas wasn't bad-looking, if you liked red hair. He had fine gray-green eyes and, if his sister was anything to go by, probably a nice smile too. But he was still a stranger, and an intimidatingly old one at that.

Which was preferable, she wondered? An arranged marriage, even a "great match," or never being married at all? Staying at Briarvale year in and year out, unwed and unsought, like Lady Bronwyn ... Nemain felt a little chill as she contemplated this future, the only one she could envision for herself. *She* had no hope of marriage, arranged or otherwise. Who would marry a girl with Outland blood and with hands like hers?

They went out to the courtyard together, Monessa talking cheerfully, Nemain making occasional absent replies. While Monessa sat on the stone bench to make a daisy chain, Nemain hunted in the dirt for a wood louse. She had just caught a large one, and was watching in fascination as it crawled up her arm, when she became aware of some commotion behind her and stood up.

All the servants had gathered outside, as they usually did to await an announcement. Then Lord Winworth came out with a boy Nemain had never seen before. He was about fifteen, tall and slender, with dark curly hair and refined, almost delicate features. Judging by his clothes, he was probably a merchant's son. But Nemain thought he had the look of a young prince in disguise.

"This is Swayne Merksam, my new squire," Lord Winworth introduced him to the row of servants, who each gave their name and bowed or curtsied in turn. Then he nodded toward the girls. "My daughter, Lady Monessa, and my foster-daughter, Nemain."

Monessa curtsied, and Nemain should have done the same. But she just stood there in discomfiture, aware that her hair was untidy, her feet bare, and her skirt dirty from kneeling on the ground. She felt a tickle on her arm and hastily shook off the wood louse.

"Pleased to meet you." Swayne nodded politely to both girls, but when his eye caught Nemain's, his mouth twitched in suppressed laughter.

They all filed inside once more, leaving the girls in the courtyard. Monessa grinned at Nemain. "Isn't he handsome?"

"He's all right," Nemain conceded, annoyed to feel a blush creeping into her cheeks. For once she wished she had taken to heart Lady Bronwyn's constant carping about cleanliness and deportment. How must she have looked next to Monessa, who was impeccably neat and lovely as always, with not an ash-gold curl out of place?

Then she looked down at her own gloved hands, and her shame deepened into bitterness. It didn't matter, she realized. No matter how tidy or well-behaved she was, she could not change her hands or her parentage. She would never be on the same level as Monessa, who already had the advantages of beauty and charm, and who was entitled by birth to every other advantage as well. *She was born to have everything,* Nemain thought, looking at her. *And I nothing.*

It was the first jealous thought she had ever had, and she quickly repressed it. But it rankled in the back of her mind for a long time.

Chapter 4

ONE AFTERNOON THAT summer, she went farther than usual on one of her lonely walks: over the hills surrounding Briarvale and into the dark fringe of woods beyond. She had always had a secret hankering to explore them—the shadows and silence at their edge were deeply beguiling to her—but had never done so before. The servants sometimes told odd tales of the woods; and she knew that Lord Winworth, not a superstitious man himself, had cautioned Monessa to avoid them for the very sensible reason that she might get lost.

But Nemain was not in a sensible mood. She hungered for something new to do, to see. Neither her books, nor her music, nor even Monessa's company was enough to satisfy her today. She wanted to strike out on her own and go somewhere—anywhere—she'd never been before. Supper was hours away, and no one would miss her. Why not walk a little farther on?

So she plunged into the woods, drawn onward by the singing of birds, the scent of moist earth and moss and ferns, the sunlight threading down through the trees. She walked as if in a dream, paying little attention to the passage of time, until the light had faded from afternoon gold to twilight blue.

Presently she shivered; the air had suddenly grown cold. She stopped, looked around, and realized she had no idea where she was. In every direction as far as she could see, there was nothing but more woods, and the woods in twilight were an uncanny place. Strange shadows crowded around her, and the sounds of teeming unseen creatures filled her ears. She clenched her gloved fists, fighting down a wave of panic, and continued on.

At last she came to a clearing. In front of her was a little stone cottage, its walls greened over with ivy and moss. As she approached, a huge dog sprang out from behind the cottage, barking wildly, and knocked her down. She felt its hot breath and slavering jaws close to her face, and screamed.

"*Béira!*" said a scolding voice. "*Tar ayns shoh!*"

The dog backed off, growling, and Nemain saw a woman standing in the doorway. She was tall and thin, dressed in a plain dark kirtle, and her long fair hair was tied back by a scarf. Her face, though not pretty, was arresting: strong-featured and full of intelligence.

"Get up, lass," she said, not unkindly. Her voice was unusually deep for a woman's, and her accent was distinctly Northern. "Béira's got no manners, but she won't hurt you. Come inside."

"Thanks, but I'd better get home." Nemain rose and dusted off her skirt. "Can you tell me the way back to Briarvale? I'm lost."

"You're not lost. I've been expecting you."

"What?"

"I know who you are," she said. "Lord Winworth's ward. I've wanted to meet you for some time. And you're not that far from Briarvale—you've just been walking in circles."

The hair on the back of Nemain's neck stood up. How could she know that?

"I'll take you home, but why don't you come in and have a cup of tea first? I've got it ready."

The woman went inside, and after a moment's hesitation, Nemain followed. As she entered, her fear was forgotten. She had never seen such an interesting-looking place. The walls were lined with shelves, and every shelf was crammed with books, as well as bottles and jars of every description. Bunches of dried herbs and flowers hung from the ceiling, lending a dusty-spicy smell to the air. The dog, a great black bitch, was skulking in a corner.

"Who are you?"

"My name is Rhiannon," said the woman as she poured the tea, "but you may call me Caillagh. Names like ours should only be spoken with care."

"What do you mean?"

"Don't you know? You were named for one of the Good Folk, as was I."

"Wait ... the Good Folk? You mean faeries?"

Rhiannon, or Caillagh, sighed. "Lowlanders," she muttered as she handed Nemain a cup. "Aye, faeries—but not your little men in green. Look, I haven't time to explain to you the forces that govern the Three Worlds. That's not why I brought you here."

"You *brought* me here? How?"

"I'm what's known, in these parts, as a witch."

Nemain gasped, and Rhiannon chuckled. "Oh, relax. You carry a name of power; I couldn't harm you even if I wanted to."

"What do you want with me?"

"I want to help you."

"How? Why?"

Rhiannon set down her cup of tea and gazed into Nemain's eyes. Nemain found herself unable to look away.

"We have a lot in common," she said. "Your element is fire, as is mine; it shows in your eyes and features. You're clever—very much so. And you are marked"—she looked at Nemain's gloved hands—"by powerful magic."

Again Nemain felt a crinkling at the back of her neck. But she was more fascinated than frightened now.

"I know what it's like not to belong," Rhiannon went on softly. "To feel that you have no future where you are. I can offer you a path, if you're willing to take it."

"A path?"

"As my apprentice." Her blue-gray eyes sparkled. "There's so much you could learn … so much I could teach you."

Nemain thought about it. In spite of her apprehension, Rhiannon's words awakened a lively curiosity in her. She liked this lonely cottage deep in the woods, with its heaps of books and aroma of herbs—liked this strange woman whose eyes seemed to be reading her very soul. Looking into those eyes, she had a peculiar sensation of looking at an older version of herself. She *could* see herself in a setting like this, ten or twenty years hence, living the quiet, studious, solitary life of a mystic.

A witch.

And perhaps—

She took off her gloves and laid her hands on the table. "Can you cure this?"

Rhiannon looked grave, but not horrified or disgusted. She picked up Nemain's hand, studied the palm, traced its erratic lines with her fingertip.

"If there's a way"—her fingers clasped around Nemain's for a moment—"I promise you I'll find it."

Nemain smiled, filled with unaccustomed hope and joy. "Then yes. I'll be your apprentice."

"Very well. I'll write to Lord Winworth about it."

Meanwhile, the black dog had padded softly over and laid her head in Rhiannon's lap. "*C'red t'ou laccal, Béira?*" Rhiannon murmured, stroking the dog's head. "Shall we show her your babies?"

Nemain's smile broadened. "Oh, yes!"

They went into the next room, where sleepy animal squeaks and snuffles sounded from a large blanketed basket in the middle of the floor. Rhiannon uncovered it to reveal eight squirming black puppies to Nemain's delighted gaze.

"They're too small to leave their mam yet," she explained, "but if you like, I can save one for you."

"Would you? Really?"

"Pick one."

Nemain looked them over, hardly daring to believe it. They were all adorable, glossy and perfect, except one. The runt of the litter had been shoved against the edge of the basket by his siblings and was trying to wriggle his way free. His breathing was labored, as if he had a cough.

She pointed to him. "How about that one?"

"That one's a bit sickly, I'm afraid. He may not last long. Are you sure he's the one you want?"

"Can I hold him?"

Rhiannon lifted him out and handed him to her. So seldom was she allowed to touch anything without gloves, that the warmth of a living thing in her hands—a tiny, helpless, trusting creature—brought sudden tears to her eyes. All she could do was nod.

"Well, you never know," said Rhiannon brightly. "Sometimes the weakling grows up big and strong after all. We'll call him Moddey-Dhoo: the great black beast of the North."

Nemain laughed.

She could hardly bear to put him down, but she knew she couldn't delay her return much longer. So she put her gloves back on while Rhiannon lit a lantern, and they set out into the woods together.

"If your people ask where you were," said Rhiannon, "what will you tell them?"

Nemain shrugged. "The truth."

"How much of it?"

She frowned as she pondered that question. "Well … I suppose it would alarm them if I told them I met a witch."

"It would indeed."

"But if I'm to be your apprentice, won't they have to find out then?"

"Not if we choose our words carefully. If anyone asks, say I'm an apothecary. That's how I'll represent myself when I contact Lord Winworth."

"Oh." A pause. "I don't like to lie."

"It isn't a lie. Much of what I do *is* apothecary's work, which you will also learn. Beyond that, Lowlanders won't care to know. Tynan will know better, of course, but—"

"Oh! You know Tynan?"

"I used to, long ago. I doubt he remembers me. The point is, little sister, there are many secrets in my line of work—and you'd best be in the habit of keeping them. Understand?"

"Yes."

They walked on in silence. Eventually Nemain saw a light bobbing in the distance and heard a voice calling, "*Inneen! Inneen!*"

"Go on then," said Rhiannon. "*Slaynt-lhiat!*"

Nemain knew that was how Northerners said "farewell." She turned to respond, but Rhiannon had already vanished, lantern and all, into the woods.

She broke into a run towards the light ahead. It was carried by Swayne, and beside him was Tynan. When the latter saw her, he gave a hoarse cry of relief and embraced her.

"Are you all right? Where were you? What happened?"

"I'm fine. I got lost, that's all."

"Never wander in these woods again! Have you any idea what could have happened to you?"

She shrank back a little, stunned by his emotion. "I'm sorry."

"It's all right," said Swayne. "She's not hurt, you can see. Let's just get her home."

"Aye." Tynan turned away, wiping his forehead with his sleeve. "Tell Winworth that she's found, and make sure she gets some supper."

He said nothing more until they reached the castle, and then he abruptly headed for his quarters behind the stables. Nemain was sorry to have upset him so, but secretly pleased that Swayne had come out to look for her as well.

"How long have you been searching for me?"

"We set out at suppertime."

"Oh!" She suddenly realized that her stomach was rumbling—she had had nothing but a cup of tea since midday—and she was shivering, partly from the chill of the night and partly with suppressed excitement. "I'm sorry."

"It's all right," he said again, looking at her curiously. "You *are* all right, aren't you?"

"Oh, yes, quite."

He led her to the presence chamber, where Lord Winworth was waiting. Monessa was pacing to and fro outside the door. When she saw Nemain coming, she ran up to her.

"Oh, Nemain, I was so worried!" she cried, throwing her arms around her. "Where have you been?"

While Nemain told her about getting lost in the woods, the kind lady called Caillagh who lived there, and the puppy she would get to keep—leaving out certain details, of course—Lord Winworth opened his door and listened quietly. When she finally noticed him standing there, she shut her mouth in guilty confusion. Would he yell at her for getting herself lost and disrupting the household? Would she be whipped?

"All right then," he said mildly. "Thank you, Swayne. Go get her some supper. Monessa, off to bed with you." Then he shut the door again.

So she was not to be punished at all! She gave a sigh of relief as she followed Swayne down to the larder, where he piled a plate with bread, meat, and apples for both of them, and they sat down on the stone steps to eat.

"Caillagh sounds nice," he remarked.

"She is."

"I'm glad. I imagine you could do with a friend."

"I have friends. Monessa is my best, and there's Tynan, and Master Ives …" She trailed off, unable to list any more.

"And me, I hope."

She smiled in pleased surprise. "If you like."

"Must be hard for you," he said around a mouthful of apple. "You an orphan, and having to wear gloves, and nobody around here paying you much mind."

Nemain thought to herself that there were worse things than being ignored— like being watched and checked all the time by, say, Lady Bronwyn—but she did not say so. She could tell that Swayne pitied her, and it was rather nice to be pitied for a change.

"I have seven sisters back home," said Swayne. "I'm the only son. Nobody paid me much mind, either. Couldn't wait to get out of there. But I guess having too much family is better than having none at all."

He patted her head as he stood up. "Anyway, next time you feel like wandering off, you can come talk to me."

"Really?"

"Sure. Anytime."

After Swayne had gone to bed, Nemain remained sitting on the steps for a long time. A plan—the culmination of all the strange and wonderful things that had happened that day—was beginning to take shape in her mind. Someday, when she was grown up, and when her hands had been cured of their deformity— oh, joyous possibility!—she would marry that boy. Nothing seemed beyond her reach anymore. Monessa could keep her red-headed Northman and her castle by the sea! She, Nemain, would be better off after all, with a man of her own choosing and a future of her own making.

For a moment she wondered uneasily just how Swayne would fit into that future. Would he want to marry a witch? (Would anyone?) And what if Rhiannon couldn't cure her hands after all? Would she still be happy as she had envisioned herself earlier, living alone?

But she pushed her doubts aside. Who knew what powers she would have as a witch? If she wanted something badly enough, surely she could make it happen. She would learn all she needed to know.

As she lay in bed that night, too happy to sleep, she tried to remember just what Rhiannon had said about the Good Folk, the Three Worlds, and so forth. Whoever and whatever they were, she felt for the first time that they were on her side, and that this world, at least, had something marvelous in store for her.

Chapter 5

LADY BRONWYN CAME home a few days later, and life returned more or less to normal. There was no more playing in the dirt, and no more wandering over hills and fields, but Nemain didn't mind too much. She had hope that Rhiannon would send for her any day now, and that made it easier to obey Lady Bronwyn with good grace, even without fear. Which was well, because the hot springs of Senuna had not improved either Lady Bronwyn's temper or her liking for "the Outland girl."

Nemain made herself as scarce and docile as she could. She wore her gloves at all times except when fiddling, and then she stood behind a latticed screen. She took care to restrain her appetite at meals, to be neat in her appearance, and to speak softly and politely when spoken to, at least when Lady Bronwyn was around. For two weeks she was ceaselessly, painfully good.

Yet she still did not manage to get by without a whipping. That was the day Lady Bronwyn had caught her emerging with Swayne from an old, disused passageway that led up to the minstrels' gallery in the great hall—admittedly, not the most decorous place to be caught with a young man. Nemain insisted that she had only wanted to show him what the sound quality was like up there—she had only half an idea of what Lady Bronwyn suspected her of, anyhow—and Swayne apologized profusely for any misunderstanding. But it was no use. Nemain was whipped, not for wrongdoing, but for the appearance of wrongdoing, which in Lady Bronwyn's eyes was the same thing.

"My brother will hear of this," she warned as Nemain stumbled, tear-blinded, from the room. "You'd better mind the example you set for his daughter, or he may not be disposed to keep you anymore."

Nemain was at first too angry to care about the threat. But suppose it was not an empty one?—and at that thought, her anger was replaced by the old, accustomed chill of dread. Suppose Lord Winworth *was* finally persuaded to get rid of her, and Rhiannon had not yet sent for her?

I must hear from her soon, she thought fervently. Surely she would not be forsaken ... surely, if whoever governed the Three Worlds had any interest in her fate, they would manage things better than that.

The next day, in the middle of her lesson with Master Ives, Lady Bronwyn put her head in the doorway and announced that Lord Winworth wanted to see her.

Nemain felt cold and sick. Yet a struggling little hope shot up in her heart as she followed Lady Bronwyn. "Is there anyone else?"

"What do you mean?"

"Is it just Lord Winworth who wants to see me, or is anyone else with him?"

"There's no one else. But that's no reason why you shouldn't be presentable." She looked Nemain over with a critical eye. "There's a grease spot on your dress. Go and change it."

"It's the only one I can wear."

"What's happened to your others?"

"They're too tight."

Grumbling, Lady Bronwyn propelled her to the castle wardrobe. She opened up chests of clothing, fragrant with southernwood and lavender, and finally picked out a dark blue gown, plainly made, but of finer material than Nemain had ever worn. It took her a moment to recognize it as one of Lady Bronwyn's own.

"That'll do." She tilted her head and frowned at Nemain. "Stand up straight, and try not to scowl. And don't—"

"Why are you doing this for me?" Nemain asked suddenly.

"I beg your pardon?"

"You've never liked me." She was stunned by her own frankness, but she went on, "You'd be delighted if your brother decided not to keep me anymore. Why do you bother making a lady of me? Why have you ever bothered?"

Lady Bronwyn gave her a sharp look, and Nemain flinched, fearing a worse punishment than that of the day before. But Lady Bronwyn merely compressed her lips tightly for a moment and then said, "I do my duty. As we all should. Whatever my feelings about it, no one will ever say I didn't do the best I could for you."

Without another word, she led Nemain to the presence chamber and knocked on the door. "Enter," said Lord Winworth.

He was reading a letter at his desk. On the wall hung the portrait of Gavin mac Airleas and his sister, Nairne, and Nemain felt encouraged at the sight of it. Nairne seemed like a friend, and Gavin a useful person to have on your side. What a fine, strong chin he had! She had not noticed that before.

Lady Bronwyn gave her a none too gentle push forward. "You wished to see the Outland girl?"

"Ah, yes. Nemain." Lord Winworth put the letter aside. "You're looking vastly improved."

Nemain flushed. The last time he had seen her was just after her adventure in the woods, and the time before that was in the courtyard while he was introducing Swayne. She had not exactly looked her best on either occasion.

"How old are you now?"

"Eleven and one half, my lord."

"I've had good reports of your lessons. Master Ives tells me you're clever."

"I am."

His mouth twitched briefly in a smile. Nemain had never seen Lord Winworth smile before.

"Humility is not among her virtues," Lady Bronwyn said dourly.

"At least false modesty is not among her faults," he countered. "Leave us, sister. I want to talk to her alone."

Lady Bronwyn made a stiff curtsy and withdrew. Lord Winworth folded his hands and regarded Nemain with eyes that were appraising, but not unkind.

"You're well, I trust?"

"Well enough."

"Is Bronwyn plaguing the life out of you?"

She dared to smile. "No, my lord."

"Good." He held out the letter to her. "This is what I want to talk to you about. It came to me from that friend of yours, Rhiannon of Gwehara, called Caillagh."

She took it from him with trembling fingers. It was written in an odd, slanting, loose-jointed hand, almost as difficult to read as the script in Tynan's books, but it was unmistakably the summons she had been hoping for. *It has come to my attention that your ward, Nemain, is approaching the age at which she might be fitted for a trade—I hereby offer to undertake her education and living expenses until such time as she becomes independent—I am satisfied as to her character and capacity.* Nemain vowed she would not disappoint in either respect.

Her reading was interrupted by a chuckle. Was Lord Winworth actually laughing? "I've never seen your face light up like that," he remarked. "I take it you want to go to this woman?"

"Yes, I'd very much like to go to her." She looked over the letter again and noticed the date for the first time. "Why, this came over a week ago! You didn't tell me!"

Lord Winworth's eyebrows went up at her accusing tone, and she subsided.

"There was little point in telling you until I'd found out more about her myself. And I had to talk it over with Tynan."

"Tynan?"

"He knows her. He's from that part of the North Country. And he has an interest in your welfare, as I'm sure you're aware."

"Well, what does he say? What do *you* say?"

He shrugged. "I say you can please yourself. She's right, this Caillagh; you *should* be fitted for a trade of some sort." His gaze fell on her gloved hands, and his brows knit together for a moment. "Tynan approves as well, provided you come home for visits at least every few months. I know Monessa will be glad of that."

Nemain grinned, resisting the urge to jump up and down with glee. "Thank you, my lord."

"I'll send word to Caillagh to expect you in a few days. Oh, and before I forget"—he rummaged in his desk—"Swayne felt very badly about getting you in trouble with Bronwyn the other day. He asked me to give you this."

Lord Winworth tossed a small object to her, and she caught it, surprised. It was a little packet of sugared almonds from a vendor in the village. Nemain was fond of sugared almonds and deeply gratified by this gesture. As she examined the packet, she heard Lord Winworth chuckle again.

"It doesn't take much to make your face light up, does it?" he said. "Well, run along, and don't let Bronwyn see you eating those."

⸱⸱⸱⸱⸱⸱

Tynan was playing his fiddle in the courtyard. The slow, poignant notes of a Northern lament filled the evening air, mingling with the voice of an unseen nightingale beyond the garden wall.

He did not notice Nemain at first, and as she watched him it struck her how *old* he looked—weary, haggard, unutterably sad. Yet he was not an old man. Was he ill, or … ? A dreadful thought crossed her mind, and she hastily pushed it away before it could find words.

But when she caught his eye, he put his fiddle down and smiled. She saw then that his frail appearance was only a trick of the twilight. He looked just as he always had.

"Are you well?" she asked.

"Just tired. I've been training that new gray hunter all afternoon. He's withy-cragged."

"He's what?"

"Too loose in the neck. Not fit for the hunt yet, but I'll have him up to it in a few weeks. What is it you want, *inneen?*"

"I was just wondering, how do you know Rhian—er, Caillagh?"

"Ah, yes. Spindle." He frowned faintly. "I knew her of old, though not very well."

"Spindle?"

"That was her nickname before she became a *caillagh*. She was the daughter of my father's steward, and little more than a child when I left home."

"What was she like?"

"Clever." His frown deepened. "A bit odd, but nice enough."

"How was she odd?"

"Oh, just … not like other children. Those with names of power never are."

"What *is* a name of power? She said that I had one too."

Tynan looked around as if he thought someone might overhear, even though the courtyard was empty. Then he went over to the stone bench. "Come."

She sat down beside him, and he began to explain in a low tone. "A name of power is a name shared with one of the Good Folk. You, *inneen*, were named for a great warrior queen—Her we call the Raven. Because you carry Her name, you are under Her protection."

Nemain's eyes widened.

"Such a name is a safeguard in all Three Worlds," he went on. "Anyone who dares to cross you will meet with a sure vengeance in one world or another. But there's a price attached. One never knows how the Good Folk will respond to the use of Their names. And the children who bear them are always a little peculiar—set apart, as it were, from others. *You* know."

"It was you who gave me my name, wasn't it?"

Tynan nodded.

"Why did I need so much protecting?"

"Why do you think?"

She looked down at her gloved hands. "Because I was marked," she realized aloud. "By powerful magic."

He patted her shoulder.

"But you never use my name. You always call me *inneen*."

He nodded again. "Out of respect, we don't invoke the Good Folk too often. We give nicknames to keep them at a distance. Lowlanders, of course, know no better. ... But on the other hand, perhaps it's better for a child with such a name to grow up hearing it. Perhaps that makes it more yours—and you more Hers."

Nemain was silent in wonder and a little fear. The nightingale, too, had fallen silent, and for a moment the courtyard seemed full of unseen, listening presences. And yet she liked Tynan in this rare talkative mood—was fascinated by the lore he touched upon, which was obviously close to his heart—and she wished he would go on. But he abruptly got up from the bench, and the moment passed.

"Anyway, your *caillagh* will teach you all about these things," he said in his accustomed tone. "*Caillagh* is a holy title—a good path. I'm glad for you."

Are you? Nemain thought. In his eyes she saw that same look she had seen once years ago: sorry and yet not sorry, full of things he wished he could say.

"I'll miss you," he said, "but Winworth's right. It's your choice. And a good one it is."

He headed back to his quarters, leaving her alone in the darkening courtyard.

Chapter 6

A WEEK LATER, after all the goodbyes had been said—a tearful one from Monessa, jovial ones from Lord Winworth and Swayne, a cool one from Lady Bronwyn that smacked of I-told-you-so, and a glum one from Master Ives, who was unexpectedly sore over losing his chatterbox of a pupil—Nemain left the castle to begin her apprenticeship.

Tynan accompanied her to Rhiannon's cottage in the woods. He carried the small sack of her belongings in one hand and his fiddle-bag in the other—though why he had brought the fiddle, she didn't know—and was unusually quiet even for him. His straight-ahead gaze and the tense set of his jaw made her uneasy.

"What is it?" she asked. He merely shook his head.

When they arrived at the cottage, he strode up to the door—ignoring the great black dog that barked and strained frantically at her tether—and Rhiannon opened the door before he knocked. She was wearing a heavy black hooded robe, though the day was warm. A red and white plaited cord was knotted around her waist, and her hood was pulled up, casting a shadow over her features.

"Caillagh." Tynan bowed and set down the bags, and Nemain thought she saw Rhiannon blush. "May I have a word with your apprentice before I leave?"

"Of course," said Rhiannon quietly, withdrawing to the other room.

Tynan laid a hand on Nemain's shoulder. He looked as if he would like to say a great deal, but hesitated. Were there tears in his eyes?

"Stay in practice," he said finally, nodding toward the fiddle.

"Oh, I can't take that!"

"Take it. I want you to have it."

He took a deep breath and turned to go.

"Tynan, wait!" She caught at his sleeve, suddenly afraid. "Please, tell me—"

"I can't," he cut her off. "Don't be afraid, *inneen*. Trust in the Raven, as I do. You'll be all right."

He left without another word. She watched him from the doorway until he vanished from sight beyond the trees.

She found Rhiannon standing with her arms folded, staring morosely out through the tangle of ivy that covered the window. "Is he gone?"

"Yes."

"Go untie Béira and let her in."

Nemain obeyed somewhat nervously, half expecting to be knocked down again. But Béira bounded past her without so much as a sniff and went straight to Rhiannon, who knelt down and embraced her, as if in need of comforting.

"Is everything all right?"

"Aye. Of course." Rhiannon hastily stood up, brushing the dog hairs off her robe, and Béira settled herself down near her puppies. "I wanted to show you this. This is a *caillagh*'s robe, which you'll earn when you complete your apprenticeship. The colors black, red, and white are symbolic ..."

"He spoke well of you," Nemain interrupted gently.

"Did he?"

"He said you were clever. And nice."

Rhiannon looked away. "I think I'd rather he'd forgotten me," she said softly. "Better to be forgotten than to be remembered so—*kindly*. But never mind. Come, little sister, we've a lot to do."

⋅→▻═◉ ◉═◅←⋅

The first few weeks of Nemain's apprenticeship were the most stimulating and challenging time of her life thus far. She adopted Rhiannon's schedule, staying up long into the night, poring over books and spells or observing the moon and stars. She was often tired and sore, but she soon grew accustomed to the odd hours as well as the plain food and hard work. And all the while, under the influence of Rhiannon's conversation and the texts she was given to study, her mind was awakened and expanded as never before. Magical lore was very different from anything Master Ives had ever taught, and it satisfied some deep mystic strain she had not known she possessed.

The Three Worlds, she learned, were those of human existence: the realms of the living, the dead, and the unborn. But there were also the Three Worlds of land, sea, and sky—the realms of nature—as well as any number of other, purely notional worlds in time and space. And the Good Folk inhabited the spaces in between, where anything could happen: thresholds, crossroads, the turning points of the seasons, the twilight, the gray hour before dawn, and even puns and riddles, the flickering intersections of language.

Among the many books Rhiannon gave her to read was the Book of Dark Sayings, a hotchpotch of Northern riddles and proverbs, from which she had to study a portion every day. "All the good and evil in the world are contained within that book," Rhiannon said. A Dark Saying could be interpreted on multiple levels, each one integral to the ancient wisdom at its core. Nemain, accustomed to devouring the facile prose of Lowland authors, had to learn to slow down with magical texts, to examine each word and phrase and attune herself to their varied resonances.

Along the way she picked up bits and pieces of the Northern tongue, which was rich in ambiguity. *Caillagh,* for instance, was a respectful term for "witch," but it also meant "hag." (Since most *cailleeyn* were, in fact, older women— Rhiannon herself being considerably younger than most—this sort of made sense.) Another word she frequently encountered, *ashlins,* could refer to a ghost, a dream, or second sight. All three meanings were tied together in the notion of things invisible to the natural eyes—"dark" to ordinary vision in the same way that a Dark Saying was dark to ordinary reasoning.

Names, too, were loaded with meaning, especially names of power. "My name means 'Great High Queen,' " Rhiannon told her. "And so does yours, some say."

"I still don't see where the power comes in," Nemain confessed. "Tynan said that anyone who crossed me would meet with some kind of vengeance. But

I've been called Nemain all my life, and I've been crossed plenty of times, and nothing ever happened."

"Are you sure?" Rhiannon leaned forward, her eyes gleaming. "What exactly happened that day a few years ago when those boys followed you and beat you?"

"You know about that?"

"Everyone does. Don't you know why folks in this village are so afraid of you?"

"Because of my hands."

"Not entirely. Do you remember what happened?"

Nemain shuddered and shook her head. "It's fuzzy."

"Well, they say those boys all ran back to their homes in a panic, screaming about a great black bird." Rhiannon smiled grimly. "Fancy that. ... What's the matter?"

"I don't know. It frightens me, almost."

"*Ommijys!*"—Nonsense!—said Rhiannon. "If the Raven Herself came to your aid just to scare off some no-account lads, you've nothing to fear, little sister, in this world or any other."

Nevertheless Nemain remained, if not frightened, deeply sobered, and was glad when Rhiannon changed the subject. It was one thing to study and speculate about the Good Folk; it was quite another to accept Them as a force in one's own life, especially if They were in the habit of appearing in such terrible forms. And yet part of her, that mystic strain, rejoiced in the very strangeness and terror of it—in the idea of being guarded and guided by such power.

There was much about ordinary mortals, too, that she had never suspected. Facial features, the lines in the palm, and the shape of the fingers all revealed a great deal about a person's character and destiny. By certain subtle signs, Nemain learned to recognize a person's dominant element—fire, water, earth, or air—which influenced their temperament, their decisions, and their relationships. She was both pleased and somewhat bewildered that her own element was fire.

"Fire people are natural leaders," said Rhiannon. "Strong, brave, clever, stubborn—that's us. Loyal, sometimes to a fault. Intense in love and hate." Nemain only partially recognized herself in that description, but she liked it nonetheless.

Water people, by contrast, tended to be gentle, pliant, sensitive souls—rather like Monessa, who also possessed water's sparkle and grace. Air people were also natural leaders, steady, clear-eyed, decisive, ruled by their heads rather than their hearts—now that was Lord Winworth all over. As for earth characters, she had no close acquaintance with any, but they sounded like a jolly lot: blunt, pragmatic, often crude, but funny, warm and generous as often as not. Nemain, who generally shied away from people in the flesh, now found them fascinating in the abstract.

Oh, there was so much to learn, so much to fit into her scheme of things! When Tynan came to bring her home for her first visit a month later, she felt as if she had been away for years, and yet the time had passed in a twinkling. Everything was fresh and vivid to her senses—the red and gold brocaded hills surrounding Briarvale, the crisp autumn air with its tang of wood smoke. She gave a happy sigh, feeling that life was infinitely rich and interesting.

"You've grown taller," Tynan remarked.

"Have I?" She wasn't sure if she actually had, but she sensed that she was walking with a straighter back, her head held higher.

"Is she good to you?"

"Oh, yes."

He nodded curtly and said no more. But he no longer seemed tense or unhappy about her situation. He seemed resigned to it—and, Nemain thought with surprise as she caught a sidelong glance of his, not ill-pleased. Why, he was proud of her—as proud of her as he had been, perhaps, worried about her. She found Tynan's approval very sweet.

And yet ... being at home again was curiously unsatisfying. Monessa was happy to see her and was just as dear as ever, but something was missing from their companionship. For Monessa, the past month had been uneventful, if somewhat lonely; it had not changed *her* at all. And Nemain, bursting with new ideas, found herself at a loss to share them.

"How is your apprenticeship going? I suppose you're learning about healing herbs, and things like that?"

"Yes," said Nemain truthfully—"and a lot else too," she almost added, but stopped herself. What could she share that would be interesting or even comprehensible to Monessa? She couldn't very well bring up the Good Folk; Monessa would laugh and accuse her of superstition. Nor did it seem appropriate to mention divination, Dark Sayings, or multiple worlds. Monessa, like her father, was under the impression that Nemain was studying to be an apothecary and nothing more.

"That's splendid. *I* wouldn't have the head for it, I'm sure, but you're certainly clever enough. Come out and see my new palfrey. Her name's Russet, and she's the sweetest creature. If you'd like, you can take her for a ride. Oh, and what do you think of this new gown? I just adore this shade of blue. See how it turns silver in the light?"

She got on slightly better with Master Ives, who offered to lend her some books on botany and medicine that might be useful to her, and with Swayne. Swayne was learning to play the guitar, along with other courtly skills that Lord Winworth felt he should have, and had taken to practicing in the great hall when it wasn't in use. On the evening of Nemain's return he was playing his guitar there, thinking himself alone—and got a good scare when he heard a ghostly fiddle up in the minstrels' gallery playing his tune back to him, note for note.

"Oh, it's you!" he laughed. "Say, we should have a concert one of these nights. You and me, and Master Ives on the lute. Lady Monessa could sing, perhaps. We could have dancing."

"That sounds like fun." Nemain smiled, savoring his offhand pairing of "you and me." And they did put on one or two impromptu concerts—Nemain playing her fiddle behind a screen, as always—which were attended by everyone at Briarvale (except Lady Bronwyn, who invariably had a headache). Performing was still one of the keenest pleasures Nemain had ever known. With her fiddle in hand, she no longer felt lonely, out of place, or compelled to hold back.

Still, it was with a mixture of sadness and relief that she returned to Rhiannon: sadness at leaving her friends again, and relief at returning to what was beginning to feel like her real life, her true self. It was hard to believe she had ever *not* aspired to be a witch.

Chapter 7

OVER THE FOLLOWING months, Nemain's relationship to Briarvale and its inhabitants continued to evolve. Her apprenticeship was the hub of her existence; her periodic visits "home" were just that—visits, not homecomings. She went to Briarvale not as a returning dependant, but as a young woman in her own right, and was tacitly recognized as such. She was not required to attend lessons or anything else, but could spend her time however she wished.

Her companion on these visits was Moddey-Dhoo, Moddey for short. From the time he was weaned, Nemain tended and trained him herself under Rhiannon's direction, and the sickly pup thrived. He never grew as big or as handsome as the rest of Béira's litter; his black coat was mottled with gray, and his eyes were mismatched, one brown and one blue. But what he lacked in beauty and size, he more than made up for in loyalty, protectiveness, and ferocity. He adored Nemain, tolerated Rhiannon, and had absolutely no use for anyone else.

This was a bit of a problem whenever they went to Briarvale. As long as no one approached too near him or Nemain, he behaved all right; but once that one- or two-pace boundary was crossed, he would tense up and growl alarmingly. The servants learned to leave him alone after he bit one of the kitchen maids, who had unwisely nudged him out of her way with her foot. Lady Bronwyn tried to whip him for that, but Nemain, enraged, grabbed the switch from her and flung it out the window.

Amazingly, she was not scolded for this. Lady Bronwyn merely gave her a tight-lipped look and left the room. But later that day, as Nemain was passing by the presence chamber with Moddey at her heels, she overheard Lady Bronwyn arguing the matter with Lord Winworth.

"*You* know all I've done for that girl, for all the thanks I ever got. And now when she behaves disgracefully, I can't say a thing about it! I can't even lay a hand on that wretched mongrel of hers when it attacks one of my staff!"

"Una's fine," said Lord Winworth in a tone of strained patience. "And she shouldn't have kicked the dog."

"That's hardly the point! It's absurd to have the Outland girl here at all, now that someone else has the keeping of her. If you'd only let me send for some young ladies to keep Monessa company ..."

"Monessa doesn't need ladies-in-waiting just yet. You've already taught her well about sewing and deportment, and you can teach her all she needs to know about running a manor. There'll be time enough for her to acquire a retinue and learn about vanity and gossip as well. As for company, right now Nemain is the company she wants."

"She's not fit to be my lady's guest."

"Then think of her as *my* guest." Lord Winworth's voice was very quiet now, but unmistakably angry. "And stop trying to poison me against her. I will not turn her out, Bronwyn. I keep my promises."

There followed a brief exchange of harsh whispers, and then Lord Winworth said clearly, "Now go and fetch her. I want to speak to her."

Nemain froze as Lady Bronwyn came out into the corridor. She hadn't meant to eavesdrop, at least not at first, but it was obvious that was what she was doing. Moddey immediately moved in front of her as if to defend her.

"She's right here." Lady Bronwyn sniffed. "Mongrel and all."

"Good. Leave us."

Nemain whispered to Moddey to stay put, then went in. Again she noticed the portrait of Gavin mac Airleas and Nairne, and again the thought struck her that she would like to get to know them. Someday perhaps, when Monessa was married—but Nemain still didn't like to think of that.

"How are things?" Lord Winworth inquired.

"Very good, my lord." She bowed slightly. "I thank you for having me back, as always."

"Have you seen much of Tynan lately?"

"Er—now and then." She frowned as she thought about it. Now that she knew the way to and from Rhiannon's cottage, Tynan no longer accompanied her through the woods. Nor had she had much occasion to go to the stables. When they did see each other, they hardly spoke, but there was nothing abnormal in that.

"He's unwell," said Lord Winworth. "Hasn't been well, really, for months—not since last autumn. First he insisted nothing was wrong; then he insisted he'd be better when the warm weather returned. But it's nearly summer, and he's not showing any improvement."

"What's wrong with him?"

"He's getting pale and thin. He tires quickly, and coughs a great deal. I don't want to worry you," he added quickly as Nemain's hand went to her heart. "It may not be that serious. Only I don't think it's the sort of thing that will go away on its own."

"Has he seen a physician?"

"No. You know how stubborn he can be. I even offered to send him to Senuna, thinking the air and the waters would do him good, but he refused to go."

"I'll help, of course, if I can," she said tentatively, "but I really don't know enough yet ..."

"Oh, I know that. I don't expect you to cure him. But you might persuade him to see someone—consult with your mistress, perhaps. If he'll listen to anyone, it'll be you."

Nemain nodded slowly, though she wasn't at all sure of her own influence over Tynan. If he refused to listen to his master—even, possibly, at the peril of his life—why should he listen to her?

"Anyway, do what you can. And keep him company while you're here. That would mean more to him, and possibly help him more than all else."

She nodded again, and he dismissed her. As she turned to leave, he asked, "Did you really throw that switch out the window?"

"Yes," she admitted.

"I'm sorry I missed that," he said. "You may go."

She went to Tynan's quarters the next morning, bringing herbs that she knew would help with a cough. As an afterthought, she brought her fiddle as well.

Tynan had stepped out, leaving his door ajar. Nemain went over to his medicine shelves and examined the herbs he used to treat the horses. Most of them she recognized from Rhiannon's training: mugwort, fennel, comfrey, wild chervil. ...

"What are you looking for, *inneen?*" said Tynan behind her.

She turned, and could not repress a start of alarm at the sight of him. Again, as for that brief moment in the courtyard all those months ago, he looked unwell indeed—even at death's door. His face was ashen, with deep shadows under the eyes, and his clothes hung ragged on his wasted frame. It was no trick of the light this time. A terrible fear gripped her heart.

Then she blinked, and again the vision passed. He didn't really look as bad as all that—no worse than one suffering from a head cold and a poor night's sleep. And he sounded like himself, if a trifle hoarse.

"Just wondering if you had any lungwort," she said as casually as she could. "Or cowslips."

"No, why?"

"Good thing I brought some, then." Smiling, she held up the little pouch of herbs she had brought with her. "Sit down. I'll make you some tea."

"Oh, *inneen,* there isn't any need—" He interrupted himself with a fit of coughing. When it subsided, he gave her a wry look and sat down. "Really."

"Can't you rest today?"

"Aye. I was just telling Swayne and the stable lads what needs to be done. They can get on for a day without me. It's just rest I need—that's all."

He sat down at his table, wincing.

"Lord Winworth says you've been ill since last fall. Why haven't you seen a physician?"

Tynan rolled his eyes. "Winworth worries over nothing."

"That cough doesn't sound like nothing. Why don't you come and see Caillagh?"

"I'm not that bad off. I just have a bad day now and then." He smiled gently. "I promise you, *inneen,* you needn't worry. Now, tell me what you're learning these days. How are you getting on with the Dark Sayings?"

Nemain grinned. "You know the Dark Sayings?"

"No one *knows* them," he reminded her with a wink.

"But you've studied them?"

"Aye, a bit. All children in Gwehara are given some instruction of that sort." He coughed again. "But the highest learning belongs to the *cailleeyn,* of course. How far along are you?"

"I've gotten as far as the triads," said Nemain, excited to discuss such things with someone besides Rhiannon for once. "I love to read them. They're beautiful, like poetry. But most of them don't make any sense."

"Have you got a favorite?"

"I like the one that goes,

Thrice nothing is everything.
Thrice darkness is light.
Thrice silence is wisdom.

And also,

Of riches, three: a gift ungrudged,
a good deed unseen,
a heart that is never filled.

What does that mean?"

"I couldn't say," Tynan smiled. "But they're a good deal more than poetry, you know."

"Oh, I know. I try to understand them. I just feel like I never will."

"You won't—not completely. But that's all right. Remember them—carry them in your heart—and understanding will come little by little."

He fell to coughing again, and Nemain laid an anxious hand on his shoulder. "I'm sorry to keep you talking. You can stop."

"I'm all right. Let me have that tea."

He drank it down, grimacing as he did so, for there was no honey to sweeten it with. Then he lay down on his pallet and drew a scrap of blanket over himself. "Thanks."

"Is there anything else I can do? Shall I play for you?"

"Yes."

Nemain played him a soft, sweet tune, and he fell asleep quickly under the sedative effect of the cowslips. For a while she watched him sleep, wondering how to help him. Then she left, closing the door softly behind her.

→═◉ ◉═←

"Is that you, little sister?" Rhiannon called from the other room. "I wasn't expecting you until next week."

Nemain went in and told her about Tynan's illness. When she mentioned the two brief visions of Tynan she had had, Rhiannon paled.

"It sounds as if he's fey," she said grimly. "Has he told you?"

"Told me what?"

"Why, the truth about himself. Why his family cast him out."

"No, he's never told me that. What has that got to do with it?"

Rhiannon looked puzzled. "I thought he might have broken his *geasa*. But if he's never told you …"

"*Geasa?*"

"A *geis* is the most binding of oaths, thrice death to him that breaks it. Tynan is under bonds of silence; his family placed them on him when they cast him out. Lord Winworth knows why, of course, and it's no secret in Gwehara either. But he's forbidden to speak of it to you."

"Why? What's it to do with me?"

"My dear," said Rhiannon, "it's everything to do with you. Do you really not know?"

Nemain's heart was beating rapidly with sudden dread. She took a step back. "I know nothing," she cried. "He's never told me. Don't *you* tell me, either. If silence will protect him, I never want to know."

She buried her face in her hands. Moddey, alarmed, came closer and pawed at her skirt, making a whingeing noise in his throat.

"I thought you knew," said Rhiannon softly. "I thought you would have figured it out long ago, or some prating servant would have told you. Lord Winworth must run a tighter ship than I thought. My dear, have you never wondered at Tynan's fondness for you? Never noticed anything peculiar about his eyes?"

"Don't talk of it," said Nemain in a choked voice. "I don't want to hear it. I don't want him to die."

"It will make no difference if you hear it from anyone else. The *geasa* are on him alone." She added in a not very hopeful tone, "And I could be mistaken. Perhaps this is a simple illness and not a fey one. Perhaps your *ashlins* meant nothing; sometimes they don't."

Nemain felt a kindly arm around her shoulders. "Go to him," said Rhiannon. "Lord Winworth was quite right that you should keep him company. We'll suspend your studies until he's better, or—well, until we know."

"Will you come with me?" Nemain sniffled. "You'll know better what to do."

Rhiannon shook her head. "Make sure that he doesn't work too hard, and keep on treating him with the herbs. I'll give you more to take with you. They'll ease him for a while, if nothing else. That's as much as I would do if I were there. But it's you he wants, not me."

She turned her face away as she said this.

Chapter 8

FOR A TIME that summer, it seemed as if Tynan was improving. He was still pale and gaunt, and moved very slowly even on the days when he could work; but he coughed less and slept better, thanks to Nemain's treatments, and he was in good spirits. Nemain spent as much time with him as she could—playing the fiddle for him, helping him with small tasks in the stables, or just talking to him in his quarters—and he seemed glad of her company, though, as usual, he had little to say. For a while she allowed herself to hope.

But at the first chill of autumn, he went into a rapid decline. Lord Winworth had him moved into the castle and summoned a physician against his will, but by then it was clearly too late. His cough was worse than ever, sometimes accompanied by blood; and for many nights, unable to breathe lying down, he struggled to sleep sitting up, flushed and twitching with fever.

"Lord Winworth shouldn't have waited so long," said Nemain in despair, feeling as if she must blame someone, as she brewed yet another herbal remedy at the fireplace in Tynan's room. "He should have summoned that physician long ago, and *made* you see him, no matter what you said."

"It wouldn't have made any difference," Tynan said between labored breaths. "There's no cure for broken *geasa*."

Up till then neither of them had made any reference to *geasa*. Nemain, who had determinedly believed that Rhiannon was mistaken about the cause of Tynan's illness, began to tremble. "I don't know what you mean. You haven't broken any *geasa*, and you're not about to."

"I have kept them—and not kept them—since they were laid on me." He took a few more rasping breaths and added wryly, "There's a Dark Saying for you."

"Don't." Nemain flew to his bedside, ready to shut his mouth forcibly if need be. "Don't talk of *geasa*. You never broke them. You never told me. *You never told me!*"

She burst into tears, overwhelmed by fear and a grief she hardly understood. Tynan reached out to touch her hair and could not quite manage it.

"You'd better not swear to that, *inneen*," he said hoarsely. "I've been telling you since you were born."

She shook her head, not comprehending.

"It's all right," he went on. "I've known this was coming. After you left—for your apprenticeship—She came to me, and gave me a year."

"Who?"

"She—whose name you bear. The Raven."

Nemain stared at him, stunned into silence.

"She was very beautiful," he added, "and very kind. She's always been good to us—looking after you—giving me a better place—than I deserved. She promised—I would be here—as long as you needed me—and then 'thrice death'—would come as a friend."

"It won't be thrice," said Nemain. "It won't even be once." Yet even as she spoke, she recalled that she *had* seen Tynan twice, already, as one dying.

He smiled. "It's all right," he repeated. "I'm ready—now that you don't need me—anymore. You're just as I always wished you to be—strong—brave—wise—a *caillagh* in the making. It's so much less than you should have had—but still—"

He stopped, overcome by a violent spasm of coughing. "I'm so sorry, *inneen*."

"Don't talk anymore," said Nemain anxiously.

"I'm sorry," he repeated firmly, "for denying you—what you should have had. You've no idea—what your birthright—should have been."

His breath was coming shorter, rattling in his throat. For a moment he managed to raise himself on one elbow, looking past Nemain at something only he could see, and smiled faintly. Then he fell back and was still.

The next few days were a nightmarish blur to Nemain. She avoided Monessa, who was sorry about the farrier's death but didn't know why Nemain should take it so hard. She could not relieve her feelings in music; she doubted she would ever be able to take up her fiddle again. At night she clung to Moddey, who licked the tears from her face and slept with one paw laid protectively on her, like Béira with an oversized pup.

It seemed such a waste, after so many years of believing herself quite alone in the world—unconnected to anyone by blood—to discover that she *was* connected to someone, only to lose him. She railed at herself for her own foolishness in not having seen the truth sooner. She hated Tynan's family—*her* family, whoever they were—for casting him out and forcing him to keep his identity a secret from her. And she hated Tynan, too, for breaking his vows and letting himself die. How had he done it? *Why* had he done it? And could she have stopped him if she had known?

Some of her questions were answered by Lord Winworth. On the day of Tynan's burial, he called her into his presence chamber.

"How are you?" he asked. His eyes were keenly sympathetic.

She shrugged. "Well enough."

"I would have told you long ago," he said, "but it was his express wish that you not be told. I always said you'd figure it out eventually, being such a clever girl."

She managed a wan smile. "Not so clever, it seems."

"Oh? So someone told you after all?"

"Yes and no." She hesitated, not sure how to explain, then gave an odd little laugh—partly a sob—at how very Northern that answer was.

"I suppose you think he was very heartless in not telling you."

"I don't know what to think."

"Then let me explain, on his behalf, as best I can. Sit down."

She obeyed, folding her gloved hands on her lap.

"It certainly *was* heartless of his family to exact those vows from him, in addition to casting him out," said Lord Winworth. "As much as I respect Northerners, I cannot fathom treating a son in that manner. But it's the custom in Gwehara, when a man gets a child out of wedlock—" He stopped abruptly and looked at her. "I'm sorry, I keep forgetting how young you are."

"I'm studying to be an apothecary," she reminded him. "I know how such things happen."

"Ahem! Well, in Tynan's case, his family would have been more lenient if the woman in question had not been an Outlander. He would have married her, and that would have been that. But intermarriage between Outlanders and the ancient clans of Gwehara is strictly forbidden. So they disowned him, and you, at one stroke. They made him promise to give you up, never acknowledge you as his own, and never act as a father to you.

"He did his best to obey. He left the Outland woman with her own people and came here to the Lowland, where no one knew of his disgrace. He didn't expect her to follow him. But she did—alone and pregnant, all the way here. And then you were born."

"And he gave me up to you."

Lord Winworth nodded. "On his own terms: You were to be my foster-daughter, an orphan I took in on charity, and he would repay me by working as my farrier, with only the smallest recompense on which to live. You've seen his quarters. He insisted that was all he needed, and whatever more he earned should be laid aside for you."

Nemain was shaking her head. "I don't understand. You mean he lived that way on purpose?"

"I didn't understand it either," said Lord Winworth ruefully. "I would have been happy to take you in without such sacrifice on his part. I told him vows that went against flesh and blood were better broken than kept. But no; he told me he'd sworn on his life, and that you were better off not knowing his 'shame,' as he called it.

"So he provided for you, in his way, and looked after you as best he could. He even gave you your name. All that a father without a father's rights could do, he did for you—keeping his vows in letter, if not in spirit."

"That explains a lot," Nemain murmured.

"As to your inheritance," Lord Winworth continued, "it isn't much. Five hundred gold staters, set aside from his wages, and his books. The money will be kept for you for some years yet, but I suppose you'd like to have the books?"

She nodded, somewhat in shock. Five hundred gold staters!—not much to Lord Winworth, to be sure, but twelve years' worth of hard work and scrimping for Tynan. She could not bear to think of taking it.

"Now, will you be going back to your mistress straightaway? Or would you prefer to stay here for a while?"

"Straightaway, I should think."

"Ah, well, perhaps that's best. There's nothing like work to ease sorrow." He smiled. "But you're welcome here at any time, Nemain. I hope you know that."

She thanked him mechanically.

"And don't judge Tynan too harshly," he added. "He was raised differently than I, but we had one thing in common: there's nothing we wouldn't do for our daughters."

⊷⊶

Rhiannon took the news of Tynan's death calmly, and she refrained from talking about it or offering sympathy, for which Nemain was grateful. Outwardly she seemed not affected by it at all, until the day Nemain found her examining one of Tynan's books. She was turning the pages with oddly reverent hands and weeping silently, with an expression so distorted by pain that Nemain made an involuntary sound of alarm.

"I'm sorry," said Rhiannon, putting the book down and wiping the tears from her face. "They're yours; I shouldn't have ..."

"No, it's fine," Nemain hastened to assure her. "That's why I put them on the shelves. I can't read them, after all. But you're welcome to."

"He loved those books so," Rhiannon said quietly. "I often saw him reading them. I can see him now, as he once was—oh, he was splendid. So handsome, kind, gifted ... a very prince."

"You loved him, didn't you?"

"We all did. We had such hopes for him—he had such a bright future—and he threw it all away for—"

Nemain stiffened slightly, and Rhiannon abruptly shut her mouth. For a moment they faced each other—the bitterly grieving woman who had loved Tynan, and the young girl looking coolly back at her with Tynan's eyes—each sensing that the future of their relationship depended on how they handled this moment. Then Rhiannon bowed her head to Nemain, in silent concession to things that must not be spoken of, and set about preparing their midday meal. It was clear that the conversation was over.

"Do you want any help?" asked Nemain, relieved that there would be no quarrel. She really didn't want to quarrel with Rhiannon. But she knew that if Rhiannon had dared to say one word against either her father or her poor, unknown Outland mother, she, Nemain, would have walked out the door and never returned. She had not known she possessed such passionate loyalty, but there it was.

"No, thank you. Why don't you work on the Dark Sayings."

Nemain obediently opened up that tome but could not keep her mind on the arcane phrases. She thought of Tynan, who had once been a promising, much-loved youth, and of Rhiannon—"Spindle" of old—who had been "little more than a child" to him, but had loved him. Nemain suddenly felt as sorry for Rhiannon as she had been ready to do battle with her just a moment ago. Probably Tynan had never known of Rhiannon's love. Or had he suspected it? Was that why he had looked troubled when he spoke of her?

Oh, there was so much she would never know about him. Even his speech on his deathbed—when there was surely no more need to keep secrets—had been mysterious. What had he meant when he said, "I've been telling you since you were born"? ... And then, as her eyes scanned the Dark Sayings in front of her, understanding came.

Inneen. Why had it never occurred to her that her nickname, like so many Northern words, might have more than one meaning?

"What does *inneen* mean?" she asked Rhiannon, as if it were just another Northern word she had picked up from the pages.

"It means 'daughter,'" said Rhiannon, not looking up from the pot of soup she was stirring.

"Oh." A pause. "I thought it just meant 'little girl.'"

"Well, it means that too."

Nemain smiled sadly. "Of course it does."

Chapter 9

As LORD WINWORTH had predicted, Nemain did find that hard work eased sorrow. She threw herself into her studies, and with time she found it easier to laugh—to sleep at night—even to play her fiddle again. But Tynan's death had left a pain at her heart, like a scar that ached in rainy weather, that she could sometimes forget but that would never be wholly gone.

She thought a great deal about his dying words, especially about the Raven. So, She had a fair and kindly, as well as a fearsome aspect; She had shown Tynan mercy when his family had shown none, and if She could not lift his death sentence, at least She had made it somewhat easier for him. It was all right, he had said, now that Nemain didn't need him anymore—but didn't she? She knew now that she had needed Tynan all her life, without knowing it, and was not at all sure she could do without him now. If only the Raven would appear to *her!*—but she wasn't sure she really wanted that, either.

Outwardly she was not much changed: a little more sober and quiet, a little more withdrawn. But few would have noticed that, and fewer would have guessed at her deep unhappiness. Monessa did not; Lord Winworth, if he did, left her alone. Only Swayne—who rarely spoke to her at all these days for fear of provoking Lady Bronwyn—reached out to her, and only once, in passing, during one of her visits to Briarvale.

"Hey, I'm sorry about Tynan," he said in a low voice. "I know we weren't supposed to know, but—well, I sort of figured. Anyway."

He patted her arm and quickly walked away just as Lady Bronwyn came up the corridor. She gave Nemain a sharp, questioning look, but Nemain brushed past her, barely noticing. Her eyes filled with tears of mingled pain and gratitude.

She hated to be reminded of Tynan's death—hated to have her hard-won composure disturbed in that fashion—but she was a little glad, all the same, that someone cared enough to say *something*. And she was glad it was Swayne.

With Tynan gone, she began to realize just how few and superficial were the friendships in her life. Lord Winworth was an ally, but she was under no illusions about him; he was Monessa's father, not hers, and so far above her that she could never relate to or confide in him. Master Ives was a friend—at least she thought of him as such; he had known her from childhood, and he prized her quick wit and intelligence. But the following spring, to her surprise and hurt, he left Briarvale without warning.

"Just like that?" Nemain said in disbelief. "He's been gone a whole fortnight, and no one told me?"

"Father dismissed him. He says I have all the education I need." Monessa shrugged. "I'm sorry, dear. If I'd known it would distress you, I'd have asked Father to keep him on. But he wasn't your tutor anymore, so I didn't think …"

Nemain went straight to the presence chamber and rapped on the door. Lord Winworth had scarcely said "Enter" before she strode in and demanded, "Why have you dismissed Master Ives?"

"He asked me to," said Lord Winworth, his pen suspended above some document.

"Oh." She frowned. "Monessa said—"

"What I told her."

"But why did he ask to be dismissed?"

Lord Winworth looked at her for a long moment before replying. "He'd been in rather low spirits since you went away. There was little for him to do here; Monessa has neither the need nor the inclination for much book learning, and you'd found a new teacher. We agreed a change of scene would do him good."

"But why didn't he even say goodbye? He could have waited till my next visit, or—"

"Because *I* asked him not to."

Nemain stared at him, feeling a nasty, confused sense of guilt. He lifted a hand to keep her from protesting. "Now, now, I know you've done nothing wrong. I'm not

Bronwyn. But I'm no fool, either. A man of his age does not form a connection with a girl of yours. If he's not your tutor, he should be nothing to you."

"But—oh, it was never like *that!*" Her nasty sense of guilt became an even nastier sense of indignation. "You can't think he would even *want* to—well, really! I mean, look!"

She pulled off one of her gloves.

Lord Winworth looked pained. "Even so. Now do stop making a scene. I'm sorry you're upset, but believe me, it's better this way."

Nemain wanted to ask him how it was better, but she gritted her teeth and put her glove back on, blinking away a few tears. Despite her Northern and Outland blood, she was still Lowland-bred, and shared all the Lowlander's distaste for "making a scene." Especially in front of Lord Winworth.

"If it helps," he said hesitantly, as if against his better judgment, "he left you some books. They're on the table in the schoolroom."

He bent his head over the papers on his desk, signaling that the conversation was at an end.

As Nemain entered the schoolroom and saw the little pile of books on the table, her mouth fell open in shock. Why, these were her favorites from Master Ives's collection: a treatise on music, another on philosophy, and several volumes of poetry. How dear of him!—and yet it saddened her, for she knew he loved them at least as well as she did. If he would make a gesture like this for her, couldn't he have been bothered to say goodbye?

For a moment she wondered if Lord Winworth was right—if there really was something inappropriate in Master Ives's fondness for her. Then she looked down at her gloved hands and dismissed the thought. Of course not, she told herself. He had never had any intentions of *that* sort. What man would, for heaven's sake? In leaving her these books, he was just being nice. He had always been nice.

Still, she wept as she gathered them up. There went another friend out of her life—a kind heart and a living mind that was akin to hers, that had even helped shape hers. No number of books could replace that.

Chapter 10

TWO MORE YEARS went by: busy years, filled with discovery ... and yet curiously empty. Or so it seemed to Nemain, who spent her days studying texts and assisting Rhiannon, and her nights either in the dead sleep of exhaustion or in discontented wakefulness.

She had acquired Rhiannon's habit of drinking strong tea at all hours, and that may have accounted for her frequent insomnia—that and, perhaps, adolescence. By age fifteen she was fully grown, almost as tall as Rhiannon, and considerably stouter: a full-fleshed, long-limbed, Northern-built woman, and rather self-conscious about it.

"*Ommijys*," Rhiannon said. "You're strong, and your health is good. That's all that matters. Stop taking the tea, though, if it robs you of sleep." But Nemain didn't want to.

She wondered sometimes about Rhiannon's own health. Rhiannon was naturally thin—the nickname "Spindle" was apt if somewhat cruel—but she had grown thinner of late, and her strength seemed to be dwindling. Nemain tried to avoid seeing these things; she told herself that Tynan's death had made her morbid, looking for fey symptoms that weren't there. But she worried nonetheless, especially on nights when she couldn't sleep. If Rhiannon was ill, what was ailing her? (Her only answer to inquiry was "I'm well enough.") If she took a turn for the worse, would Nemain know what to do?

And she was lonely—oh, horribly lonely. She had thought, as a child, that she knew what loneliness was; but at least in childhood her friendships, though few, were uncomplicated. She had not known this restless yearning for companionship (specifically, male companionship—the only male creature close to her was Moddey). And she had not had to stifle her jealousy and resentment of one of the few friends she had.

For Monessa had grown up, too—grown into the beauty everyone had known she would be, with her luminous skin, delicate bones, silken hair and blue, blue eyes. Though not tall, she was well-proportioned and carried herself with a grace that made Nemain feel like a plodding carthorse beside her. She had acquired a lady's maid to dress her hair and lace her into her fine gowns, and a retinue of ladies-in-waiting, who, as far as Nemain could tell, did nothing but fuss and gossip and squeal all day long. Or, worse yet, attempt to sing or play instruments.

Visits to Briarvale were tedious torments now, but Nemain kept going for two reasons. One was Monessa's continued kindness in inviting her. And the other was Swayne, who usually came in person to relay the invitation.

Swayne was about nineteen now, old enough to be courting, but so far Nemain had not heard his name paired with any girl's. She was too well-bred to ask him about it and too proud to ask anyone in the village. But as he was still friendly towards her—neither more nor less than he had ever been—she decided that as long as he remained unattached, she might as well hope.

And hope, and dream, she did incessantly. Swayne's occasional calls at the cottage were the highlight of her days. He always brought something nice, in Monessa's name—some fruit or sugared almonds—and always asked her to play the fiddle, which she did gladly. And Rhiannon (so blessedly unlike Lady Bronwyn in every way!) never even pretended to chaperone. She would bow politely and withdraw at once, giving them a few cherished minutes of private conversation. For, alas, Swayne never stayed longer than a few minutes.

Nemain knew quite well she was being a fool, but she took care not to act the part, at least. She never pressed him to stay longer than he wished, never went out of her way to encounter him or ask about him, never let on by word or look that she was in love with him. She had learned at an early age to hide her feelings; life and Lady Bronwyn had taught her that kindness and affection were privileges, not rights, for the likes of her. She felt she would die of shame if Swayne ever found out just how badly she wanted *his* affection, for he would almost certainly reject her. Almost.

But for the sake of that "almost," she kept going to Briarvale. And she dreamed of the day when Rhiannon would discover a cure for her hands.

→▶■◉ ◉■◀←

On one of her visits to Briarvale, her hopes received a crushing blow. She heard Swayne's voice in a part of the castle where he rarely went—one of the shadowy, out-of-the-way passages that she knew well—and she headed over, thinking to say hello. Perhaps, happy thought, he was looking for her! Then she stopped cold when she heard Monessa's voice as well.

Cautiously she peered around the corner of the passage. Swayne was holding Monessa's hand, and his expression was both eager and aggrieved. Monessa's face was turned away.

"Can you not at least ask him?" he said.

"I can't. I can't." Monessa sounded as if she were crying. "It's been arranged since I was a child. If we backed out of it now—"

"Don't you think he'll understand? I know your happiness means everything to him—as it does to me."

"But suppose he doesn't? You'll be thrown out without a copper stater to your name, and then what will become of you? Of your family?"

Swayne hesitated, and Nemain noticed detachedly that his element, like Monessa's, was water. It showed in his tender mouth and pleading, beautiful eyes, which seemed on the verge of tears; it sounded in his voice, ever so soft and gentle despite his strong emotion. But he did not have the indecisiveness associated with water, flowing every which way. No; as he looked into Monessa's eyes, Nemain saw water's steadfastness—the patience and determination to erode any obstacle in his way, even if it took years.

"I'll make him understand," he said. "Whatever it takes, however long it takes, I'll prove myself to him. I promise."

With a sob, Monessa pulled away from him and ran right past Nemain without seeing her. After a minute Swayne left as well, with only a glance in Nemain's direction, barely registering that she was there. She stayed behind, trying to face this unwelcome revelation.

As yet she did not feel pain—only a dull emptiness, and a sense of wonder that she had not seen this coming. Of course Swayne and Monessa were in love. How could she have ever imagined it might turn out otherwise? No girl could help loving Swayne, and Monessa would steal the heart of any young man with eyesight. Never mind that she was already betrothed and would someday be mistress of the grandest estate in the North Country. Never mind that Swayne's heart would never be of any use to her—for of course his suit was hopeless. ("There's nothing we wouldn't do for our daughters," Lord Winworth had said once; but a man who so prized his daughter would hardly give her away to his squire!) And never mind that Monessa already had everything else Nemain had ever wanted. Why shouldn't she have that, too?

Ah, now there was pain.

She left Briarvale that afternoon, cutting her visit short. Monessa seemed vaguely sorry to see her go, but she wouldn't lack for company, surrounded by gabbling ladies-in-waiting. For a moment Nemain felt an unreasonable sense of hurt that Monessa had never spoken to her about her feelings for Swayne and clearly wasn't about to. Weren't they best friends? Didn't best friends talk about such things? But even she knew that was unfair. After all, she hadn't exactly confided much in Monessa over the past few years—and certainly not her own feelings about Swayne. No, their friendship had already worn thin, and it was she who had let it happen.

Another friend—two friends—lost to her.

She sat down in the woods to have a cry before heading back to the cottage. Moddey sat beside her, sympathizing heartily if inarticulately. Good old Moddey! He did not know or care what a fool she had been. The Good Folk willing, no one would ever know.

It was twilight by the time Nemain was sufficiently composed to return home. Rhiannon was sitting at the table, meditating. She was dressed in the black robe, which she only wore during meditation (or for the rare, eccentric customer who actually wanted the services of a witch rather than an apothecary). In front of her were a candle, a stick of incense, and a bowl filled with pebbles and water.

"Sorry," Nemain whispered, tiptoeing past her.

Rhiannon grunted and got up. As she took the candle and lit two others with it, Nemain noted with unease that she was moving very slowly. "You're back early."

"Yes. I think I've done with Briarvale."

"Oh?"

Something in her voice told Nemain that *she,* at least, had seen this coming.

"You already know, don't you?"

"Know what?"

"About Swayne."

"That you're in love with him?" Rhiannon gave her a shrewd look. "Or that he's in love with that little friend of yours? Both are fairly obvious."

"Does *he* know?" Her voice cracked.

"Of course not. He's a nice lad, but a bit thick, I'm thinking."

"Why didn't you tell me that they—? Why didn't you stop me from being stupid?"

"You wouldn't have listened," said Rhiannon. "And you weren't so very stupid. You've behaved quite well on the whole."

"Yes," said Nemain glumly, sinking into a chair. "I'm nothing if not well-behaved."

Rhiannon chuckled. "So you've found out, and you've done with the Briarvale folk. What now?"

"What do you mean?"

"What are you going to do about it?"

"What can I do about it? They're in love. I can't very well undo that."

"My dear," said Rhiannon with a mysterious smile, "it hasn't even occurred to you—has it?—that you are in a position of power here."

Nemain's eyes widened.

"All you have to do is go to Lord Winworth with whatever tale you care to tell. He knows you for an honest girl. He'll believe anything you say."

She shook her head. "That would ruin Swayne."

"It would serve him right, *nee shen myr t'eh?*"—Is that not so?—"And young Lady Monessa, too. I can't help thinking, little sister, Fate hasn't dealt quite squarely with you two."

As Rhiannon spoke, Nemain felt the repressed anger and malice of years welling up within her. Fate hadn't dealt squarely? Talk of understatement! Her gloved hands clenched in her lap. But even then she could not muster enough ill-will to make anyone else suffer as she was suffering, especially two people who had always been kind to her.

"I won't do that. They've been good friends to me. And they'll have enough grief from this without my help."

Rhiannon's face softened, and Nemain suddenly had the feeling that she had just passed a test. "You're a good girl," said Rhiannon. "But you've done with them, all the same?"

Nemain nodded. "To spare myself, not to punish them."

"Well, take all the time you need, little sister. But don't burn any bridges just yet. One of these days, you may want to go back to Briarvale after all."

"Why should I?" A dreadful thought occurred to her. "You *are* well, Caillagh, aren't you? Not—er—fey, or anything like that?"

"You needn't worry about me."

"But you're not strong. You should have a rest."

"Actually …" She eased back into her chair and clasped her hands under her chin. "I've been thinking about an *immram*."

Nemain looked at her in puzzlement and some alarm. An *immram* was a ceremonial journey, a pilgrimage of sorts, although the destination mattered less than the journey itself. Indeed, on a proper *immram,* you set out with no specific destination in mind, trusting in the Good Folk to provide for your needs and guide you to wherever you were meant to end up. (Presumably, when you arrived at your journey's end, you'd know it.) But any journey could be an *immram* if undertaken with an eye of faith and a readiness to accept whatever circumstances you found yourself in—even if it meant never going home again. If Rhiannon was considering such a venture, some grave matter must be at hand.

"But you'll need all your strength for that."

"Not for me. For you."

Now Nemain turned very pale. An *immram*, she knew, was an important part of a *caillagh*'s education—the step that would qualify her for the black robe—but she had comforted herself with the assumption that it was a long way off yet. The very thought of setting off into the unknown, throwing herself completely on the mercy of the Good Folk, was beyond terrifying.

"I can't! I'm nowhere near ready."

"I'll be the judge of that. And no, you're not ready. But you will be before long."

Before Nemain could say anything else, Rhiannon dismissed her with a wave. "Now get yourself some supper. And over the next little while, be thinking about your direction."

"My direction?"

"The direction in which you want to start your *immram*. Also think about what you want to take with you. Remember: only what you can't bear to part with, and only as much as you can carry."

She gave a hollow laugh. "How can I possibly decide that?"

But Rhiannon had already lapsed back into meditation.

Nemain ate in distracted silence and then sat up half the night, alternately crying over Swayne, worrying about the *immram*, and trying to take her mind off both by reading. When she finally crawled into bed to get what sleep she could after such a day, it occurred to her that Rhiannon had not really answered the question about her health at all.

Chapter 11

FOR THE NEXT several months Rhiannon said nothing more about an *immram,* and Nemain dared not bring it up. But she thought of little else. She pored obsessively over texts she had already studied many times, wrestled anew with the Dark Sayings (many of which she heartily hated at this point), and was constantly on the lookout for clues as to whatever she was supposed to know by now. For Rhiannon *must* be mistaken about her being almost ready for an *immram.* She had never felt less ready for anything in her life.

She even studied her own palm, which she had thus far avoided doing, as she had hoped that her hands would eventually have a new form and thus new lines. But since she had no idea if Rhiannon was any nearer to a cure or not—and, as she admitted to herself, there might never be one—she examined the lines that Fate had given her and found them illegible. They were fractured, incoherent, and strangely resistant to scrutiny; as she stretched out her hands to see them properly, she opened a number of tiny cracks in her skin. Rhiannon gave her a salve for her hands but offered no advice on how to read them.

Rhiannon, too, was preoccupied these days. She spent a great deal of time shut away in meditation or poring over texts and spells of her own, leaving Nemain to look after customers. And while Nemain was quite capable of treating minor injuries and prescribing herbs for simple complaints, it was a cheerless business, for the villagers still looked at her with deep distrust and could hardly bring themselves to speak civilly to her. She bore it quietly, not wanting to hurt business for Rhiannon, and not wanting Rhiannon to think she wasn't equal to the work. But she felt hurt and frustrated nonetheless; and the more time Rhiannon spent absorbed in her own mysterious pursuit, giving only the most evasive answers to questions, the more Nemain struggled and despaired in se-cret. It was as if they were both fighting a battle—though perhaps not the same one—against time.

⇥⇤

On Midsummer Eve she went into the village on an errand. She ought to have known better, but she had never been in the village during a solstice festival; Lord Winworth had never allowed her or Monessa to go. And for a solitary *cail-lagh,* the solstices were times of quiet reflection and devotion, not revelry. So she was unprepared for the drunken carousing taking place on the village green.

Her instinct was to slip away quickly before anyone noticed her. She had never forgotten the boys who had taken away her gloves and beaten her all those years before, and she trembled to think what a drunken man or group of them might do. But for the moment at least, no one seemed inclined to violence. Women as well as men were laughing, dancing, singing, sprawled in various postures and stages of consciousness. It looked rather dreadful to Nemain's sen-sibilities, but she acknowledged that it also looked like a good time.

She watched from the shadows with aloof curiosity, wondering how these people could enjoy themselves with such abandon (especially knowing how they would feel in the morning!) and why she did not feel remotely tempted to join them. What made her so different from them? Was it her blood, her upbringing, her unconventional education? Or was it some inherent weirdness of her char-acter, a deformity like her hands, that imposed a barrier between her and people of any sort? She folded her arms and shivered in the warm evening air, feeling very sorry for herself.

What did it take to be ready for an *immram?* If it was thorough disgust with one's current situation, Nemain thought that she was pretty well there after all.

She felt a touch on her arm and whirled around, instantly on the defensive, to see Swayne standing there laughing.

"I barely touched you! What's the matter?"

"Nothing." Her face reddened deeply.

To her delight, and somewhat to her terror, he put his hands on her waist and drew her closer. She realized then that he, too, had been drinking. Rather heavily.

"It's good to see you," he said. "We've missed you at Briarvale. What have you been doing with yourself?"

"Oh …" She had difficulty finding words. "I've been busy."

"Well, tell that old harridan to give you a holiday."

She laughed. "Don't call her that."

"Sorry. I don't know where my manners have gone. Anyway, you must come see us again soon."

He smiled as he spoke, and there was a teasing light in his dark eyes. But Nemain, looking into them, also saw a deep sadness, a hunger and frustration that matched her own. She knew he did not want her or anyone to see these things, but there they were, as plain as day to a *caillagh*'s eye. And it did not take a *caillagh* to guess at the cause of his distress.

"How is—?" She intended to say "How is Lady Monessa?" but before she could finish, Swayne's mouth was suddenly on hers.

For a moment she was wonderfully happy. She forgot about her loneliness and discouragement, her anxiety over Rhiannon and the *immram*—forgot all vexing and complicated things. In that moment everything was pure, simple, lovely; when their eyes met again, she was no longer a *caillagh* in training or even a well-bred young lady, but an eager girl who would have followed him anywhere, said yes to anything.

The change that came over Swayne, however, was somewhat different. He blinked, and his hands dropped from her waist. His eyes were now furtive, troubled—repulsed? She could not tell.

He gave her a fraternal pat on the shoulder. "Have a good night," he said, and walked away.

"I have what you want," said Rhiannon as Nemain walked in the door.

Oh, I don't think you do, thought Nemain miserably. She sat down to pet Moddey, who flung himself at her as if she had been gone for ages. "What's that?"

Rhiannon pointed to a small bottle on the windowsill, gleaming darkly in the half-light. "It needs time to steep, but it'll be ready by the next full moon. By which point, I think, you'll be ready for a visit to Briarvale."

Nemain looked from her to the bottle, hardly daring to hope. "What will it do?"

"Put a few drops on a young man's pillow under the full moon, and when he wakes up in the morning, he'll love you and none other."

Nemain went over and reverently took the bottle in her gloved hands. Such a little thing ... and yet it held the fruition of all her hopes. The power to recapture, for good and all, that beautiful moment that had ended so cruelly earlier. Carefully she set it down.

She had a crazy impulse to embrace Rhiannon, but neither of them was the embracing type. So she merely gazed at her, her great shining eyes filled with a gratitude she could not express.

"Is this what you've been so secretive about? Why could you not tell me?"

"Not just this." Rhiannon looked away. "In what I have been trying to do—what I promised you—I've failed thus far. But I can offer you this." She smiled ruefully. "I am bound to help you in any way I can."

"Oh, it doesn't matter! *This* is enough."

"You care for him that much?" There was an odd, strained note in her voice. "So much that you don't mind living the rest of your life with *that*"—gesturing at Nemain's hands—"as long as you can have him?"

"Yes." She was surprised there could be any doubt of it. What did it matter what her hands looked like if Swayne loved her? What did anything else matter?

Rhiannon gave a laugh that sounded like a sob. "Have it your way, little sister. May it truly be enough."

—◦═◉ ◉═◦—

Accordingly, she prepared to return to Briarvale at the next full moon. Rhiannon had warned her that the potion would not keep for much longer. Nevertheless, as she took in Rhiannon's pallor and slow movements—the wasted appearance of her once strong, sinewy hands and arms—she changed her mind.

"I can't leave you."

Rhiannon settled into her chair with a grunt. "*Mollaght*, girl! I've told you I'm not fey."

"You're not well!"

"I promise you I'll be alive when you get back," she said dryly. "Do you really want to miss this chance?"

Nemain looked at the bottle and bit her lip. Her concern for Rhiannon was not the only thing holding her back.

"I don't know," she said. "Now that it comes to it … I mean, yes, I want him—but I don't know if I want him *this* way."

"You were sure enough before. What's changed?"

"Is it right? When you were making this potion, did *you* feel right about it?"

Rhiannon shrugged. "Think of it this way. Is he happy, pining for wee Lady Monessa?"

"No."

"Do you intend to make him happy?"

"Of course."

"Then you're doing him a favor. *Nee shen myr t'eh?*"

As Nemain considered this, Rhiannon added softly, "Are not two happy people better than three unhappy ones? As for Lady Monessa, she can't be with him anyway. So who will be any worse off for this?"

"No one, I suppose."

Rhiannon nodded. "Now go. I'll look after Moddey for you." Hearing his name, Moddey whined as if in protest.

Nemain made it to the door and again hesitated. "What about the *immram?*"

"What about it?"

"Won't this complicate things?"

Rhiannon made an impatient gesture. "We'll talk about it later. See if your mind has any more changing to do."

Back at Briarvale, Monessa greeted her warmly. "Goodness, how long has it been? You really must come out more often!"

"I've been busy." Nemain smiled, ignoring a tiny twinge of guilt.

She let Monessa lead her to what had become "the ladies' wing" of the castle, where the ladies-in-waiting idled away their time under the pretense of needle-point and music, and Lady Bronwyn kept watch over all their doings. The latter cast a baleful glance at Nemain as she entered, but said nothing. Nemain in turn looked coolly through Lady Bronwyn as if she weren't there.

She spent the afternoon chatting with Monessa whenever she could, and sitting in patient silence through the ladies' inane nattering. At supper she had no appetite, which was just as well, as she had to share a trencher and dipping bowl with one of the ladies and didn't feel up to exposing her hands. All the while she kept an eye on the lowering sun through the western windows.

"Poor dear," said Monessa in a low voice as they filed back to her rooms. "Did you get enough to eat?"

"Yes, thank you." Then, snatching at the opportunity, "Will you excuse me for a bit?"

"Of course."

Outside the ladies' wing, she heaved a sigh of relief. Lady Bronwyn would not follow her; Lord Winworth was probably in his presence chamber—yes, she could hear his voice behind the closed door, and Swayne's as well. But there was still the possibility of a servant passing by. She tried to look casual so that if anyone did pass, she could pretend to be on her way back from the privy or something.

When the sun had set and the moon was on the rise, she slipped into Swayne's room and took out the bottle of potion with trembling fingers. Uncorked, it released a mossy, woodsy odor, pungent but not unpleasant. She could not guess what herbs were in it.

Again she hesitated.

Was love reducible to this? A full moon, a few drops of potion—was that really all it took to bind a living heart to hers? Even if it was, who had the right to exercise such power? Not she, surely.

Still, that kiss ... it had felt so good. So right.

She heard footsteps coming and knew she had better decide quickly. In an agony of conscience, she dropped the potion back into her pocket and left the room just before Swayne entered it.

Could he have missed seeing her? She shrank against the wall of the corridor, her heart pounding. He stopped, sniffed the air, looked around in apparent puzzlement, and then closed the door behind him.

He hadn't seen her. She sighed again, this time with perverse disappointment.

No longer caring if anyone else saw her, she went out to the courtyard and emptied the bottle onto the cobblestones. That kiss hadn't been real anyway, she told herself; it was wine that had made him kiss her. And what was this potion but merely a stronger wine? Still, she felt as if she were watching her own heart's blood trickle away.

She felt ashamed, too, though she was sure she had done the right thing. Ashamed for getting her hopes up in the first place, for the pains Rhiannon had taken to help her, and for the fact that no one would see any benefit from her sacrifice. Swayne was still free to love Monessa, for all the good it would do him. Monessa was still bound in betrothal to another man. Rhiannon would be disappointed, perhaps angry. And she, Nemain, did not even have anyone to pat her on the back and say, "Well, at least you did the right thing." *Had* she done the right thing after all?

If only Tynan were alive! He would have sympathized; he had certainly understood how hard it was to fight the inclination of one's heart. And something told her he would have also agreed with her conscience. He had been proud of her for becoming a *caillagh,* and surely a *caillagh* ought to be above stealing anything, including love.

Stealing. That was it; that was why she could not use the potion. Her heart, ahead of her mind, had recognized it as an act of theft. So why hadn't Rhiannon viewed it as such? The awful thought crossed her mind that perhaps Rhiannon could not be trusted. Oh, was there no bright side to any of this? No one to whom she could turn for either guidance or comfort?

"Help me," she sobbed—not addressing anyone, and of course not expecting an answer. But curiously, she began to feel a little better. A warming, steadying influence stole into her veins, quieting her sobs, enfolding her heart like a handclasp. She closed her eyes and listened to the crickets, sensed the twilight deepening around her.

Then, unmistakably, she heard the caw of a raven.

Her eyes flew open. It was just a raven—not *the* Raven—perched on the garden wall. But in her current state of mind, desperate for help and alert to signs from anywhere, she watched it carefully. It gave her a passing glance, uttered another caw, and then flew away, heading north.

A raven flying north. Was that an answer? Certainly it was as cryptic and unhelpful as any Dark Saying. She considered it.

What lay to the north? The North Country, of course: Tynan's country and Rhiannon's. It was also her own, in a way, and not just by blood. In the North Country were people who spoke two languages—one that was her own and one that was rich and mysterious, which she could not speak but which she loved. There were people who believed in the Good Folk and the Three Worlds; people to whom the black robe of the *caillagh* was a mark of high honor. If there was anywhere she could hope to find greater understanding—acceptance—love—surely it was there. ...

"Nemain?" Monessa was behind her. "Are you all right?"

"Oh. Yes." She hastily wiped her eyes and turned around. "I just came out to see the moon."

She followed Monessa back into the castle, feeling a sense of peace beneath her sorrow. Only a few more days at Briarvale—the last, she hoped, she would ever spend here—and then when she returned home, she would tell Rhiannon she was ready for the *immram*.

Chapter 12

NEMAIN CAME HOME to find Rhiannon slumped at the table, her head in her hands. She had not been meditating—no incense or candles were lit—and the shutters were closed, leaving the cottage in darkness. At her feet Moddey and Béira whined nervously, unheeded.

"Rhiannon!" Nemain hurried to her side. "What's wrong?"

Rhiannon started as if from sleep. She lifted her head and smiled faintly. "Did you just call me by name?"

"Well, you gave me a fright!" She scrutinized Rhiannon's white face and dark-circled eyes. "You're worse off than before. Have you even eaten today?"

"First things first. How did it go?"

"No, supper first. Eat, and convince me you're not dying, and then I'll tell you."

Rhiannon laughed softly and laid her head on the tabletop. After she had laboriously consumed what Nemain put in front of her—some bread, cheese, and an egg cooked in butter—she asked again, "How did it go?"

Nemain sighed as she sat down. "I couldn't do it."

"I know."

"Then why did you ask! You knew all along, didn't you?"

She nodded with another small smile.

"Was it a test? Just to see what I'd do with it?"

"It was." Rhiannon pushed her dish away. "And you passed—but I failed."

"What do you mean? There's no harm done."

She gave a short, bitter laugh. "I knew you wouldn't do it, little sister, but I rather hoped you would, all the same. I thought that if I could not give you what

I owed you, I could at least give you your heart's desire, and then I might have peace. But you didn't take it, so …"

"Caillagh, please don't think you owe me anything," Nemain said earnestly. "I know you promised to help me with my hands, and you tried. It's all right."

Rhiannon winced. "Now then, what about the *immram*? Have you decided which way you want to go?"

"North."

"Why north?"

Nemain told her about the raven that she had taken for a sign. As Rhiannon listened, a frown gradually darkened her features.

"Are you going to look for your father's people?"

"No, I'm not going to Gwehara."

"If your path should lead you there …"

"I can't forgive them for what they did to him."

Rhiannon winced again.

"Where do you hurt?" Nemain asked in concern.

She shook her head. "I'm just surprised you chose north. In *immrama*, you know, directions are not just directions; they have symbolic meaning. I should have thought your affinity lay with the west or the south. You know the text: 'In the west, learning; in the south, music …' "

" 'In the east, treasure; and in the north, battle,' " Nemain finished. "But you know, sometimes 'battle' in that passage is rendered 'ancient lore.' And that does sound like me. I suppose the west represents one kind of learning—Master Ives's kind—but the north represents the kind I want."

Rhiannon gazed at her for a moment. In her eyes Nemain saw pride, fondness, and above all an inexpressible sorrow.

"For whatever you hope to gain up North, you'll have to do battle all the same," she said. "Do you think Northerners will treat you any better than Lowlanders?"

"Won't they?"

"Think, my dear. How is every oath, every contract sealed in the North Country?"

Nemain looked down at her gloved hands, knowing where this was going. "With a handclasp."

"And we take our oaths very seriously. We believe in signs and omens. How do you expect to be received by people who place such significance on hands? The very fact that you wear gloves all the time would be suspect. As for love—"

"Who speaks of love?" cried Nemain.

"You may not speak of it, but I know you want it. If love is what you hope to find, remember that marriage, too, is a contract, and taken more seriously than any other. No Northman would take the hand of one marked as you are."

In the silence that followed, Nemain began to weep.

"I don't tell you these things to hurt you," said Rhiannon in a gentler tone. "I hoped I would never have to. But you have a right to know what the curse of your hands really means. It's not just ugliness; it's loneliness. You'll always be a stranger, even among your own kind."

"I understand that." Nemain sniffled, but her voice was calm. "I still want to be among them."

Rhiannon reached over and stroked her hair. There were tears in her own eyes as well.

"For what it's worth, little sister, *I* love you," she said quietly. "And I'll die loving you, though you curse my name."

Nemain smiled wanly. "Now you're talking rubbish."

"It's the truth. I love you like my own bairn—which, in a way, you are. And you will hate me before the day is out. But it can't be helped."

From her pocket Rhiannon took a much-folded scrap of parchment. "I have not been idle," she said, all emotion gone from her voice. "I've spent all my energy searching for a cure for you. But I kept running into stone walls. I've written this down for you in case you might succeed, in time, where I failed. Read the first line."

Nemain unfolded it. The first line was a Dark Saying: *What was done in darkness must be undone in the light.*

"I don't understand ..."

"Wherever I turned, I seemed to find variations of that saying. It was as if all the texts were screaming it together—reminding me of what a coward I was to keep the truth from you. So I'm telling you now, my dear." She took a deep breath and said, "It was I who cursed you in the womb."

For a long moment Nemain could not speak.

"*You?*" She felt a dark, choking sensation in the back of her throat, as if she were swallowing blood. "You did this to me? Why?"

"I hated your mother, and I hated you for existing," Rhiannon replied, brutally frank. "You know how I felt about Tynan. And I was young—not much older than you are now. I didn't know my own power. If I had known then exactly how it would turn out ... no, I don't think I would have done it. At least I hope not."

She fell silent for a while. Nemain kept on weeping, though as yet she felt somewhat numb; the truth had not fully registered.

"Did Tynan know?"

"No," said Rhiannon, "but I think he suspected."

"And yet he let me come to you."

"I know. I marveled at that myself. He would have sought an omen before letting you go; he must have received a good one. And he always had great faith in the Raven's protective power. But if he had *known* that I was the one who— No, I doubt his faith could have withstood that. He would have taken you and run, no matter what the omens said."

Nemain slowly shook her head. "If you hated me so much—and yet you say you love me—"

"Well, there were some ... shall we say, side effects." She smiled grimly. "When I was a child, I used to have *ashlins*—quite vivid ones—that had a habit of coming true. That was why my parents allowed me to be trained as a *caillagh* so young. That and I was clever, like you, and strange, like all children with names of power. Not likely ever to marry.

"After I—did what I did—I found I didn't have the *ashlins* anymore. My gift had been revoked. She whose name I bore had turned Her face away from me, and it has never been turned to me since. I still have some skills; I know my texts, I know my herbs, and I can read signs and omens that any fool with a bit of training can read. But the power I once had is all but gone."

Her mouth quivered as she spoke, and Nemain felt an odd stab of pity—yes, pity for this woman who had ruined her life before it had even begun. She tried to remind herself of that fact, but it still didn't seem quite real.

"In place of the *ashlins*, I found that I now had a connection to you. I saw you as a child; I saw how you suffered from what I had done to you. I could feel your emotions. Your music—oh, you'll never know what that has meant to me. I could hear it as *you* hear it before you play: in my head, as pure essence. For that alone I would have loved you.

"Yet even with that connection, I would not have expected you to turn out so much like me! You have my element; you have my cleverness and strangeness; you even have some of my looks, my manners. I shaped you, unknowingly, as a parent shapes a child. And I loved you for what you *didn't* get from me: your brilliant gifts from your father's side, and your honesty, your trusting heart—I don't know where you got that—probably from your mother. Aye, I've been richly rewarded for an evil deed. I gained a daughter who wasn't mine, a blessing and a torment every day of my life since.

"So, little sister, do you still say that I owe you nothing? That you cannot forgive your kinfolk in Gwehara, who did only what they thought right, and grieved to do it? I know where that must leave me in your eyes. Say whatever you will—I deserve the worst you could possibly say—but then go away, please, because I'll be dead by morning."

Under this new shock, all of Nemain's feeling returned. She sprang to her feet with a cry, causing the dogs to retreat in alarm to their corner.

"You said you weren't fey! You promised me!"

"No faery doom is sealed on me. I brought this on myself." Rhiannon shrugged as if it were of no consequence. "I told you I've spent all my energy ..."

"Not for this!"

She grasped Rhiannon's thin wrists, her eyes blazing. "You can't be dying! You can't tell me these things and then die! Tell me what to do for you!"

"There." Rhiannon nodded weakly toward the parchment on the table. "Read the rest of it."

Nemain snatched it up. After the Dark Saying, there was only a verse:

Between two hands, a tie is formed;
All other ties are severed.
Cleave mother's flesh from father's bone
And run our blood together.

"What is this?"

"The cure, if you can make sense of it." Rhiannon shrugged again. "It's from a text I never gave you—believe me, you're better off not knowing it. But that verse is the key."

"It'll save you?"

"No, you little fool, it'll save *you*. Haven't you been listening?"

She made an effort to rise from her chair and failed. Nemain took her by the arm and half led, half carried her to her bed. How light and frail she had become!

"Go on," Rhiannon said hoarsely. "Decide what you want to take with you—get some rest, if you can—but please be out of here before dawn. I want to know that you're safely on your way—under the Raven's wing—before I go."

"You think I'll leave you to die alone?"

Rhiannon looked up at her. Love, wonder, and gratitude shone in her sunken eyes.

"You would stay with me?"

Nemain nodded. No word was said of forgiveness—she wasn't at all sure if she *could* forgive—but Rhiannon seemed to take it that way. Overwhelmed with contradictory emotions as she was, Nemain saw no point in withholding peace from a sick woman's last hours—could not bring herself to express anger over her lifelong pain or her current sense of betrayal. For the moment, at least, none of that seemed very important beside the fact that she loved Rhiannon and Rhiannon was dying.

"Dear little sister." Rhiannon's eyelids fluttered closed. "Who would have thought you could still surprise me?"

Chapter 13

NEMAIN RETURNED TO Briarvale with a heavy heart. She would have preferred to start her *immram* immediately, as Rhiannon had urged her to do. Perhaps when she was far from home, on her own at last, she could start to heal. But she could not leave without making sure that Rhiannon's affairs were settled, her burial was arranged, and Béira found a home. For that, she needed Lord Winworth's help. And meanwhile—having nowhere else to go, and knowing he would object to her fleeing to the North Country—she must bide her time under his roof.

"You'll always have a home here," Lord Winworth assured her. He gave her a room away from the ladies' wing so that she would not be bothered by noise, and so that she and Lady Bronwyn hardly crossed paths at all. Nemain was so grateful to him that it pained her to think of running away. Both he and Lady Bronwyn would see it as a rash, nasty, ill-bred deed; he might even join Lady Bronwyn in blaming Nemain's Outland blood for it. But to think of staying at Briarvale indefinitely—feared and disliked by the servants, as ever, and looked down on by the ladies—so close to Swayne, who would never be hers—surrounded by people with whom she could never share the beliefs and ideas closest to her heart—no, better to face the terror of the *immram* than the certainty of such an existence.

Time was running out. Autumn was not far off, and to delay a northward journey much longer would be foolhardy even under normal circumstances. And so, on the night she deemed would be her last at Briarvale, she stayed up late to decide what to take with her—only the belongings that she couldn't bear to part with, and no more than she could carry—and to plan ahead as far as she dared.

Moddey would go with her, of course. (An *immram* was generally a solitary venture, but there was no rule against an animal companion.) Her fiddle, obviously. A couple of extra shifts, worn atop one another. A pouch of linen rags and another of herbs to hang from her belt. A handful of copper staters to put in her skirt pocket.

Rhiannon's black robe. She carefully unfolded it and laid it out. It would serve for warmth and cover, at least into the autumn. By the time she reached the mountains, she would need more, but for that she would have to depend on the Good Folk. Now was not the time to worry about it.

She touched the fringed ends of the plaited belt. White, red, and black: the colors of Maid (*caillin*), Mother (*moir*), and Crone (*caillagh*). Three stages of a woman's life, and three aspects of the same Being: the many-named Great High Queen of the Good Folk. A reminder that within apparent contradiction were wholeness and harmony. As she put it on and pulled the hood over her head, she felt momentarily transformed; it gave her a glad sense of integrity, of being part of something grand.

Then she turned her attention to the problem of her books. She could not carry more than one or two, yet how could she part with any? There were Tynan's books, which he had loved—Master Ives's books, bound up with many happy memories—and the veritable mountain of Rhiannon's books, which had shaped so much of her thinking over the past four years. After a few minutes of agonized indecision, she chose the Book of Dark Sayings.

Next she sneaked down to the larder, where she got a loaf of bread, apples, and some dried meat and put them in an old flour sack. She filled a bottle with water from the pump and added that to the sack, too. By the time she was fully ready, with her fiddle-bag slung across her back, the Book of Dark Sayings under one arm and the sack of food in the other, she was trembling within the limit of what she could carry.

Go now, she thought. The sky was clear and the moon was bright; she could be on the drovers' road before dawn, miles away before anyone noticed she was missing. It was the perfect moment to leave.

And then she thought of Monessa.

Shouldn't she at least say goodbye? It would be awkward and painful, all the more so because she must bind Monessa to secrecy about her leaving. And since they had not been close for so long, there was really nothing to say *but* goodbye. Still, Monessa, who had always been unfailingly kind, and who was not to blame for the waning of their friendship, or for the fact that they loved the same man … surely Monessa deserved the courtesy of a farewell.

Nemain groaned inwardly at the thought of tiptoeing through the ladies' wing, past the rooms were the ladies-in-waiting slept (or whispered or giggled through the night), in the hope of waking Monessa and no one else. She would as soon have trodden over a nest of vipers. Suppose she left a note instead? But even as she had that thought, she abandoned it in disgust. If she was to say good-bye at all, she would do it honorably, face to face.

She set down her things and made her way to the ladies' wing. Luck was with her; Monessa still slept in her old room and, thank the Good Folk, slept alone. A light sleeper as ever, she responded to Nemain's faint, fearful tapping on the door.

"Nemain?" She blinked in the light of Nemain's candle. "What's wrong? Why are you dressed like …"

"I'm sorry to wake you. Can I come in?"

Monessa drew her inside and closed the door. "What is it?"

"I have to go away. I just came to say goodbye."

"In the middle of the night? Where are you going?"

"Up North. Beyond that, I don't know yet."

"What? Why?" Monessa's eyes grew very wide. "What kind of trouble are you in?"

"None; this is just something I have to do. I'm sorry, I can't explain why. Please don't tell anyone."

Monessa was slowly shaking her head. "You're not making any sense. Why don't we talk to my father in the morning? I'm sure he can …"

"No! Please, no one else can know." Nemain's gloved hand gripped Monessa's, Northern-fashion, to plead for her word. "Promise you won't tell him."

Monessa looked torn, but she said in a small voice, "All right."

"Thank you."

"But—but you're going alone, on foot? Anything could happen to you! How will you get by? How will we know you're safe?" Her eyes suddenly swam with tears. "Are you ever coming back?"

Nemain sighed. "I don't know. I'll send word when I can. Don't worry about me. I just wanted to say goodbye, and"—oh dear, now her own eyes were welling up—"I'm sorry I haven't been the friend to you that you've been to me."

"Don't be stupid."

Monessa surprised her by embracing her. She had not done that since they were children.

"Be careful," she said. "Send us word as soon as you can. Oh, I wish you wouldn't do this."

"I have to." Nemain mustered the ghost of a smile. "Goodbye, then."

⋅→▣◉ ◉▣←⋅

It was a quiet day on the drovers' road. Nemain dimly recalled that there was a fair going on at Kell's Crossing, several days north of Briarvale, and she ought to encounter more activity as she went farther on. But for now the road was deserted in both directions as far as the eye could see.

She supposed she should have been nervous—it didn't take much imagination for a solitary traveler on a vast and empty track to be nervous—but she felt glad, even giddy, to be on her way. *Goodbye to Briarvale!* her heart sang with every step: goodbye to old fetters, snubs, and heartaches. Whatever lay ahead of her, it had to be better than what she was leaving behind. Its very unknown-ness had ceased to be terrifying and now held a certain charm.

To be sure, that question of Monessa's—"Are you ever coming back?"—had stung. Nemain had not the least intention of going back. She would miss the comparative ease and security of life at Briarvale, but not its emotional and intellectual emptiness. She would miss Monessa's kind heart and loyalty, but not her own smothered resentment, guilt, and sense of inferiority in Monessa's presence. She would miss Swayne ... no, she had better not think of Swayne.

Around midday, hunger and lack of sleep caught up with her. She stopped under a stand of willow trees, where she ate an apple and a hunk of bread, gave Moddey some of the meat, and then stretched out to sleep in the shade.

Towards evening, she was startled awake by the sound of horses. Two men had ridden up to her and were now peering down at her from their mounts. She recognized them as Briarvale servants, and her heart sank.

"You're to come back directly. Lord Winworth's orders."

One of them dismounted and moved to lift Nemain forcibly onto his horse, but Moddey leaped between them, barking and snapping savagely.

"I'll walk behind," she said.

The men looked warily at the dog, then at each other, and relented. "Well, don't try anything stupid," one of them warned.

"Bit late for that, innit?" the other remarked.

And back to Briarvale she went, this time under guard. She could have wept at the loss of the few miles she had gained. Who knew when she would have another opportunity?

Realizing she was walking hunched over, she forced herself to straighten up. An *immram,* she reminded herself, didn't stop just because you got waylaid or thrown off course. It didn't go as you expected; it wasn't supposed to. And it wouldn't be over until it was over. As long as she stayed in the *immram* mindset, trusting in the Raven, she would be on the right path no matter where it led.

Still, she was unprepared for the meeting with Lord Winworth that awaited her that night. As she approached the presence chamber, flanked by her guards, she saw Monessa waiting outside, biting her nails.

"I had to tell him." Monessa choked back a sob. "I was afraid for you. I'm sorry."

"Leave us," said Lord Winworth from within, in a voice that sent everyone else running. Nemain gulped and went in to face him alone.

She had never seen Lord Winworth righteously angry before. It was not a thing that happened often. But looking at him now, even before he started yelling, Nemain suddenly understood why all his people obeyed him without question— understood, too, why she had always been secretly intimidated by him. Even the steadiest and most quiet-spoken of air characters, when pushed to their limits, were capable of furies matching those of fire.

It did not occur to her that he was angry because he cared about her—that if it were Monessa who had done something so foolish and dangerous, he would have reacted the exact same way. She bore it meekly and tried not to snivel, but gazed levelly back at him through the tears that had begun to flow under his tirade.

"What were you thinking? Hiking up to the North Country alone—do you even realize how far it is?"

"Well, the Middle Cantrefs are about fifty miles off, and then the mountains are ..."

He flung out more rhetorical questions. "Do you have any idea what could have happened to you out there? A lone girl, on foot—are you insane? What possessed you to do such a thing?"

Nemain was silent, not wanting to provoke him further, but it seemed to have that effect. He strode up to her as if to shake her like an errant child, and she froze; but he stopped just short of it.

"Why?" he said in a lower voice. "Why would you run away and break Monessa's heart? You've hurt her with this, and frightened her badly. You've hurt me too."

That was worse than all else he had said. Oh, *mollaght*, suppose he started weeping! He looked capable of it.

"My lord," said Nemain, gripping the back of a chair to steady herself, "say all you want, and when you're ready I'll explain."

"I'm ready now." Lord Winworth sat down at his desk once more. He still had a face like thunder, but his tone was a shade closer to reasonable. "Explain to me what makes a clever girl do something so stupid."

She took a deep breath. "I'm very sorry for the trouble ..."

He waved her ahead impatiently.

"You should know, first of all, that I'm not—strictly speaking—an apothecary."

"Yes, yes, you're a witch. I know."

Her mouth fell open in consternation.

"Oh, stop gawking, girl. Tynan told me all about Northern 'apothecaries'—spiritual guides, or some such. What's that got to do with it?"

"Well, part of my—er—education is to make a journey called an *immram*."

As she explained the concept, his frown deepened. When she had finished, he shook his head.

"That *is* insane. Who sends a fifteen-year-old girl on such a quest?"

"Begging your pardon, my lord, there are not many fifteen-year-old *cailleeyn*."

He barked a laugh. "I daresay not. But even so, *some* allowance must be made—some adjustment to this absurd rite. Your mistress can't possibly have intended this for you. Either you misunderstood her, or she was an unfit guardian."

"My lord, the texts are very clear on the nature of an *immram*, and the choice was mine. She was keen for me to start; she tried to send me off the very night she died." Nemain's voice cracked. "I could not leave her—just like that—not until I had seen her buried. And I could not tell you because I knew you would stop me."

"Then why did you burden my daughter with this? You must have known she would tell me."

Nemain shrugged. "I thought it better than saying no goodbye at all. I felt I owed her that."

Lord Winworth was silent for some minutes, still watching her from under lowered brows. His expression had not noticeably changed, but she could tell his anger was gone.

"If I understand correctly," he said, "you believe that if you go on this journey, the faeries will look after you."

Nemain barely flinched at the word *faeries*. "Yes."

Another silence. His eyes flickered toward the portrait of Gavin and Nairne on the wall. What was he thinking? Was he wondering if all Northerners were this crazy? Regretting that he had formed an alliance with them?

"And if I let you walk out of here now, you'll get right back on that road."

"Yes."

"Well, I'm not going to do that."

"I didn't expect so."

He reached for pen and paper. "A horse," he said, making a list. "Fifty gold staters—I wouldn't travel with more than that if I were you—and three days' provisions. That'll get you as far as Kell's Crossing. After that you're on your own. Now, will that satisfy your ridiculous conditions?"

Nemain's jaw dropped again. "My lord! It's too—I couldn't—"

"The money's yours anyway," he reminded her, "a small part of what I hold in trust for you. And the rest you have not sought, so by the rules of this game, you have a right to it. Consider it a gift from the faeries."

Her eyes overflowed again. She pressed a gloved hand against her mouth to keep from sobbing, or laughing. "Why are you doing this for me?"

"Because I'm morbidly curious to see how this venture will end up," he said. "That, and—perhaps against my better judgment—I have a great deal of respect for your people. And for you."

Nemain bowed her head. "Thank you, my lord"—uttering silent thanks to the Raven as well.

Chapter 14

IN LATER YEARS Nemain would frequently try to recapture those first days of her journey. They were physically hard—long hours in the saddle, chilly nights on the ground—and emotionally unsettling; the road was so vast, the solitude so complete for many hours at a time. But underneath the strain, the weariness, and the constant low-level apprehension, she felt a paradoxical sense of security. There seemed to be an unseen power surrounding her, like a magical net; she could feel the tension of it supporting her, yielding as she moved, opening before her path a little at a time. And when she lay down to sleep, cold, saddle-sore and hungry (for she allowed herself only meager rations and almost no meat, saving most of it for Moddey), the moon glimmering through the trees was like the face of a beloved friend. Shelterless and alone, she had never felt less lonely.

How good it was to *be* alone! Unnerving, yes, to be so far from everyone she had ever known, but refreshing at the same time. The part of her soul that always thirsted for solitude and space could now drink its fill. She could think expansively, talk to herself, or simply enjoy the perfect company of sun and wind as she rode along on Keeley, the little mare Lord Winworth had given her. The peddlers and herdsmen she saw on the road passed her without a word; only one, a Northman, raised his hand to her and called out, "Safe journey!"—perhaps guessing by her black robe the nature of her journey. Nemain was so absorbed in thought that she did not realize he had addressed her until he was long gone.

But on the third day, the road became crowded and noisy. Ahead of her was Kell's Crossing, the site of the largest fair in the Lowland. From east to west, the broad River Kell gleamed like a silver ribbon in the afternoon sun. There was no way to cross it without going into town and paying the toll at the bridge.

Nemain's courage failed her at the sight of so many strangers. It wouldn't be so bad, she told herself. She would buy some supplies, find lodging for the night, and be on her way at dawn. Why, this was just the normal business of traveling!—nothing to fear here. But the feeling of dread persisted, and her fists clenched as if she expected someone to take her gloves away.

She closed her eyes briefly, trying to sense the invisible net around her. It was still there; it would hold, even in a crowd of people. And there really was no way to go but forward.

When she finally reached the bridge, bracing herself for trouble—one hand clutching Keeley's bridle, the other hovering over the purse concealed beneath her robe—she was astonished to be told, "Go on. Your way's been paid."

"What? How?"

The toll collector shrugged. "Earlier, some fellow paid double for a girl in a black robe, with yellow eyes, carrying a fiddle. Oh, and I'm to give you this." He handed her a sealed note. "Now move along."

"Er—thank you."

Once she was off the bridge, she led Keeley and Moddey a little ways off the road, away from the press of fellow travelers, and opened the note. It read, in a familiar black, businesslike hand:

> *Go to the Speckled Ox Inn. They'll put you up for the night and supply you with whatever you need. Don't concern yourself about the man I've sent ahead to pay your way. You don't know him, but he can be trusted.*
>
> *After this you really will be on your own. —W.*

Nemain shook with quiet, nervous laughter as she dropped the note into her pocket. Dear Lord Winworth! Someday she would repay him for all this.

She looked around and quickly got her bearings. The Speckled Ox Inn was impossible to miss; its sign was just down the road. And in the immediate vicinity, there was quite a lot going on—minstrels playing, tumblers dancing, customers haggling at the merchants' stalls along the roadside. The aromas from a dozen cook fires sharply reminded her how hungry she was. It was scary, but also exciting in a way, to be surrounded by so much color and noise.

She felt vaguely for the net around her, but could no longer sense it. Perhaps it had merely slackened; perhaps that meant she might go where she liked, do as she liked, at least for now. And surely there could be no harm in walking around and seeing the sights before retiring to the inn.

So, after seeing that Keeley was stabled for the night—which was simple enough, as even the stable hands at the Speckled Ox had been told to expect her—she set out with Moddey to explore the fair. She admired textiles and handicrafts and gazed with open longing at a stall filled with books. She listened, fascinated, to snippets of conversation in various accents: the flat drawl of peasants, the measured cadences of the high-born, the brisk burr of the North. She spent a few copper coins on some fried pork dumplings and thought it the best purchase she had ever made.

As the evening wore on, however, she became aware that she was getting some odd looks, even hostile ones. At first she couldn't think why. No one in these parts knew about her hands or her Outland blood. But the black robe *was* rather witchlike … that would be off-putting to Lowlanders … and Northerners, who would respect the black robe, would be put off by her wearing gloves in the summertime without the excuse of working or riding. And Moddey, the poor dear, wasn't helping. He, too, sensed something amiss; he growled continually, and his fur stood in an angry ridge along his back.

When she actually heard the word "witch," spat like an insult through clenched teeth, she stopped and turned slowly to face the speaker. It was a woman, who had drawn her two little children to her side. Nemain looked thoughtfully at the children—a boy and girl, their eyes round with fear and fascination—and decided it was not worthwhile to respond.

"She's a *caillagh*," said a Northern voice. "She won't harm you. Show some respect."

A middle-aged man approached her. He was handsome and looked well-to-do, if somewhat dissolute; his face was unshaven and his collar unlaced, disclosing some dark chest hair.

"Why, you're rather young for the robe," he remarked kindly. "Your first *immram*, is it?"

Nemain gave him a tiny smile, grateful for his intercession, but still not feeling quite safe enough to speak.

"Come, I should like some counsel from you. It's long since I spoke with a *caillagh*. Let's go into that pavilion."

He extended his hand, and she was on the verge of following. But she saw that he had the little finger of a liar, and palm markings that made her uneasy. She immediately stepped back. "No."

"No?" He smiled. "But you *cailleeyn* live by certain rules, do you not? You cannot refuse a request for counsel."

"An honest request," she corrected.

Something ugly crossed his face for a moment, but then he shrugged. "Oh, very well," he said, and turned away with a sneer. From the corner of her eye Nemain saw a man in the crowd, a man-at-arms, take his hand off the hilt of his sword. But he vanished before she got a good look at him.

The evening was spoiled for her. She headed back to the Speckled Ox, intending to go straight to bed without speaking to anyone. Unfortunately, she entered the dining hall right at the hour when it was most crowded. As she tried to make her way through, the din of conversation and clinking dishes was suddenly hushed.

"What's she doing here?" someone said nervously.

The innkeeper shrugged. "Her way's been paid."

"She's a witch, is she not?"

"It's no business of mine."

"No? Go and look in your till-box, man! I'll wager you'll find it full of dust."

"Hush, fool!" said a Northman sharply. "She's one of the *cailleeyn*. They're honest folk. Leave her be."

"She's too young for a *caillagh*," another Northman objected. "And she's wearing gloves—that's an ill sign. Oi! If you be honest, show your hand."

Moddey growled, and Nemain shrank within herself. "No."

An angry murmur rippled through the room. One of the customers headed for the door. "If she stays, I leave," he said loudly, and there was a chorus of agreement. "There's more than one inn in this town."

Nemain turned to the innkeeper for help, but he shook his head. "I'm sorry, lass. I'll give you the money that was paid, but I can't have you driving away customers."

"Sir, I'm a stranger here. If you turn me out, who will take me in?"

"That's not my concern. I've an inn to run and a family to feed."

Nemain thought quickly. "What if I could make more money for you, just for tonight? I could have this place full, and then some."

He laughed shortly. "Can you conjure up more rooms and beds? I've only got so many."

"They won't need them. They'll pay anyway."

"With real gold? That'll stay solid?"

She sighed in exasperation. "Of course."

"How will you manage that?"

"I'm a fiddler." She took off her fiddle-bag. "I'm very good. Now close the windows, open the door, and have someone stand guard. Let no one in without payment. —You, there! You wanted to see my hand?"

The Northman looked startled by the tone of command in her voice. "I don't want any trouble," he said as he came forward. "And I don't want to think ill of a *caillagh*. It's just that …"

Nemain pulled off her gloves, taking a perverse pleasure in his stricken face and sudden, appalled silence. "Go sit down," she ordered, and he obeyed, stumbling over his own feet in his haste.

She began to play, trembling with indignation and suppressed fear; and that intensity of emotion, that tremor in her fingers, caused her to play better than she ever had. Before long a crowd of curious passers-by, drawn in by a faint but irresistible strain of music, were jostling at the door, eager to pay for a space to stand within. The long trestle tables had to be taken down and stacked along the walls. The room was crammed to capacity and the innkeeper's till-box filled to overflowing, but Nemain heeded the cries of "Play on!" far into the night.

At last she stopped, exhausted, and swayed on her feet. She was conscious of a steadying hand on her arm, and then of someone—a man-at-arms—taking her fiddle and bow before they slipped from her fingers, and placing them in her fiddle-bag. Seeing that the concert was over, the audience (those who had not been lulled to blissful sleep on the floor, like Moddey) began to file out into the night. Nemain saw with satisfaction that several of them were weeping openly.

"Thank you," she murmured to the man-at-arms. "And give my thanks to my lord as well."

He half smiled. "Get some rest," he said. "And listen—why don't you just leave off the robe? That's what bothers people more than anything else."

Nemain smiled ruefully. No use explaining to a Lowlander that she was soliciting the protection of a higher Being and that to leave off her robe, for fear of what people might think, would signal a lack of faith. She merely bowed, and he took his leave.

Chapter 15

THE NEXT MORNING she departed from Kell's Crossing in high spirits, with fresh supplies, provender for her animals, and a generous share of the profits from her fiddling. "It's the least I can do," the innkeeper had said fervently, and she had accepted his goodwill in lieu of an apology. She could tell that he was sorry he had nearly turned her out the night before—perhaps even sorry on her own account, and not just for the money he would have lost. But Nemain, despite her good mood, was far from forgiving.

"Come back for the next fair, or anytime," he said; and she merely smiled, thinking, *Not a chance.*

She forgot all about him once she was on the open road again. Ahead of her stretched an area known as the Middle Cantrefs—rolling meadows, fields, and scattered farmhouses—and far beyond, deep green and hazy purple on the horizon, were the mountains that bordered the North Country. Her *immram* sense settled around her once more, like a web of warmth and light, and filled her with a solemn joy. Somewhere beyond those mountains was *home* ... at least the nearest thing to a home she could hope to find.

The farther north she went, the fewer Lowlanders and the more Northerners she encountered on the road. The Lowlanders passed her by without a word, either ignoring her completely or looking askance at her witch's robe. But Northerners would hail her with "Safe journey!" or, occasionally, "*Cair vie!*" (Fair wind!)—a relic of ancient times when an *immram* meant a sea voyage in a craft without rudder or sails. A death sentence that was not a death sentence. Oh, there was such depth and richness in the lightest utterances of the Northern tongue!

But though she relished hearing the language, she dared not try to answer in kind. Her education had taught her how to interpret Northern mystical texts, but not how to hold a conversation. And she feared to use her limited vocabulary lest she make a mistake or, conversely, make people think she was more fluent than she really was. So she responded to their greetings with only a shy smile, and no one attempted to draw her out further than that.

Once or twice she even encountered groups of Outlanders straggling along the roadside. She had never seen any Outlanders except for the beggars who sometimes approached the Briarvale gatehouse, and she regarded them with a mixture of fascination and shame. They looked like other people for the most part, but they were immediately recognizable by their accent, their motley clothing and general slovenliness, even the way they walked—bowed forward, as if constantly carrying a heavy load.

Watching them, Nemain could not help thinking of that poor, nameless Outland girl who had trudged all the way from Gwehara to Briarvale, alone and pregnant. Come to think of it, had she ever seen an Outlander traveling alone? They always seemed to be in groups. Outland families stuck together, you had to say that for them. ...

She sat up a little straighter in the saddle and tried to ignore them. Having been raised with all the Lowlander's scorn of Outlanders, she could not muster much kindness or fellow-feeling for them. But possessing a keen sense of honor, she felt she owed respect, at least, to her mother's people—*her* people, uncomfortable as that thought was. It was preferable just to not think about them at all.

⟶⟫◉ ◉⟪⟵

A peculiarity of the Middle Cantrefs was its intermingling of Lowland and Northern ways, so when Nemain knocked at a door to request shelter for the night, she could not predict how she would be received. One old farmer, seeing her black robe, shut the door in her face without a word; another, a Lowlander, took her in kindly and sent her on her way with additional food. (His late wife, she learned, had been a Northerner and very devout, so he was well acquainted with *cailleeyn*. And being a Lowlander, he didn't even notice that Nemain never showed her hands.)

One stormy night, a Northern couple had let her in and were just sitting down to supper when they saw that she had still not removed her gloves.

"I can't," she said, seeing the direction of their eyes. "Please don't ask."

They exchanged a look of suspicion bordering on alarm, a look that told Nemain everything. To these people, to deny hospitality to an ordinary *caillagh* would be a great wrong. But a *caillagh* who refused to show her hands might well be a rogue—a liar, a charlatan, a worker of dark magic. And their baby was asleep in the next room.

"What if I told you my name was Nemain?" she said.

They exchanged another look, a shocked one this time. Surely even a rogue *caillagh* wouldn't dare tell such a lie. "*Is* that your name?" said the wife shrewdly. "No riddles."

"It is."

They quickly withdrew to a corner, but Nemain still heard every word. "*Ta blayst yn irriney er*"—It sounds like the truth—said the husband. "I dare not put her out in this weather. It'd be terribly unlucky."

"But do we dare keep her under our roof? With the baby?"

Nemain picked up her bowl of stew and stood up. "I'll stay in your barn."

They smiled at her, united in graceless relief. "We'll rest easier," the man admitted. "We mean no offense, you understand—"

"I do."

So she spent the night in the hayloft—not too uncomfortably, despite the wind whistling through the cracks in the walls—with Moddey curled up beside her. Better to sleep here, she told herself, than in a room with a squalling infant. She was more at home with dogs and horses anyway!

Nevertheless, as soon as it grew light enough, she crept down and rode away without saying goodbye to the couple, resolving to sleep in the open as often as the weather allowed.

⋆⟞⊙ ⊙⟝⋆

Another peculiarity of this region, mostly in the foothills, were the arrangements of rocks—a cairn here, a ring of boulders there, an occasional standing stone or group of them—that had been there since time immemorial. The locals had given some of them names: the Faery Pillars, the Giants' Hearth, the Peepstone (this was a solitary upright with a perfectly round hole through it). Who had placed them and for what purpose, no one knew.

The first set of standing stones Nemain saw was on a hilltop: starkly beautiful in the late sunlight, like the columns of a ruined temple. Something about them—something beyond their sheer size, or the *how?* and *why?* of their presence there—drew her irresistibly toward them.

She tried to ride up the hill, but Keeley balked. After dismounting and tying the horse to a tree, she turned to Moddey; but he, too, whimpered and would not budge. So she went up alone.

The stones were arranged in a ring. Their weathered faces were covered with engravings: jagged lines, wavy parallel lines, circles with rays (wheels? sunbursts? stars?), circles broken into sections (the phases of the moon?). Whether they were illustrations, abstract designs, or some form of writing, she could not tell.

She took off her glove and placed her hand on one of the stones. There was some indefinable energy in the contact—an immediate sense of communion, almost of nostalgia. It was like the first time she had picked up one of Tynan's books and traced the design on its cover. It was like the time they had sat in the courtyard and he had told her the origin of her name. She felt close to something that she could not quite understand, but that was nonetheless very real and very relevant to her. As if this silent, lifeless stone were somehow steeped in life, reverberating with voices.

The sun disappeared behind the mountains, leaving the hilltop in shade, and she shivered. Evening was coming earlier, the warmth of the day slipping away faster. She hurried back down to her waiting animals, anxious to find a place to sleep before it grew quite dark—perhaps, too, a little afraid to linger at the stone circle in the twilight.

In the mountains, autumn had already set in. The densely forested slopes were turning rust and gold, and the peaks were dusted with snow. Though Nemain lived in daily terror of the myriad fates that might overtake her on the steep trails—getting caught in a snowstorm, getting attacked by wolves, her horse stumbling and breaking a leg—she was still keenly alive to the beauty of these wild heights. There was nothing like this in the Lowland; the whole country was as flat and tame as a walled garden in comparison. And the views! Lakes like silver mirrors; serrated ranks of evergreens; distant peaks like layered watercolors, receding into mist. Like so much of the North Country, the mountains were difficult to inhabit, difficult to traverse—but oh, the beauty was worth it.

Here she was more aware than ever of her dependence on the Good Folk. She was rationing her food severely now, supplementing it with whatever edible herbs, roots, and berries she could find; somehow it was always sufficient to stave off exhaustion, if not hunger. Lord Winworth had given her a thick woolen cloak, which was warm enough for any weather in the Lowland but hopelessly inadequate for the mountains this time of year; and yet she somehow found enough strength in her half-numbed extremities to keep going day after day. Every morning she woke up stiff and sore all over, but grateful to have survived another night.

Curiously, above all other comforts—good food, warmth, a soft place to sleep—what she yearned for was soap and water. She had never been the fanatic for cleanliness that Lady Bronwyn was; but after days in the mountains, where the lakes and streams were too cold for anything but a brief and partial dip, she could hardly stand herself. What she wouldn't give for a bath, a little vinegar to wash her hair, some clean clothes, and then, the Good Folk willing, a cup of strong tea! ... But rather than let herself pine for such things, she shoved them to the back of her mind and pressed grimly onward.

Then, one day, came the marvelous moment when she reached a high overlook and saw a landscape of hills and moors: a stark, strange landscape, gray and mauve under autumn frost, but lovely to her eyes all the same. There—*here!*—was the North Country at last. She descended the last mountainside with a joyful heart, feeling that she had as good as made it.

At the foot of the mountains, she reached a milestone marking a three-way fork in the path. To the northwest lay Gwehara, and beyond it, the resort town of Senuna. To the northeast, many miles away on the coast, lay Northwaite. And due north were several places whose names meant little to her—Elmwold, Defena, Slogh-Chlagh. A little chill came over her as she contemplated those names, no longer abstractions on a map but real, accessible entities. Options.

Gwehara was out of the question, and so was Senuna, if she had to cross through Gwehara to get there. Her heart hardened at the very thought of it. Set foot on the land of her lost inheritance, the land whose owners had ruined her father? Never!

And Northwaite? Could she stomach living on the land that would someday be Monessa's? No, that would be a sort of continuation of her life at Briarvale: doomed to obscurity in the shadow of Monessa, the perfect lady. Of course that thought immediately made her feel guilty, but there it was—her jealousy of Monessa was just as strong as her affection for her. Besides, in five more years' time, when Monessa would become Lady mac Airleas, what would be left of that affection to salvage anyway?

Due north it was, then. To the unknown, unhampered by any baggage from her past.

She urged Keeley onward, and immediately a strange thing happened. She felt a ripple of resistance in the unseen net—ever so faint, but it made her stop. It wasn't like the way the net usually shifted as she changed course, so subtly that she was not quite sure if it was directing her or if she was directing it. *This* was a gentle but definite "no," and it was coming from a will not her own.

Experimentally, a little fearfully, she let Keeley take a few more steps, then reined her in, ignoring her snort of impatience. There was that resistance again! What did it mean? Was it not the will of the Good Folk that she move forward?

She looked at the roads on either side, which she had no intention of taking, and resentment began to build up in her along with unease. Well, what did it matter! She had accomplished her goal of reaching the North; her *immram* was basically over. Wherever she chose to go now was just a matter of details.

So she moved forward once more and kept on going. There was no sense of resistance this time. *Ha!* she thought, trying to feel relieved. *I guess it really is all right.*

As she rode along, she tried to distract herself from her uneasiness. This region was lovely in its austere way. It wasn't a bit like the Lowland, which had been the rich emerald of summer when she left, and must now be clothed in even richer autumn color; but the moor's sober hues of misty violet, gray, and fawn were more to her liking. Elmwold sounded like a pretty place; Slogh-Chlagh, not so much. And what was the name of that other place? Anyhow, this stretch of road was a very pretty one, lined with hawthorn trees and late-blooming heather. How nice it must be in summer, all this shade … but at the moment it was decidedly chilly, and the sun had gone down almost before she knew it.

She tied up the horse, ate a scanty supper by the roadside, and lay down to sleep next to Moddey. Tomorrow she should reach Elmwold; by tomorrow night she might actually have a hot meal, a bed to sleep in, a bath … ah, wonderful thought! She burrowed her face under the blankets and, despite her unacknowledged anxiety, fell asleep almost at once.

At some point in the night, she heard a rustling in the trees and then the soft whickering of her horse, but these sounds only mingled with her dreams. It was a human voice that woke her, causing her eyes to fly open and her heart to pound.

"Come on, there's a love," the voice whispered, then chuckled. "Soft mouth on this one. Worth a lot, I'd say. She'd probably follow our lead without the bit."

"Well, hurry. Let's not wake the lass."

Outlanders. Horse thieves! Oh, *mollaght mynney,* they would take everything— the food, money, and medicine in the saddlebags, even the Book of Dark Sayings! All she had by her were her fiddle-bag, her blankets, and Moddey.

She reached out for the dog, willing him to be silent and still, but such was not his nature in the face of danger. He sprang up, barking, only to be viciously kicked aside. He struck a tree and lay still, momentarily stunned, and Nemain scrambled to her feet with a cry.

"Hullo, lassie." In the light from the man's lantern, she saw a broad, whiskered, leering face. "Does your mother know you're out here all alone?"

"Give me back my horse."

"Now, now, we didn't follow you all this way for nothing. But"—he came closer, and his breath was hot and foul—"now that I have a good look at you, I might be open to a trade."

Her blood turned to ice water. "A trade?"

"Stop talking rubbish, Arran, and let's go," said his companion, grabbing the horse's bridle.

"Aye, a trade," said Arran, ignoring him. "We'll still take the horse, but we'll leave you whatever you can carry from those saddlebags—and in return ..."

His hand clamped around her arm, and suddenly her blood flowed hot and strong again. She spoke in a low, savage voice that was not her own, a voice that shook her whole frame.

"Touch me, and I swear by your mother's flesh and your father's bones, *I will rend you.*"

Amazingly, he dropped her arm and stepped back, turning pale. But he quickly regained his composure, covering his retreat with a sneer.

"Have it your way. Oi, Mawg, take the lot! We're going."

They left her standing there, shaking with rage and suppressed fear. When she had recovered enough to move, she gathered poor Moddey in her arms and tried to sleep once more—tried not to think about how she would get anywhere with no horse, no food, no money, and the threat of cold weather setting in.

⟶⟨⟩⟩ ⟨⟨⟩⟵

Three things she learned that night. First—on the bright side—she had an effective defense against Outlanders. She had no idea what that oath meant to them, but obviously it was a fearsome thing. She didn't even know how it had occurred to her to use that clue of Rhiannon's as an oath (quite the stroke of luck, that!). But she had some idea of where that dark, powerful voice had come from. The memory of it chilled her to her bones, not with fear exactly, but with awe.

So, second—and also on the bright side—the Raven's protection was still in force. But third, she could not count on it to keep her out of every scrape. She may have escaped one dreadful outcome, but she was still facing another: the possibility of dying of hunger or cold before she could find refuge. It was clear now why she shouldn't have taken this road, but it was too late to go back. And her sense of the guiding net around her was utterly gone.

At the first gleam of dawn she rose and, before searching for food, searched for some pebbles. She arranged them in a circle on the ground, then gathered some frost-covered flowers, warmed them in her hands, and squeezed a few drops of water onto the pebbles. Next, after much painstaking work with some twigs, she succeeded in igniting a pitiful little blaze.

Earth, water, and fire—so far, so good. Now, how could she represent air? Rhiannon had always used incense for her meditation. But if a fragrance could perform that function, being carried on the air, couldn't music do just as well? It wasn't the approved method, but it was worth a try.

She got out her fiddle and began to play. Moddey, sensing that breakfast was still a long way off, settled down resignedly to listen. The sun was well up by now; the magic hour of dawn, when the barriers between worlds were thin, had passed. But she played on, striving for a sense of oneness with the gathered elements, pouring all her hope and fear and regret into the music as it flowed from her throat to her fingertips. *Help me,* she willed as she played. *Put me back on course.*

At last, feeling physically and spiritually depleted, she put the fiddle away and extinguished the fire. There was nothing to do now but keep moving and hope the Good Folk were merciful.

⋆⇒⊜ ⊜⇐⋆

Elmwold took two days to reach on foot. By that time Nemain, ready to collapse, would have taken any shelter that was offered. But Elmwold—a pretty, prosperous little village, much like the one attached to Briarvale—offered her none. Here it was not the black robe that condemned her, nor even her gloves, now that she had the excuse of chilly weather. It was simply her wild, desperate, dirty appearance. Elmwold was no haven for beggars.

"If you've no money, I've no room," said the innkeeper shortly.

"Oh, please! I'll sleep in the stable, I don't care."

"That you will not. You're a horse thief for all I know."

"I am not!" she cried, her temper flaring up. "I'm a *caillagh*."

"And a fine one, by the look of you. *Ersooyl lhiat!*"—Away with you!

As Nemain left the inn, her eyes filling with bitter tears, a young man stopped her. "Wait," he said, touching her shoulder gingerly, then wiping his hand on his tunic. "You said you're a *caillagh?*"

"I am. I'm on an *immram*. Will you please help me?"

She lifted pathetic eyes to his, and his tentative sympathy immediately became decisive. "Of course. Don't cry! I'll take you to our *caillagh*. She'll know what to do."

"Oh yes, please. Thank you!"

The local *caillagh* lived in a handsome cottage by the village green. She was a solid, well-preserved woman in an immaculate black robe and kept a fat black cat—an unfortunate circumstance for Moddey, who was half-crazed with hunger. As soon as the cat appeared, Moddey gave chase; but the cat, in spite of his fatness, moved quite nimbly up a tree, hissing and spitting from the safety of a high limb.

"Well, well," the *caillagh* said witheringly. She sent the young man away, then gave Nemain a long, cool stare. "You're rather young for the robe."

"I'm on an *immram,* and my name is Nemain. Will you help me?"

The *caillagh* stiffened. "That's a bold claim. Show me your hand, and I'll know if you speak the truth."

Nemain hesitated. "Can you not tell by my face?"

"Faces can lie, but hands do not. If you don't show it to me, I can't help you." The door began to close.

"Wait! I'll show you—only don't shut me out!"

As Nemain peeled off her glove, the *caillagh* gave a horrified gasp. "*Livrey shin veih olk!* This is beyond anything I've ever seen. What did you do to cause this?"

"Nothing! I was cursed from birth. I'm telling the truth, can't you see that?"

"I can see nothing in such a hand as that, but I know black magic when I see it. It renders things unreadable. No, sister, I'll give you a piece of bread, but you'll not stay under my roof."

The door closed with a vengeance. A moment later, the *caillagh* opened a window and flung out some bread and meat. "There. Now be gone."

Nemain and Moddey fell upon the food, but it did little to assuage their hunger. As the sun set, she considered looking for that nice young man, then gave up the idea in despair. If the local *caillagh* didn't trust her enough to take her in, who else in Elmwold would? And would any other settlement welcome a traveler as desperate and disreputable as she—assuming she could even make it to the next settlement?

"I've failed us," she said bleakly to Moddey, as they huddled beneath the elm trees just outside the village. "I ruined this *immram* when I got on that road, and now I might as well give up. I'm so sorry."

She began to cry, and Moddey licked her face as if to assure her he had no hard feelings. And then she thought of something Rhiannon had said, seemingly ages ago: "For whatever you hope to gain up North, you'll have to do battle."

Yes, she thought. And having only just begun to do battle, she could not give up now. Fight she would—fight the elements, fight hunger and fear, fight for every scrap of human kindness that came her way—until she had found a home.

Or until death. Whichever came first.

⇥⊜ ⊜⇤

At dawn she was off again, trudging along at a snail's pace, heartsore, empty, and bone-weary. How far away was this next place? She couldn't remember what the milestone had said, either the distance or the name.

Moddey, too, was at the end of his endurance. He loped dutifully alongside her, his head and tail hanging down. His breathing had taken on a raspy quality that worried her. He had had difficulty breathing as a pup; Rhiannon had feared he wouldn't survive. *Oh, please not him! Send me into the next world if You must—it's my own fault I've come to this—but not him! Not yet!*

By now she had only two objectives: Moddey must not die, and the first house they came to, she would ram against the door until she was allowed in.

As the day wore on, she began to lose awareness of her surroundings. She kept on walking, but she had no sense of the terrain, the weather, the time of day. Nothing that wasn't a house registered in her bleary vision. Several times she fell down, and each time, she lay on the ground a little longer, finding it harder and harder to persuade herself to get back up.

The moon must have been bright that night, because when she finally reached the house, she could see it with arresting clarity. Or perhaps it was the onset of delirium that made the house unnaturally brilliant and sharp to her eyes. At any rate, she *must* get in—and she threw her weight against the door, beating it with all the strength left in her fists.

"All right, all right!" said a grumpy female voice, and the door opened. "No need to wake the dead. What's the matter?"

"Don't take my gloves," said Nemain … and fainted.

"Mercy on us!"

"*Hysht!* We're trying to sleep!"

"Somebody quiet that dog!"

"Take her upstairs, and keep that animal outside."

Chapter 16

SHE HEARD VOICES in the dark: a man's and a woman's, far away at first, then gradually more distinct.

"Rois, are you sure about this?" the man was saying. "We know nothing about her, save that she's marked …"

"Hnh! That's all *you* know. I know that she's very young and very ill, and she'll die if we turn her out. She ought to weigh nine or ten stone, judging by the bones of her; but she's starved near to death, poor thing. She's got no food, no money—nothing but a fiddle, and no companion but that mongrel outside."

"But she had on a *caillagh*'s robe under that cloak. What if she's a rogue *caillagh*?"

"If she is—and you know I don't believe in all that—wouldn't you rather she was on our side?" Rois said dryly.

"I'm just saying, it's best to be cautious."

"Oh, we'll keep the children away from her, of course. But she'll stay with us until she's well. I'll not leave a poor girl to die on our doorstep. *Ta shiu toiggal, nagh vel shiu?*"

"*Ta mee toiggal dy mie.*"

Nemain sank gratefully back into unconsciousness. She didn't know where she was or who was deciding her fate, but she gathered that she wouldn't be cast out immediately.

When she opened her eyes again, it was broad daylight. She was in a small, plain, but tidy room, and lying in a bed with a straw tick. At once she was gladly conscious of cleanliness. Someone had gone to the trouble of removing her filthy clothes and washing her, and she now had on a linen shift considerably too large for her. But her gloves—*where were her gloves?*

Panicking, she struggled to sit up, then fell back against the pillow. How nice it was to have a pillow! She had never felt so weak, so sore, so relieved and terrified at the same time.

"Morning, lass! Well, afternoon, more like."

The woman—Rois?—had a Northern-peasant accent, rich and strange to Nemain's ears. She was in her thirties, big and capable-looking, with a mop of russet hair and twinkling hazel eyes.

"My gloves," Nemain croaked.

"Oh, yes. Sorry, I had to burn them—burned all your clothes, actually. They were past saving. But *you* aren't, so just you rest easy."

She lifted a spoonful of porridge to Nemain's lips. After about three spoonfuls, Nemain grabbed both spoon and bowl and started wolfing the stuff down.

"Oi! Steady," warned Rois. "We don't want it coming back up again."

"Where am I?"

"The Deep Valley Inn, in Defena. I'm Rois, and I run this place with my husband, Henry. What's your name, dearie?"

"Nemain."

Rois's eyes widened. "There's a name you don't hear often. Shall I call you that, or something else?"

"Call me anything you like." Nemain smiled faintly. "Thank you for taking me in."

"Oh, it's nothing. Henry was a mite nervous about it at first, but—"

"Mam!" a childish voice shrieked from the next room, causing Nemain to cringe. "Ita's spilled porridge all over the floor!"

"Well, clean it up, Bess! You've got two hands!" Rois bellowed back. "And don't let the baby crawl in it! ... So what's happened to you, dearie? Were you robbed, or hurt?"

"Robbed, yes. My horse was stolen. And my dog? Is he all right?"

"He's fine and fed, but a nasty-tempered beastie, I must say. We've got him tied up out back."

Nemain sighed in relief. Of course the poor darling was upset, not knowing who these people were or what they had done with his mistress. "May I see him?"

"Aye, when you're up and about. I'll not have him in the house with my little ones."

"That's probably best."

"You're a Lowlander, aren't you? You've got that pretty accent. What are you doing this far north?"

Nemain wondered if Rois knew what an *immram* was, then decided she didn't feel up to explaining it.

"I wanted a new start," she said finally. "It's not easy being a *caillagh* in the Lowland. Well, it hasn't been too easy for me anywhere."

She spoke matter-of-factly, not looking for sympathy, but Rois's eyes softened. "Poor little soul. What about your parents?"

"I just have a foster-family. Actually, is there any way I can send a message to them, just to let them know I've made it this far?"

"Not for a while, I'm afraid. We don't get many southbound travelers this time of year, not until the mountain snows melt. But if you'll write up a letter for your people, we'll hold onto it until we can pay someone to pass it along."

"Oh, I haven't any money but—"

She was about to say, "I can earn some with my fiddle while I'm here," but Rois interrupted her with a scoff. "*Ommijys!* I said *we'd* pay."

Nemain flushed, grateful but embarrassed. "You're very kind. You must let me repay you when I can."

"For now, you should only concern yourself with getting well." Rois took the bowl from her and tucked the covers up around her with a gentle but uncompromising hand. "And don't be afraid, or feel you need to hide. Gloves or no gloves, no one will meddle with you under *my* roof."

"I believe you," Nemain murmured drowsily. "You're an earth character, aren't you? ... I think I shall learn a lot from you."

"Whatever you say, dearie." Rois left the room, closing the door behind her.

⊷⟞⟠ ⟠⟝⊶

During her recovery, Nemain did learn a great deal from Rois and Henry—one always thought of them in that order—of the Deep Valley Inn. She quickly grew to like them both in very different ways.

Rois was the earthiest of earth characters, a cheerful, vulgar, warm-hearted soul you couldn't help liking. She was a tireless nurturer, the kind of mother who mothered everyone, and Nemain resigned herself to being coddled and scolded like one of the children. As long as she was bedridden, she had very little choice in the matter.

"I'm sorry to put you to all this trouble," she often said, as much to maintain her dignity as anything.

"Oh, never fear. As soon as you're up and about, I'll put you to work. I can use every pair of hands around here."

"Even mine?"

"Aye. No special treatment for you just because you're a *caillagh*," Rois grinned.

She was a different type of Northerner, having no belief in the Good Folk, no reverence for *cailleeyn*, and no concern with any world but the one she inhabited. And yet she held a certain fascination for Nemain's mystical side. Richly experienced in wifehood and motherhood—the whole sphere inaccessible to Nemain, who had, in a sense, gone straight from maiden to crone—Rois represented a lore unavailable in books, a wisdom blind to itself. Nemain found her an interesting and worthwhile study, if a puzzling one at times.

Henry was a contrast to his wife in every way: mild, soft-spoken, very much an air character. On first meeting him, Nemain noticed that he had a diplomat's thumb—narrowing below the knuckle—and thereafter observed how his children came to him, not their mother, with their little sorrows and worries; how shrewdly he compromised with his wife, always seeming to give in to her will; how skillfully he smoothed the ruffled feathers of neighbors who had been offended by Rois's blunt tongue. Whatever outsiders might think, there was really no question as to who wore the breeches in this family.

A pious man—again, very unlike his wife—he had a great regard for *cailleeyn*, and took a liking to Nemain once he got over his initial suspicion of her. Satisfied that she posed no threat to his family, and that the condition of her hands was the mark of a victim rather than a perpetrator of dark magic, he surmised everything else about her quite easily. She was clearly of mixed blood, with her Lowland accent and her Northern build, so he did not ask about her parentage. She was clearly unmarriageable, with those hands, so he did not ask why she had become a *caillagh*. She couldn't have had an easy life in the Lowland, so he did not ask why she had come up North. And he rightly guessed that she did not want to talk about any of these things. But Rois was not so perceptive.

"You're not bad-looking, dearie, now that you've fattened up a bit," she said approvingly on the day that Nemain was well enough to come downstairs.

Nemain smiled wanly. She was wearing one of Rois's old dresses, which was still too large for her, and hiding her hands awkwardly in her apron. "That's kind of you to say."

"I mean it. She's got fine eyes, hasn't she, Henry? And well-bred and clever to boot—why, you're wasted as a *caillagh*, my dear."

"Now, Rois, she's not wasted," Henry put in. "Different people are suited to different work."

"Well, time spent over books and spells is time spent away from young men. And you're young yet, dearie. There's plenty of time to change your mind about this *caillagh* business."

Nemain's eyes met Henry's, and she pressed her lips tightly together to keep from laughing.

"You do fancy young men, don't you?" Rois said with a raised eyebrow.

"In theory."

"Well! Mark me, dearie, there's *always* hope."

Rois left the room then, in response to the baby's cries, and Nemain let herself laugh. Henry smiled as he returned his attention to the inn's account books. She might be troubled, but at least she had a sense of humor. There was no living with Rois without that.

⇥▸◉ ◉◂⇤

Nemain was never quite sure when it was decided that she would stay indefinitely at the inn. At first Rois decreed that she couldn't possibly travel until the weather warmed—a decree that made sense, for winter in this region was bitterly cold. Then Rois enlisted her help in laying out the garden, with special attention to the medicinal herbs. And then one day Henry came home with a new *caillagh*'s robe and several pairs of gloves for her.

"Thought you'd be wanting these," he said. "For when we have more company."

Nemain took them, stunned into silence, her eyes suddenly full of tears. How thoughtful—and how expensive! A busy innkeeper, the father of a large family, would hardly acquire such things for someone he didn't consider part of that family.

That night she lay awake for a long time, torn between gratitude and uncertainty. To leave Rois and Henry now would be to hurt them, as she had hurt Lord Winworth; she could not bear that thought. And even Moddey was used to the place. He was well fed, he left people alone as long as they left him alone (which they quickly learned to do), and he was allowed to sleep on Nemain's bed. For his sake alone, she would be willing to stay.

But was her *immram* really meant to end here? Had she found the home that she wanted, the learning she had sought? A home of sorts, yes; she did not deceive herself that she might be better treated anywhere else—though her introverted soul shrank from the noise and bustle, the constant presence of strangers at the inn. And learning, too, she had found, though it was not quite what she had had in mind. She hungered for texts, for intellectual conversation, for the quiet enlightenment that came with solitude and meditation. Flesh-and-blood was ruder stuff to learn from, and required an uncomfortable degree of interaction.

Although her inclination was to stay, she dared not trust her own feelings on this. She would go out at dawn and meditate. But the moment she had that thought, she realized that it *was* dawn, and there was a bird singing—or rather, cawing—on the windowsill. And for the first time in months, she felt that inward flicker of warmth and light again: the sense that she was on the right track at last.

She laughed softly to herself as the raven flew away.

Chapter 17

FIVE YEARS PASSED at the Deep Valley Inn: years that slipped by seamlessly, unmarked by any major event or aspiration in Nemain's life. She was happy here, or told herself she was. It was preferable to Briarvale in many respects. She had a recognized profession; she was treated as an adult, never bullied, lectured, or punished; and she had security, if not comfort. Certainly she had no right to complain.

She did her share of the work ungrudgingly, including the wearisome tasks of tending children and waiting on customers. With the exception of baby Henry, who was glad of any attention he received and too young to be frightened of Nemain's hands, the children held her in awe and fear. Rois found this a convenient thing—"They're much better behaved when you're around!"—but Nemain found it depressing. The customers were no easier to deal with, always glancing suspiciously at her gloves. Some of them became downright hostile, at which point either Rois would come out to eject them from the place, or Henry would come out to calm them down.

Henry suggested that Nemain be relegated to housework and gardening during the day, and never bother with customers at all unless the services of a *caillagh* were requested. As for the children, his oldest daughter, Bess, could look after them just as well. To this Nemain gladly agreed—not least because Henry made the suggestion so tactfully that she did not feel in the least ashamed or inadequate.

These days she had little time for music, snatching a few minutes with her fiddle whenever she could, usually out in the garden so as not to disturb the guests. She didn't think anyone was listening, but one day she turned around to see Henry standing in the doorway, arms folded, an unreadable expression on his face. She stopped in confusion, thinking he must be displeased with her for wasting time.

"Rois! Get out here!" he called in a rare tone of command, and Rois came running.

"What is it?"

He gestured at Nemain. "Have you heard this?"

"Why, no. Let's hear you play, dearie."

Nemain obeyed, somewhat nervously. When she had finished the tune, Rois and Henry looked at each other for a moment, then at her.

"How would you feel about playing for guests, as a regular thing?" he asked.

"Oh, I'd like that! But—"

"What?"

"I don't like to be seen," she faltered.

Rois and Henry looked at each other again. "Well, that's easy enough to manage," said Rois. "We could get a screen for her to stand behind. People need not see her at all. They'd go mad wondering who it is."

Henry smiled slowly. "Aye, and she'd not be hounded the rest of the time, if no one knows it's her."

"Oh, I like that too," Nemain put in.

"Exactly. Give it an air of mystery." Rois clapped her hands in delight. "Oh, Henry, it's brilliant! I'll go have a chat with the carpenter this minute."

She left, and Henry remained in the doorway, looking thoughtfully at Nemain. "You're sure this is what you want?"

"Oh, yes! I'm better at that kind of work than any other. I'll make enough money to repay you for everything."

"I'm not concerned about that," he smiled. "No doubt you could. But you could do a great deal more on your own. You could be famous in your own right, in your own name."

"I can't be anything in my own name," she reminded him. "Hardly anyone dares to speak it. Besides, if I'm ever famous for anything, it'll be for *this*"—she raised an ungloved hand—"and I don't want that."

Henry nodded, judiciously avoiding looking at her hand. "Very well."

So Nemain became the Deep Valley fiddler as well as the resident *caillagh*, and no one could ever confirm that they were one and the same. The children were sworn to secrecy, and Rois had a little screened stage built in a corner of the dining hall. She even knocked out part of the wall behind it, giving Nemain a secret entrance so no one would see her coming or going. It was the perfect setup. She could fiddle to her heart's content at any hour of the day (that was part of the mystique; you never knew when an elfin melody would sound from the hidden stage). She could see without being seen through a cleverly worked lattice in the screen, and watch people weep or dance to her playing. Best of all, she had a tiny circumscribed space that was all her own.

When she did have to interact with people, her choice of armor was her black robe and her Lowland manners. Despite her wholehearted embrace of her Northern blood and beliefs, her Lowland accent persisted, as did the courtesies Lady Bronwyn had drilled into her from childhood. In the rude, boisterous atmosphere of a Northern inn, where men and women mingled freely and there was a great deal of drinking, laughing, and cursing, Nemain clung to her ladylike upbringing. She had no desire to blend in, and as a *caillagh*, she wasn't expected to.

As she had told Rois, she fancied young men "in theory," but Northmen didn't appeal to her much. Not that she had anything against them; there was much that she liked about them—their accent, their frankness, their spirituality that seemed not at all in conflict with their down-to-earthness. They just weren't anything like Lowland gentlemen, who were slender of build, refined in speech, elegant and restrained in movement ... which was to say that Northmen weren't anything like Swayne.

She had just one letter from Briarvale in those five years. Lord Winworth had sent her a few lines expressing gladness that she was safe and well, telling her not to worry about the stolen horse (she had apologized profusely about that in her own letter), and assuring her that her little inherited fortune would be kept safe at Briarvale until she saw fit to claim it. His letter was just like himself—kind but not sentimental, wasting no words—and Nemain was genuinely pleased to get it. But it was bound up with a closely written sheet from Monessa, which left her with mixed feelings.

I've had a letter from Gavin mac Airleas, Monessa wrote. *I was afraid he'd think me very young and stupid from the letter I sent. I even tried writing a bit in the Northern tongue, and then wished I hadn't. (I'm learning it from a Northern tutor. It's SO DIFFICULT!!!) But his letter was quite charming and kind—he's not a bit like you'd expect from his picture, if you recall!—and he said my Northern is very good. Also, right in the middle of it, his sister Nairne had grabbed the pen from him and written a few lines of her own. I thought I'd die laughing. She reminds me of you, actually. When I'm married, you must come up to Northwaite for a visit. We'll have a merry time of it!*

There was a good deal more in that vein, but no mention of Swayne, which was all Nemain really cared about. Of course there was no mention of Swayne. Why would there be? He was nothing to Monessa—or shouldn't have been anything—but her father's squire. And as far as Monessa knew, he was nothing to Nemain either. But the omission only sharpened her longing to hear of him.

She was saddened, too, by the mention of Gavin and Nairne. Just why their portrait had left such an impression on her all those years ago, she didn't know; but she had never lost that fond, foolish sense that they were her kind of people. And yet how could they be, when they were Monessa's people? It was Monessa they were writing to, Monessa they would welcome into their lives. They probably didn't even know Nemain existed.

And what business did Monessa have to be learning the Northern tongue! That was an unreasonable response, she knew, but she couldn't help it. She felt as if Monessa were encroaching on *her* territory somehow. Well, why shouldn't Monessa learn it! She *ought* to. Someday she would be mistress of Northwaite. She would speak the language fluently and overshadow Nemain in that regard, too … as she always would, in all regards but one.

Nemain took up her fiddle and played long into the evening. As always when gripped by a strong emotion, positive or negative, she played especially well. By nightfall the till-box was full, there was not a dry eye in the place, and Nemain's self-respect was restored. But she did not write to Briarvale again.

That was around the time she started getting periodic headaches—piercing ones that would begin behind one eye or at the back of her neck and leave her feeling faintly sick. Since they seemed to occur on a monthly basis, she tried the remedies she always prescribed for women with similar complaints, but without success. Only strong tea helped alleviate the pain, and it didn't help the feeling of unbearable melancholy that always accompanied it.

It was also around that time that she first had the dream that would haunt her for years. In this dream it was a moonlit night, and Swayne came in through her window to take her away. The details changed; sometimes he took her hand (ungloved!), sometimes he kissed her, sometimes he apologized for being so blind. But always, just as she climbed out the window to follow him over the hills in the silvery darkness, she awoke in tears, her arms outstretched to someone who wasn't there.

Often, in the light of day, a particular Dark Saying came to mind: *To be content with empty space is the beginning of wisdom.*

Aye, empty space she had, the crowded inn notwithstanding. A little pocket of it on the stage where she played her fiddle. The dream-space between herself and Swayne, so slight and yet insurmountable. The wide expanse of hills and moorland surrounding Defena, where she escaped every once in a while to meditate or just to be alone. And she *was* content, she thought ... or at least she was no longer fighting her circumstances. What more could she ask of life?

Chapter 18

It was Nemain's twentieth birthday—which went unremarked at the Deep Valley Inn, as she had never told anyone the date—and a bad day in several ways. First, she woke up in a gloomy mood for no reason, which most likely presaged one of her headaches. Second, she took offense at a remark that wasn't even addressed to her. A guest had been talking of some poor wretch who had somehow set fire to his clothes, rushed outside to quench the flames in a nearby brook, tripped over a stone, hit his head, and drowned in two inches of water. In response, somebody quipped, "What'd he do? Break a *geis?*"

While everyone else laughed, Nemain, white to the lips, went outside and did not come back in for quite a while.

Third, a group of Outlanders came a-begging in the afternoon. Outlanders often came to the Deep Valley Inn, as Rois and Henry were among the few inn-keepers who never turned them away hungry. But Rois, though she was generous in dishing out scraps for them, did not trouble herself to be gracious about it.

"There, now, shuffle off! *Traa-dy-liooar!*" Rois shut the door, shaking her head. "Like ants at a picnic. Well, you know the warm weather's coming back, because they'll be out in droves."

"My mother was an Outlander," said Nemain.

There was a sudden silence in the kitchen. Rois stared at her, trying to figure out if she was joking. Henry stopped discussing inventory with the head cook and turned to stare at her, too.

Now what possessed me to bring that up? thought Nemain, irritated. She had heard Rois rant about Outlanders a hundred times before and never felt inclined to defend them or to own her Outland blood. But today, for some reason, it stung.

"I can't believe it!" Rois laughed uneasily. "*You* an Outlander?"

"Indeed." Nemain poured herself a cup of tea and went up to her room.

Spring was in the air this evening. The coming of spring—the first day that she could sit by an open window without freezing—was always something of a miracle to Nemain. Winter in the North Country was so long and dark, so miserably cold, it left her with a physical and emotional craving for sunlight. Breathing the fresh air and hearing the twittering of birds in the distance, she felt her irritation being soothed away. But the feeling of gloom persisted.

It was time to start thinking of her annual jaunt. That, surely, would lift her spirits. Every spring for the past few years, having been cooped up in the inn all winter, she had disappeared for a few days to ramble over the moor with no companion but Moddey. It was a sort of birthday gift to herself, a commemoration of those first few glorious days of her *immram*. A few days of solitude, out in the open, to reconnect with the quickening earth and remember how it felt to be so young, so full of hope … the very thought of it brought tears to her eyes.

Yes, that was why she was in such a bad mood. She just needed to get out.

She picked up her latest project, a rosemary poppet to help cure little Ita's nightmares. Nemain was not skillful with her needle and the work was slow going, even without gloves. But she contrived to give the poppet's face such a droll grin that you couldn't look at it without laughing. She rather liked to hear Ita laugh.

Ita was a pale, quiet, sensitive thing, small for her eight years. Unlike the rest of Rois and Henry's children, she still had not outgrown her fear of Nemain. And yet, oddly, nothing would banish her night terrors but to have Nemain sitting by her door—presumably to ward off lesser monsters. Nemain wasn't sure whether to feel flattered by that or not.

She heard Rois's brisk tread on the stairs and braced herself for an awkward apology. Rois was always saying thoughtless things and then making the situation worse by trying to take them back. Most of the time it was funny, but Nemain wasn't in the mood for it just now.

"It's all right, Rois," she preempted her as the door opened. "Don't worry about it."

"Thank you, dearie. Come down and play whenever you're ready. Also, we've a young man in who wants to meet with a *caillagh*."

Nemain sighed. She was certainly in no mood to deal with a young man.

"Now, now, cheer up! He's right handsome."

"Oh?"

"Aye! Red hair ... and that smile ... and the way he sits his horse ..."

"Rois, listen to you. A married lady."

"Well I've got eyes, haven't I? Where was I?"

"He wants to meet with a *caillagh*."

"Right. I told him we've got our own, right here. Bet he won't be expecting a sweet young thing like you."

Nemain rolled her eyes. "Forswear the thought, Rois. No good will come of it."

"Come on, I'll point him out. You tell *me* he isn't handsome."

They went down to the stage via the secret entrance. "Over by the door," Rois whispered.

Nemain peered through the lattice at the young man, who was leaning casually against the wall. He was perhaps in his late twenties, tall and broadly built like most Northmen, but unlike most Defena men at that age, not yet bowed or weathered by years of hard work. He had red hair and a scruffy beard, and he wore a patched gray tunic, leggings, and high, scarred boots.

"So?" pressed Rois.

"Meh," said Nemain.

"Hnh! There's no pleasing you, is there?"

Nemain chuckled to herself as she took up her fiddle. Yet there was something confoundedly familiar about the man, though she couldn't think where she might have seen him before. Red hair wasn't that uncommon in the North.

She kept an eye on him as she played. To her surprise, a stricken look came over his face. He listened for a minute or two, then abruptly went outside, letting the door bang shut behind him.

Oh, well, she thought ruefully. That happened sometimes. Most people enjoyed her music even when it made them weep, but now and then there was someone who found it peculiarly painful. She could never tell who would have that response or why. It seemed that some people were mysteriously like fiddle-strings themselves, attuned to some influence in Nemain's music of which even she was unaware.

"Got no ear for music apparently," she remarked to Rois.

"Bah! What does that matter? It's a man's sense of rhythm that counts!"

Nemain laughed in spite of herself. "All right. If he hasn't wandered off, go tell him I'll be there in a minute."

She stowed her fiddle in its hiding place and went upstairs to put on the black robe. As she was tying the plaited cord around her waist, she suddenly realized who the red-headed man was.

It was Gavin mac Airleas.

Oh, surely not! What business could he possibly have here? And even if it was him, by whatever freakish coincidence, why should that make her feel as if the wind had been knocked out of her?

She put her hand against the wall to steady herself, biting her lip so hard she tasted blood. Monessa's life was intersecting with hers again, and this embittered her beyond all reason. *Why can't I have a clean break from you!* she cried inwardly. *This life is nothing grand, but it's mine, and I'll never be content with it if I'm always reminded of what you've got. …*

And yet beside all this was a certain pleasure, a friendly curiosity. She *would* like to meet Gavin mac Airleas, and now was her chance. Oh, if only she could just go and speak to him like a normal person! Why couldn't she?

"Dearie, aren't you coming down?" Rois called from the landing.

Nemain took a few deep breaths, pulled her hood up over her head, and went downstairs.

He was sitting alone at the end of one of the long tables, sipping a mug of ale. Yes, that was Gavin mac Airleas all right; that strong line of jaw and chin was recognizable even with the beard. Nemain was not much attracted to him (though she could see why Rois would be), but she liked his face—an honest, pleasant face, ten times more agreeable without the sulky expression she remembered.

He looked up as she approached. Evidently Rois had been right about one thing: she was not what he had expected.

"*Fastyr mie*," he greeted her somewhat uncertainly. "*Nee oo'n caillagh?*"

"I am." She sat down opposite him. "And I'm afraid I don't speak much Northern."

He blinked in surprise, then grinned. "Forgive me, but you look more like a *caillin*"—young girl—he punned. "And you're a Lowlander?"

"Mm," she said, not wanting to explain her background.

"Well!" His eyes darted to the screened stage. "This place is just full of surprises."

She refrained from smiling. "How can I help you?"

"I'm here for counsel."

He held out his hand, and she leaned forward to study it rather than take it in her own. It was the hand of an unusually favored man, one needn't be a witch to see that: strong, clean, and well-formed, the major lines clear and perfectly balanced. He had probably never worked a day in his life—those calluses had come from riding and archery, not from labor—but he was neither weak nor lazy. The set of his thumb told her he was used to getting his own way, not by tact or subtlety, but by force of character; no diplomat's thumb in evidence *here*. And his little finger indicated a straightforward, vigorous, and passionate nature.

"Hands cold?" he asked, staring at her gloves.

"Always."

She waited for him to object, but he did not. So he was going to trust her anyway, or at least pretend to. Was it out of regard for her feelings? (Though what kind of man would regard the feelings of a potentially rogue *caillagh?*) Or was it simply bravado?

"Are you afraid?" she said, raising her eyes to his.

He met her gaze squarely. "Why would I be?"

Ah, it was bravado *and* regard for her feelings. She let herself smile this time.

There were some very interesting qualities revealed in this hand. The fingers were long, the head line clear and deep, showing that his mind ruled his heart; he liked to reflect, to weigh decisions carefully. And the palm indicated a remarkable tenderness for a man. It was marked for affection, generosity, loyalty. This was a man who ought to be married—*wanted* to be married—wanted nothing more than to devote himself to a wife and children. ... The headache she had been trying to avoid all day suddenly struck behind her left eye, and she motioned his hand away.

"You're not much of a talker, are you?" he remarked. "Pity. I'm rather partial to a Lowland accent."

Nemain, barely hearing him, began to analyze his face. His ears had a good shape; he would not know hunger or hardship—not surprising. He had thick eyebrows and bright, fearless gray-green eyes. But again, around the nose and mouth, that puzzling tenderness. Fire was obviously strong in him, but so was water—equally so. Nemain had never met anyone who was ruled by two elements instead of one. Fire and water, at that!

Now, why was he traveling in disguise, without a retinue, and staying at an inn far below his means? Had he fallen out with his family, or was there some crisis at home? Neither—there was no sign of shame or trouble in his countenance. But why would the most powerful lord in the North Country allow his only son to travel in this foolhardy manner, unescorted? Unless ...

"So what's a Lowland girl doing in these parts?" Gavin asked.

"One might also ask, what's the heir of Northwaite doing on an *immram?*"

His jaw dropped. "You're good! Yes, well, I feel a great need for help and direction. I'm on my way to be married."

"Ah." *So it's that time already.* She half smiled, half winced, as her headache began to throb harder. "But why come to me? Are there no *cailleeyn* closer to home?"

"Aye, we have two of them at home. They've been with my family for ages. They read my stars when I was born, and they've been counseling me all my life. But they don't always agree. One sees fire uppermost in me; the other sees water. You can imagine, when it came to picking a bride ..."

Nemain nodded. Of course they would search high and low for a lady whose stars made her equally compatible with a man of either temperament. A well-born lady, fair and charming enough to hold Gavin's interest, temperate and patient enough to balance his conflicting elements. Lord Airleas had been right to choose Monessa for his son, despite the long wait. Such a lady would be worth it.

"Anyway, that's why I'm making an *immram* of this journey, and why I wanted to meet with a different *caillagh*."

"You're looking for unbiased counsel." The irony of this struck her as hilarious, but it pained her too much to laugh.

"Exactly."

"Well, I'm afraid I can't help you."

His eyes widened. "Are you refusing me?"

"It's not that." She dug her fingertips into her temple. "It's just that I don't know what counsel to give you. You don't *need* counsel, as far as I can see."

"I don't?"

"No, you're fine. You'll reach your destination safely—but you're not worried about that; you're no coward. Your bride-to-be is a jewel among women—but you know that already. I've never seen anyone so fortunate, so firmly set on the right course, as you. There's just one thing I don't—"

Nemain closed her eyes, trying to make sense of the impression that had just come to her, and also trying to ease the pain in her eyes. Goodness, this headache was a bad one. She could feel her face turning white.

"Are you all right?" He touched her hand in concern.

She opened her eyes and looked down at his hand on hers, and he quickly withdrew it.

"One thing I don't understand," she resumed. "I don't see fire *or* water uppermost in you; I see them at war. You're going to come to a crossroads, very soon, and you'll be drawn in both directions. But whichever way you choose, it seems you're destined for happiness." She smiled ruefully. "What kind of counsel is that. Anyway, I don't know what more I can tell you."

"Am I good enough for her?"

He asked this as if it were all that really mattered to him, and she answered as if it were of no consequence. "Oh, that. Yes, I can honestly say you're well matched."

She leaned back in her chair, feeling drained, wishing she had not come downstairs at all.

Finally Gavin said, "What can I give you?"—the polite way of asking, "What do I owe you?" A *caillagh*'s counsel was not to be bought and sold; technically he owed her nothing. It was an opportunity for her to respond with some trifling sum, as most *cailleeyn* did to augment their little income from cures and spells. But that had never been Nemain's way, even when her counsel was good.

"Nothing."

"Well, take this anyway." He laid a gold coin on the table. "For the fiddler."

She stared at him in consternation, and he smiled back at her. (He did have a winning smile, she had to admit.) He knew! Not just the identity of the fiddler, but *her*, Nemain of Briarvale.

"How—?" She stopped herself and shook her head. "Excuse me."

She fled upstairs to her room, overcome with shyness and dismay. It was a rude shock, after all this time, to be connected not only with her fiddle-playing but with her past. How had he recognized her? Perhaps Monessa had mentioned her in a letter—but if he had read a description of her, wouldn't he have guessed who she was right away? Something in their conversation must have tipped him off, but what?

At any rate, he must think her quite mad for bolting like that. *Well done, Nemain. That'll be how he remembers you.* She could imagine the conversation at Briarvale: "I met that foster-sister of yours in Defena. She's an odd creature, isn't she?" And Monessa, charitable as always: "Oh, you must make allowances for the poor dear …"

Nemain hung up the black robe, buried her face in her pillow, and cried.

Chapter 19

THE NEXT MORNING, she woke up with cramps and a profound disinclination to go anywhere or see anyone. Her excursion over the moor would have to wait.

"Is that all right with you, boy?" she asked Moddey, rubbing his belly. He stretched and yawned in the sunlight. "I guess you'll get over it."

She ate a quick breakfast, brewed yet another pot of tea, and then settled down to finish working on Ita's poppet. Her wretched mood had passed with her headache; she was tired and sore, but relatively content. Only the thought of Gavin mac Airleas made her sigh with regret. Most likely she would never see him again, and if he ever thought of her, it would only be in connection with the counsel she had given—which, to her mind, was no counsel at all. And yet what other counsel could she have offered? She couldn't *see* anything else.

No, there was no point in pursuing that train of thought. It would only lead her to second-guess her abilities, and that never did any good. More than cleverness or years of training, the key to a *caillagh's* power was trust, both in herself and in the Good Folk. Without that, she couldn't have much insight or give meaningful counsel anyway. She would just have to trust that Gavin had all the information he needed, and what he chose to do with it or what he thought of *her* was not her concern.

She heard footsteps coming up the stairs and stuck the needle into the poppet, then put on her gloves. It must be Rois—no one else ever came up to her room—with either bad news to report or an unpleasant chore to assign. Or at least that was how Nemain accounted for the oddly hesitant silence when the footsteps reached her door. But she could not account for Moddey, who suddenly stiffened and growled low in his throat.

The knock sounded at last. "Come in," said Nemain.

It was Gavin mac Airleas.

"Oh!" Unwarranted gladness to see him struggled with confusion and a vague sense of impropriety. "I thought you'd have left. —Moddey, *down.*"

Moddey, who had started barking at the stranger even though he was still several paces away, reluctantly subsided at Nemain's feet.

"You call him Moddey?" Gavin laughed.

"It's short for Moddey-Dhoo."

"Ah, the great black beast. Naturally." His eyes twinkled. "Though I think he was bigger in the tales my nursemaid used to tell."

Nemain smiled. "What can I do for you?"

"May I sit?"

"Please."

He sat down opposite her at her little table, ignoring Moddey's sulky growl.

"You left me too soon last night," he said. "How are you, by the way?"

"Fine."

"I thought you might be ill. You seemed ... well, you seem in better spirits now. Anyway, after you left, I had a chat with Mistress Rois that confirmed who you were." He grinned. "Why didn't you tell me?"

When she hesitated, he added, "And how did you recognize me? Was it by *ashlins?*"

"No, I've seen your portrait—the one of you and your sister. It's at Briarvale."

He looked blank for a moment, then laughed. "Oh, that one! I'd forgotten. How did it turn out? Accurately, I gather—and memorably—but in a good way, I hope?"

"You didn't look best pleased," she evaded.

"Well, can you blame me? I was nineteen, and they'd betrothed me to a child! I wasn't in a mood to cooperate. My father said, 'Have Nairne sit with him; she'll keep him civil,' and she did, but I'd be damned if I'd smile."

Nemain laughed.

"But why didn't you tell me who you were? You were actually one of my reasons for coming here—that, and to hear the Deep Valley fiddler that everyone from here to Northwaite is talking about. 'You're going south? Oh, you must go to Defena and hear the fiddler.' I thought, why not? There's plenty of time. Might as well also look for that foster-sister of Lady Monessa's, who lives in Defena. I'd been told I should meet her if I ever got the chance."

"Who told you that?"

"Why, Lady Monessa in one of her letters. She didn't give me a description, though. If she'd mentioned your eyes, or the fact that you wear gloves, I would have recognized you at once."

"No, she wouldn't mention my hands." Nemain smiled thinly. "She was always so tactful."

"She didn't mention you were a *caillagh*, either."

"In the Lowland, mine isn't a respected profession. She may not know how *cailleeyn* are regarded here. ... What exactly did she tell you?"

"Your name—which stuck in my memory—and that you were very clever, very gifted, and very shy." He smiled. "She wasn't exaggerating on any count."

"And what did Rois tell you?"

"Oh, she's full of high praise."

She's full of something, Nemain thought.

"I don't know why I didn't tell you who I was," she confessed. "I'm just not used to being recognized. That's what I like about this place—that I can earn my keep without any fuss. On my own, as either a *caillagh* or a fiddler, it would be much harder. Not many people trust a *caillagh* in gloves, and of course a fiddler can't wear gloves. And I hate taking them off in front of people. I hate being stared at."

A tremor had crept into her voice, and she stopped, blushing. Reluctantly she met his eyes, and they were entirely friendly. She felt a little less embarrassed.

"But Rois and Henry understand. They're very kind. And people like the idea of a fiddler who might also be a ghost. ... You won't tell anyone, will you?"

"I won't. And I trust you won't tell who *I* am, either."

He offered his hand, and for a moment she stared at it, puzzled. Then her blush deepened as she realized he was asking for a promise. It was so seldom that anyone asked her for a promise, or entered into any kind of compact with her, that she had forgotten how it was done. "Oh."

She gave him her hand, and he clasped it firmly. Even that brief, matter-of-fact contact through her glove was more intimate than she was used to. She withdrew her hand as quickly as seemed polite.

"So how did you know it was me?" she said.

"Well, as I said, I came to hear the fiddler. And I wasn't disappointed."

"You weren't?"

His eyes wavered. "I hope I didn't offend you by walking out."

"You didn't."

"Don't get me wrong, it was lovely. It just ... I don't know why, but it touched a nerve. I knew no happy mortal could play like that. And later, when you gave me counsel—thank you for that, by the way—"

"Such as it was."

"What do you mean? It was all good tidings! A safe end to my journey, a jewel among women ... and your assurance, at least, that we're well matched. But I wondered, how could anyone give such good tidings so sorrowfully?"

Nemain didn't know what to say.

"Also, you seemed very sure of Lady Monessa's character. As if you knew her personally."

"Ah."

"So tell me about yourself. You were fostered by Lord Winworth; what family do you come from?"

"I have none."

He looked perplexed. She supposed that he, like most Northerners, couldn't imagine life without a family.

"My mother was an Outlander; she died when I was born. My father was a Northman." She bit her lip. "Lord Winworth took me in as a favor to him. Beyond that, I can't tell you."

"I see. And how did you become a *caillagh* so young?"

Again she bit her lip. "A kind lady offered me an apprenticeship. Lord Winworth let me take it because it was apparent I would not marry."

"Because of ... ?"

"This." She lifted a gloved hand. "Take my word for it."

He nodded. "And you came here five years ago, the mistress said. How old are you now?"

"Twenty."

He gave a low whistle. "You're even younger than I thought. My little sister would have been about your age."

Nemain looked up sharply. "Would have been?"

"You don't know?"

"Know what? What's happened?"

"Nairne is dead," Gavin said slowly. "She died two years ago."

"Oh!" Nemain pressed her hand against her mouth. "No, I didn't know. I'm so sorry."

Nairne dead. Strange that it should affect her so—the death of someone she had never met, never seen in the flesh. Yet she felt as if she had lost a friend. How often she and Monessa had looked at her portrait and thought they *would* be friends someday!

"It was a fever. Very sudden." He smiled sadly. "We were quite close, especially after our mother died. I could talk to her as I couldn't to anyone else. She was so looking forward to meeting Lady Monessa, and you too. I think you'd have liked her."

"I'm sure I would have."

He looked at her thoughtfully for a long moment.

"Tell me, what can I do for you?" he said.

"Why do you ask?"

"Because I feel I'm meant to. An *immram* is a mad business, you know. You're traveling blind, in a sense, but you can't ignore what comes your way. So here I am. If there's something I can do for you, I will."

"Oh, I don't know … I mean, I don't *need* …"

"Also, you're a lady, you're unhappy, and the knight-errant in me just won't stand for that."

Nemain laughed. "You do realize I'm a witch?"

"Not the term I would use, but yes."

"Well, I don't think your knight-errant and I would make good allies. Where I come from, the witch plays rather a different role in the tale."

"You're in the North," he reminded her, "and our tales are different. You're a lady and a fiddler as well as a *caillagh*—not to mention a Northerner, an Outlander, and a Lowlander. Three in one, you might say. And your name just happens to be ..."

"Careful," she warned, and he bowed his head with a grin. "You're verging on impudence."

"I'm sincere, though. What would you have me do?"

"I really don't know. Rois would kill me if I put you to work. And she doesn't even know who you are."

"Hmm." He examined the rosemary poppet on the table, and his mouth twitched at the sight of its loopy grin. "Shall I tell you what I have in mind?"

She nodded.

"I think you miss your foster-family—don't you?"

"Sometimes." That was true on the whole. She missed Swayne, with a constancy and intensity that she dared not admit even to herself. She missed Monessa occasionally, with a poignant mixture of nostalgia and guilt. But she hardly ever thought of Lord Winworth, save to remember him now and then with gratitude, and she missed Lady Bronwyn not at all.

"Would you like to see them again?"

"You mean go to Briarvale? With you?"

He nodded.

"Oh, I couldn't possibly! That would be too much to ask."

"You're not asking. I'm offering."

"I'd only slow you down."

"I have time. The wedding's not till Midwinter Eve."

"Why are you going down so early?"

"I want to get to know her first. It doesn't do to rush things. Also, I want to get past the mountains while the weather's still warm. But even then, there's plenty of time."

Nemain considered. The thought of a long journey did not appeal to her, especially right now. And did she really want to see her foster-family again? People could change so much over five years; she knew *she'd* changed. Undoubtedly Monessa had, too.

But then she thought of Swayne, who was never very far from her thoughts. To be sure, there was no guarantee that she would see him again. He might have gone back home to his family, or he might have been made a knight and come into a little estate of his own. He might be married. (That thought made her shudder, but she forced herself to look it in the face.) And then again, he might not be. He might still be at Briarvale, pining for Lady Monessa. But with Gavin mac Airleas in the picture and Monessa irrevocably unavailable, perhaps then ...

"If I do come with you—and I'm not saying I will—can I ask you to wait a few days?"

"A few days?"

"Yes. I'm not feeling well right now ..."

"Oh, that? Sure."

She stared at him, a little surprised, and he looked back at her with equanimity. A very Northern response, that. No Lowland gentleman would have grasped her meaning so quickly and with such an utter lack of embarrassment.

"And even then, I'd be going slowly indeed. I don't have a horse."

"I can get you one."

Her eyes widened. "You carry that kind of money on an *immram*?"

"I have some, yes. But haven't you noticed how things just seem to come to you on an *immram*? If the Good Folk are willing, They'll provide a way."

Yes, that was true, Nemain reflected. That, and a wealthy nobleman's definition of "only what you can't bear to part with, and no more than you can carry" might well be different from her own.

"I would pay you back ..."

He shook his head. "Your company would be payment enough. I'd be glad to have a *caillagh* with me on this journey. So you'll think it over?"

"I'll have to talk to Rois and Henry."

"Aye. So will I."

He stood up, as if to get right to it. At the door he paused.

"I like you," he said. "You're an odd jade—in fact, I think that's what I'll call you. But I do."

So he was giving her a nickname. That was a tad presumptuous—taking for granted that they would have a further acquaintance.

"I haven't said I'll go," she reminded him.

"No, but I ought to have a name for you anyway, seeing as we're practically family. You're my soon-to-be foster-sister-in-law."

"What sort of tie is that?"

"One worth acknowledging." He grinned and bowed. "*Slaynt-lhiat,* jade, until we meet again. Whenever that may be."

She was laughing as he closed the door.

⤙▣ ▣⤚

She saw little of him over the next few days, somewhat to her disappointment, for she found him very pleasant to talk to. She missed friendly conversation with a man. Neither Tynan, Swayne, nor Master Ives had any counterpart at the Deep Valley Inn. Henry was the only man she considered a friend, and he had little time for conversation. And though Rois would have been happy to introduce her to any number of men, Nemain steadfastly refused to take her up on it, knowing what Rois was apt to read into everything. Certainly she read a great deal into Gavin's intentions.

"He wants you to go away with him!" she reported with breathless glee. "Isn't that romantic?"

"It's not like that," said Henry with a touch of weariness. "He's betrothed to a lass in the Lowland. He told me so."

"Well, betrothed isn't married. I'm just saying."

Nemain and Henry exchanged one of their looks.

"I know when a man is interested, and he's interested!" Rois went on stubbornly. "You're going with him, aren't you, dearie?"

"I'm thinking about it," Nemain admitted, reaching down to pet Moddey. "I could do with a change of scene, and Moddey here could do with the exercise. He's getting fat."

"He's getting old," said Henry.

That was true, but Nemain didn't like to hear it. She frowned.

"We'll look after him for you," Rois offered.

"Oh, I couldn't leave him. We've never been separated." She turned to Henry. "Do you think I ought not to take him?"

Before Henry could reply, Rois uttered some low, rapid-fire remarks in the Northern tongue. He silenced her with a few curt syllables.

"Tell me what you really think," said Nemain.

Henry looked at her with a smile in his eyes. "I think if you go, you won't come back," he said. "So you'd better take the dog."

Rois beamed.

"Why wouldn't I come back?"

"Heavens, dearie! Because if you've got a chance at a better life, you should take it!"

"She's right," said Henry.

Nemain looked from one to the other, stunned. "Well, then ... I guess there's no reason not to go."

"I'll go tell him," said Rois.

She danced out of the room, and Henry watched her go with a sigh. Nemain looked at him curiously.

"What about your profits from the Deep Valley fiddler?"

"Lass, it was never about the profits. You know that."

She smiled. "Well, I won't forget all you've done for me. And I *may* come back."

"If you do, you'll be welcome. But if this young man can reunite you with friends, or find you a situation more to your liking, take it, by all means. Get whatever you can from him, I say."

Nemain chuckled. Henry's cheerful pragmatism suited her better than Rois's visions of romance.

"It's likely he can do better by you than we can," Henry went on. "He's well connected."

"How do you know that?"

"Oh, you can just tell."

"And what do you think of him personally?"

"He seems decent. We went shooting earlier today—"

"Shooting?" Devout Northmen went hunting only for food, never for sport. They couldn't afford to be casual about killing, knowing that the Good Folk often assumed the forms of birds or beasts.

"Target practice," Henry smiled. "He's a champion archer. Got the keenest eye and the steadiest hand I've ever seen. ... He told you about his Lowland lass, didn't he?"

"Oh, yes, I knew about that."

"Good."

Nemain went up to her room, wishing she felt as optimistic about this as Rois and Henry did. She had no great hope of finding a more congenial situation than the one she had here. Besides, she remembered her own *immram* all too well. Long, weary days in the saddle ... not knowing where her next meal was coming from ... mistrust and hostility from strangers. No, she had no nostalgia for it except for the strange enchantment of those early, solitary days. And she had no hope at all of recapturing that in the company of another person.

She thought of Gavin's hand and scowled. He and Monessa really were perfect for each other. Fortune's pets, the both of them! What had *she* to do with a man with hands like that?

She took off her glove and studied her own hand. As usual, she could make nothing of it; the Elmwold *caillagh* had been right about black magic making things unreadable. The fingers were distorted claws, the lines darkly etched and chaotic. She could see nothing there, at least nothing in her future—merely the familiar old record of hunger, frustration, and loneliness—just as she had seen nothing but joy in store for Gavin.

Still, she found she didn't resent him as she resented Monessa. She rather liked him. And Henry was quite right. Should she not take what she could get, even if it was just a change of scene, a scrap of friendship? Not to mention the chance—a slim one, to be sure, but nonetheless a chance—to be near Swayne once more? ...

That night she dreamed of Swayne again. He and Gavin had both come to her window, but it was Gavin who climbed up and entered while Swayne waited outside. "You'll have what you want," Gavin promised, offering her his hand; and as she took it, she felt his good fortune being transferred to her. The dream left her in tears, as usual, but this time they were tears of joy.

Chapter 20

"GOOD NEWS," GAVIN said to her the next morning. "I've got a horse for you."

"Already?"

"It was Master Henry, actually. He wanted to do this for you himself." He smiled. "Things just come, you know?"

Nemain was deeply touched. She tried to hide it with flippancy. "Well! He and Rois must be anxious to see me go. May I see the horse?"

"Certainly. He's in the stall next to mine."

The horse was a brown rouncey, dwarfed by Gavin's massive dapple-gray. "What's his name?"

"Peddyr."

The horse regarded her with mild, patient eyes as she approached. "Hello, Peddyr," she said and gently scratched his shoulder. He seemed to like that.

"Are you fond of horses?" Gavin asked.

She nodded. "My father was a farrier."

Right away she wished she hadn't said that. She didn't want him to be able to deduce anything about Tynan, as he surely would if the conversation at Briarvale ever turned to Northmen and farriers. She added quickly, "Your horse is a beauty."

"His name is Thevshi," said Gavin, patting him. Thevshi nuzzled him back affectionately.

"He doesn't really help your disguise, though. No one would believe a poor wayfarer on a beast like that."

"I know, but I couldn't bear to be parted from him. You know how that is."

She nodded, glancing at Moddey, who had followed at her heels as usual. Moddey did not trust Gavin any more than at first and was extremely reluctant to leave Nemain alone with him.

"How soon can you be ready?" Gavin asked.

"As soon as you wish. And I've been meaning to ask, do you want me to wear the black robe when we're traveling?"

He frowned. "I hadn't thought about that. It's up to you."

"It's your *immram*," she said. "I wore it on my own because it felt like the right thing to do. But as we go farther south, it may cause problems."

"In that case, leave it off."

She bowed in assent. Privately she thought it was wrong of him, but part of her was relieved not to repeat the ordeal of traveling through the Lowland in witch's garb.

He studied her face for a moment. "Are you nervous?"

"A little," she confessed. "Oh, I know we'll be all right. I'm just not used to *immrama*—or traveling at all, really. I've only done it once, and it was hard."

"This'll be different," he assured her. "You won't be alone or on foot. I'll have someone to talk to, and you'll have two able protectors." He looked down at Moddey, who growled at him, and he grinned. "It'll be fun."

Nemain smiled absently at the notion of someone like her, with a name of power, needing protection at all. No, it wasn't just the journey itself that was making her nervous, but she wasn't sure what else was.

Her parting with the Deep Valley folks was brief and, for the most part, unsentimental. She did not embarrass Henry by thanking him openly for the horse, but she curtsied formally to him and Rois as she would have done to Lord Winworth. "Thank you again for all you've done for me. I warn you, though, I'll probably come back."

"I hope you don't." Rois gave her a quick hug. "And I say that with love."

The children bade her farewell cheerfully or indifferently—all except for Ita, who merely gazed up at her with anxious eyes while clutching her rosemary poppet, and small Henry, who unexpectedly burst into tears and had to be carried out by his father. Nemain would have liked to comfort him but had no idea how to go about it. After that it was rather a relief to get away.

How good it was to be out in the open, on horseback again! And in contrast to her first journey, it was both novel and reassuring to be riding alongside a man. Nemain, stealing a glance at him, admitted to herself that Rois was right—he did look well in the saddle. Northmen often did.

"So, jade," he said, "tell me about Lady Monessa."

"What about her?"

"Anything. Everything. But start with something no one else knows."

"All right." Nemain thought for a moment, then began telling him things as she recalled them—little things that held no bitterness for her. "When we were little, I stole some custard tarts from the larder, and she told her aunt *she'd* done it, so that I wouldn't be whipped. ... She always accompanies her father on the hunt, even though she hates it, because she doesn't want to hurt his feelings. ... Also, if you say the word 'mawmeny,' she'll shriek with laughter."

"Mawmeny? Isn't that a kind of stew?"

"Yes, with cheese. It was a joke between us; I don't even remember why. But say it in front of her and see what happens."

Gavin laughed delightedly. "This is all very good. Go on."

"She's a loyal friend." Nemain bit her lip. "When I left on my *immram*, I made her promise not to tell her father about it. She broke that promise within the day because she was so worried about me."

"How'd her father take the news?"

"Surprisingly well." She told him how Lord Winworth had aided her.

"That *is* surprising from an unbeliever. My father's as devout as they come, and you wouldn't believe the fight we had when I told him I wanted to make this journey an *immram*."

"Really?"

"Aye, he's a bit on the over-protective side. And I'm his grown son. If it had been his daughter, at the age *you* were, he'd have gone through the roof. ... So what else is Lady Monessa?"

"Generous. Trusting. Affectionate. Quick to laughter. A sweet singer, a tolerable lute player. Fond of walking and riding, but no tomboy. She was always a lady, even as a child."

"Is she a happy person generally?"

"Oh, yes. She cries easily over other people's misfortunes, but not her own."

"Is she as beautiful as they say?"

"I knew you'd come to that. Yes, she is."

He gave a triumphant chuckle. "She sent me a miniature portrait a couple of years ago. I carry it with me. I'll show it to you when we stop, and you can tell me if it's a good likeness."

The miniature was a remarkably good likeness, with details so fine they might have been rendered with just one hair of the brush. For a minute Nemain stared at it, marveling at how the artist had captured the exact ash-gold of Monessa's hair and the peculiar blue of her eyes, almost too blue to be real.

"Well?" said Gavin.

"Looks about right." She handed it back to him. "Bear in mind, I haven't seen her for some years. But unless she's greatly changed, that's her."

She watched him put the picture away in an inner pocket of his surcoat. He carried it next to his heart, the way any knight carried his lady's favor. It was clear that he had fallen in love with Monessa in advance, and Nemain's information accorded nicely with whatever dreams he had built up around her image. Nemain drew her cloak a little more closely about her, though the day was not cold.

"You never know with an arranged match," said Gavin. "Painters flatter—letters can be dictated—and sometimes people just lie. Lady Monessa always seemed too good to be true. But from what you tell me, she really is that lovely and that good."

Nemain shrugged.

"Did the two of you part on good terms?"

She frowned faintly, not sure what to make of that question. "Of course. As I say, she's loyal, generous, sweet ..." Privately she added, *And it's not her fault that I am none of those things.*

"Hasn't she any faults?"

"Well, there are many points on which we differ, but I don't know if I'd call them faults."

"All right. Why don't you like her?"

She looked at him sharply. He met her gaze with shrewd amusement.

"What makes you think I don't like her?"

"Just a guess."

Nemain frowned, embarrassed but not indignant. He was impertinent, but he had caught her fairly. She *didn't* like Monessa—hadn't liked her, really, for a long time. And yet—

"The truth is, I love her," she said, surprising herself. "We were best friends as children. She was as dear and sweet to me as any true sister could be."

"What happened?"

She thought of Swayne. She thought of Tynan and Rhiannon, who had shaped her character and her life in ways Monessa knew nothing about. She thought of her years here in the North, as far away from Briarvale as she could get, desperately striving to be content with emptiness.

"Life," she said. "That was all."

He nodded slowly. "You took different paths at quite an early age."

"Exactly."

He looked as if he wanted to ask her more, but he said, "Well, this has been most informative. We can talk of something else if you like."

"Sir, if you have questions, ask them. It's my job to give you answers."

"But if the answer is 'That's none of your damned business,' you can tell me so."

She smiled.

"And you needn't call me 'sir.' "

"Oh yes, I need." She took up her fiddle-bag. "Would you mind if I played for a while? I'll go to those trees over there so I won't disturb you."

"Play here. You won't disturb me."

"Are you sure?"

Gavin stretched out on the grass and put his hands behind his head. "Play."

"All right, then. Don't look at me."

She turned away from him and played a few songs, her good humor restored. As she packed up her fiddle and put her gloves back on, she saw that tears were seeping from Gavin's closed eyes.

"Forgive me," she said. "I won't do it again."

He sat up and looked at her. "It's all right."

"It obviously distresses you."

"Jade, it would be a crime to forbid you to play." He wiped his eyes. "And if you insist on calling me 'sir,' then I'm going to command you in this, and only this. At any time or place you wish to play, I forbid you not to."

"Thank you, sir." She curtsied. "Nonetheless, I am sorry."

"For what? You play beautifully, though I don't suppose you need to be told."

"I don't, but tell me anyway. I'm incorrigibly vain."

He laughed. "Well, you're quite the loveliest fiddler I've ever heard. I could listen to you all day, though you break my heart."

Nemain smiled, hoping he wouldn't notice her blushing. Certainly she had been told often enough what a good fiddler she was, but never in quite such terms before. It discomfited her even though she knew perfectly well he meant nothing by it.

Still, she couldn't help feeling wickedly gratified to have impressed him. She did not have Monessa's lovely face or catalogue of virtues, and no man would ever keep *her* picture next to his heart; but she did have one potent charm like no other, and it was nice to have a man acknowledge it. Even though—or perhaps because—it meant nothing.

Chapter 21

NEMAIN HAD FORGOTTEN how tiring traveling could be. She had been bracing herself for the discomfort of sleeping on the ground—not to mention the potential awkwardness of sleeping near a man—but the moment they lay down that first night, she was unconscious. She awoke, blinking, to late-morning sunshine. Gavin was nowhere to be seen, which was fortunate, because in her sleep she had flung her right arm up over her head, exposing her hand.

Panic-stricken, she found her gloves and got up just as Gavin returned. "Good morning," he said. "About time."

"Why didn't you wake me?"

"You looked as if you needed the sleep. Come on, let's get a move on."

They breakfasted on nuts, apples, and dried meat. As usual, Nemain gave most of her share of the meat to Moddey.

"Have you had enough to keep your own strength up?" Gavin asked as they mounted their horses.

"Oh, yes." She tossed one last scrap of meat to the dog. "What time do you normally get up?"

"Dawn. I've always felt it a waste to sleep through the early morning. You miss so much."

"Like what?"

"The light, the colors of things." He broke off abruptly, and she got the impression he didn't share this thought very often. "What about you? Do you normally sleep like the dead?"

"Normally, I don't sleep much at all," she laughed. "I stay up late, and I drink a lot of tea. I only really sleep when I'm exhausted."

"That's quite bad for your health. And you a *caillagh!* You should know better."

"Actually, my mistress was the same way. A lot of *cailleeyn* are. We keep company with the moon and stars. ... Anyway, please wake me from now on. I don't want to slow you down."

But that night she dropped immediately into exhausted sleep again, and at dawn she was still so deeply in it that Gavin's light touch on her shoulder did not bring her fully awake. The hazy thought *Someone's at my bed,* coupled with Moddey's barking, made her thrash in terror, her hands clenched into fists.

"*Hysht!*" she heard Gavin say. "I'm sorry."

"What? Oh." Awake now, she reached out for the dog. "Moddey, *down!*"

Then she froze as she realized Gavin was staring at her hands.

"Sorry," he repeated, backing away.

Nemain could have wept with humiliation. Just why it mattered, she didn't know. Over the years plenty of people had caught an accidental glimpse of her hands, and she had not felt this kind of shame. But Gavin's white face, his look of barely controlled revulsion, really hurt her. While this was a completely different situation from her childhood encounter with the village boys, her feelings were much the same.

Nonetheless, she gathered up what remained of her dignity and went over to him. "I'm sorry, sir," she said coolly, before he had a chance to speak. "I'd forgotten I asked you to wake me. Next time I won't be so ..."

"May I see your hand again?"

"What?"

He held out his hand. "May I?"

Nemain began to tremble, but she gritted her teeth and pulled off her glove. He examined her hand very gently in both his own. The revulsion was mostly gone from his face; it had been replaced by fascination and profound pity.

"Does it hurt?"

"What?" No one had ever asked her that.

"It looks as if it might be painful."

"Oh." Her skin cracked easily and was chronically chafed from wearing gloves, but she had long since ceased to notice that. "Not really."

He released her, and she quickly put her glove back on.

"Can anything be done for you?"

She raised her eyes to his. Now that her hands were covered again, she was no longer trembling and she could speak calmly.

"There's not much that can be done about a curse. The only clue I have is a riddle, and I don't know what it means."

"What is it?"

"Between two hands, a tie is formed;
All other ties are severed.
Cleave mother's flesh from father's bone
And run our blood together."

Gavin frowned. "That's not like any Dark Saying I know."

"It's not one of the Dark Sayings."

He muttered the last two lines over to himself. "I have no idea what that means. I wish I had the wit to interpret it for you."

She shrugged. "You know these things can never be solved by wit alone. I just hope the solution isn't as gory as it sounds."

He nodded, then looked past her at something that made his eyes light up. "Oh, look at that," he said, touching her arm. "See that sky? That's just the kind of thing I get up early for."

She looked, and was struck by the beauty of the dawn sky over the moor: silver, rose, and pale gold, as delicately hued as mother-of-pearl. She had not seen such a sky (or at least had not paid attention to it) since she had traveled alone in these parts. The way it illuminated the moor—that watercolor blending of light and shadow—was like visible evidence of a threshold between worlds.

"It is beautiful," she agreed, grateful both for his calling her attention to it and for the change of subject. Nothing more was said about her hands.

They camped that night in the shadow of the mountains, not far from the milestone. This was as far south as Gavin had ever traveled, and he listened in wonder to Nemain's descriptions of mountain vistas, Middle Cantref folks, and ancient standing stones. Even after they had rolled out their bedding for the night—with Moddey, the determined chaperone, curled up between them—they kept talking.

"Those stones must be the monuments of the Vanished Ones," said Gavin. "I've always wanted to see them."

"The Vanished Ones?"

"Aye, haven't you read of them? There were people living in those foothills long before your ancestors or mine arrived, but no one knows what became of them. They died out or were scattered. Some say they became the Outlanders."

"If that's the case, perhaps they *were* my ancestors."

"Perhaps." He sounded a bit sheepish. "I forget you're half Outlander, jade. You're nothing like an Outlander."

Nemain thought of her Outland mother and of Tynan in his youth. A very prince, Rhiannon had called him. What was it about her mother that had attracted such a man? She couldn't have been one of those sad, shuffling, bent-backed apparitions who traveled in packs along the drovers' road or came a-begging to the Deep Valley Inn—if that was what Gavin meant by "like an Outlander."

"Well, I don't know what my mother was like, except that she loved deeply and she was brave. I wouldn't mind being like that Outlander. And I'd like to think my own people put up those stones."

"That would be something." Gavin sighed in contentment. "What a fine night! You 'keep company with the stars'; I like that. Are they just as fair in the Lowland?"

"As bright and as numerous," said Nemain, "but I don't find them as fair."

"Why not?"

"Well … in this country, the stars *mean* something. They can be read, like the lines of a palm. There are subtle connections between them and us, subtle forces that shape and drive us … you know all this. But in the Lowland, stars are just stars."

Gavin was quiet for so long that Nemain grew embarrassed. "Am I talking too much? I'll let you sleep."

"Not at all. I was just thinking. Remind me, how old are you?"

"Twenty."

"And you went on your first *immram* at fifteen. How old were you when you began your apprenticeship?"

"Eleven."

He laughed. "That's absurd."

"Is that not the age a boy may be fitted for a trade?"

"Aye, an eleven- or twelve-year-old boy can learn to make horseshoes, or bake bread, or mix mortar. He does not learn to read the stars! You're a rare and interesting person, jade. And you've touched on something I often wonder about." He propped himself up on his elbow to face her. "What will my wife think of our mystical ways—coming from a land where, as you say, stars are just stars?"

"She'll be a good Lowland wife," said Nemain cautiously. "She'll respect your customs and adapt to them however you require her to."

"But in her heart, she'll think us quite mad."

Nemain didn't dare comment on that.

"What made you different? Apart from being freakishly clever?"

She gave a dry chuckle. " 'Freakish' is about right. I wanted a cure for my hands, and she promised me that if I became her apprentice, she'd do her best to cure me."

" 'She'?"

"My mistress. She had a name of power also."

"Ah."

Nemain took a deep breath—anxious to avoid explaining Rhiannon's entire role in the matter—and went on, "She failed in the end; all she found was that riddle. But she gave me so much else. ... Anyway, it wasn't as simple a matter as making my hands less ugly. Of the curse I'm under, ugliness is only the sign and token."

"What is the curse?"

"Loneliness. I have no family and no lineage. Everyone I've ever loved has either died, gone away, or failed to love me in return. Or else something in *me* prevents me from feeling a bond with them. I escaped one kind of loneliness back home, but I've been lonely in the North just the same. I'll never find a place where I really belong."

Gavin was silent once more.

"I'm not trying to be dramatic or anything. That's just the way it is."

"Where did this curse come from? Who would wish such a thing on anyone?"

"It doesn't matter now. She's dead."

"Who? Your mistress, or the one who cursed you?"

"Both," said Nemain shortly. "Anyway, I'm definitely talking too much. I'll let you sleep."

"Jade."

"Sir?"

He sighed. "I hope you know that you're not without friends. You have Lord Winworth and Lady Monessa, Master Henry and Mistress Rois. And I hope you can include me among them."

"Thank you, sir. I do know that."

"And don't worry about talking too much. If I didn't like to hear you talk, I wouldn't have brought you with me."

She smiled. "You're very kind."

"Not really," he said. "Good night."

Chapter 22

THE NEXT MORNING they were overtaken by a caravan of entertainers—minstrels, tumblers, magicians, and play-actors—heading south for the upcoming spring and summer fairs. While Gavin rode ahead to converse with them, Nemain hung back shyly, watching in fascination. They were a disreputable but colorful lot, men and women alike singing and joking noisily, looking as if they cared not at all what other people thought of them. It occurred to her that if she had not met Rhiannon, she might have run away and joined a merry band like this.

"Oi, lassie!" cried a man who, like her, wore his fiddle-bag slung across his back. "Care to join us?"

"No, thank you," she smiled.

"Come on! You can do better than that ginger *gowran!*"—a rather rude word.

Gavin turned his head and shouted a retort in the Northern tongue. Amid the laughter that followed, Nemain noticed an odd-looking, unkempt little man on a donkey trailing the caravan. He was young, an Outlander by the look of him, and his expression was both wistful and vacant. She guessed that he was, in Lowland parlance, "not all there."

The other travelers paid him no attention, and Nemain forgot about him until midday, when they all stopped to rest and eat. Then he was caught poking around one of the wagons, and a scuffle ensued.

"You little thief!" cried one of the players, shaking him. "Give me back what you took, and *ersooyl lhiat!*"

"I didn't take nothing."

"No? Turn out your pockets, or I'll turn you upside down!"

"I didn't take nothing!—Hey, that's *mine!* Give it back!"

138

At that point Gavin got up to intervene, but the next words from the little man stopped him in his tracks.

"Give it back! Or by your mother's flesh and father's bones, I'll—"

Gavin caught Nemain's eye and quickened his pace. The little Outlander, seeing the big red-headed Northman coming his way, panicked and fled.

"Oi! Wait!" Gavin called, running after him at a full sprint. Nemain hurried over to the player.

"Please, what was that all about? What did he say?"

The man shrugged. "Some Outland oath, I reckon. I'm more concerned with whatever he stole."

"What did you take from him?"

He pointed at a small wooden object that he had thrown contemptuously in the dirt. It was a child's toy, a cleverly carved little dog. She stooped to retrieve it and then ran to Gavin, who had caught the little man and now held him by the collar.

"Stop crying. I won't hurt you. Just tell me what you said."

"I didn't take nothing," the little man sobbed. "Let me go."

"What was that thing you said? 'Mother's flesh and father's bones.' What does it mean?"

"Gavin, that's enough," said Nemain. He turned in surprise—she had never yet called him by name—but before he could respond, a girl's voice rang out: "Jory!"

"Danu!" The little man struggled in Gavin's grip, and Gavin let him go, exchanging a stunned look with Nemain. Danu was a name of power.

"I've been looking everywhere for you!" said the owner of the name. She was in her late teens, wiry, suntanned and barefoot, with masses of dark auburn hair. Over her dingy linen smock, she wore a vest and skirt in vivid colors, with strange and beautiful designs woven into the fabric. Her eyes were green and flecked with hazel, like Jory's, but full of intelligence—and, at the moment, anger.

"There, there, love. You know you're not supposed to go off alone." She drew Jory's weeping face down on her shoulder and glared up at Gavin. "What did you do to him?"

"Nothing. We just heard him swearing, and we wanted to know what it meant. Perhaps you can tell us? 'By your mother's flesh and father's bones' ... ?"

Danu looked uncomfortable. "He meant nothing by it. I don't know where he picks these things up."

"I'm sorry to have upset him. We mean no harm."

"Oh, and here's this," said Nemain, holding out the toy dog. "It was on the ground."

Danu took it and handed it to Jory, who immediately stopped crying. "Thanks. He can't bear to be without it. Come on, Jory, let's go home."

"Wait." Gavin moved to block their path. "Please, miss, it's terribly important that we find out what that oath means. Is there nothing you can tell us?"

How neatly he did that, Nemain thought. Intimidating with his physical presence, yet perfectly respectful and gentlemanly in his manner. The girl's manner, in turn, visibly softened.

"Well ... my gran can explain it better than I can. Come on."

They fetched their horses and followed her. Nemain's hands were shaking so badly that she could hardly manage the reins. Was she about to find a cure at last?

Jory, meanwhile, saw that she had a dog, and made eager advances to him. "I wouldn't ..." Nemain started and then stopped, for Moddey didn't seem to mind being petted by the stranger. Would wonders never cease!

"So who are you then? Traveling minstrels?"

"Pilgrims," said Gavin. "My name is Gavin, and this is ..."

"Jade," Nemain introduced herself. "How did you come by your name?"

The girl frowned. "I was given it when I was born."

"And do your own people call you that?"

"Of course. It's my name."

Gavin and Nemain exchanged another look.

"Where does your gran live?" asked Nemain.

"Our village is down in that pass"—pointing at a half-obscured valley ahead, a considerable distance for a barefooted girl. "My gran is Rensa the Weaver. Maybe you've heard of her?"

"I have not," said Gavin, "but if she made what you're wearing, she ought to be famous."

Danu laughed delightedly and tossed her head. "She's good, isn't she?"

"That she is."

Nemain studied the designs on the girl's vest and skirt. They looked familiar, but she wasn't sure why. And the girl herself struck her as odd in some way, not like any Outlander she'd ever seen. It took her a while to realize the difference: Danu walked with a straight back—not with a tired, defeated slouch—and when she spoke, she looked you in the eye.

What had made her thus? She was obviously poor, but poverty had not broken her spirit. She was dirty and uncouth—Lady Bronwyn would have taken the birch switch to *her* early and often!—but there was pride in her gait and the way she held her head, a pride that no well-bred Lowland lady could match.

"She doesn't seem much like an Outlander, does she?" Nemain murmured to Gavin.

"She's beautiful," said Gavin.

Now Nemain stared at Danu in perplexity. "You think so? She's not a bit like …"

"There's more than one kind of beauty, jade." Seeing the expression on her face, he laughed. "Don't worry. My affections are very much elsewhere."

Danu's village was a scattering of stone houses along the valley floor, with a strip of communal fields just beyond. She led Gavin and Nemain into an austere two-room structure, one room of which was dominated by a massive warp-weighted loom. A young girl stood working side by side with a tall, gaunt old woman. "That's good … that's much better, Caya."

As Gavin and Nemain entered, the old woman immediately turned to face them, hands on hips. Her sleeves were rolled up, and her hands were stained from working with dyestuffs. She, too, had distinctive green eyes.

"Run along home," she said to Caya, and then to Danu: "So you found Jory. I take it he was wandering along the main road, as usual?"

Danu nodded.

"And who are these?"

"Pilgrims."

Rensa raised an eyebrow.

Gavin made a bow. "My name is Gavin, and this is …"

"Save it," said Rensa, turning back to inspect something on the loom. "You're a Seafarer and a gentleman, which means you can only want one thing. We're not selling our land, nor moving off it."

"Begging your pardon, but I'm not a seafarer. And if I were, why would I want your land?"

Danu rolled her eyes. "She means a Northman. It's what she calls all Northerners."

"And that's what you Seafarers have done for centuries, ever since you came ashore. Moved onto our land and pushed our people off it. Well, we didn't leave then, and we're not about to."

"I give you my word, that's not what I'm after."

"My wares, then? You can buy them at the Kell's Crossing fair this summer, like everyone else. I do my own trading, and I have sole rights. I'll not be beholden to any man."

"Come off it, Gran," said Danu in disgust. "They just have a question about the Old Ways."

"Oh?" Rensa faced them again, but if anything, she looked even more suspicious.

While Gavin told her what Jory had said, Nemain moved closer to the loom. Those strange designs were being worked into this fabric as well: wavy parallels, circles with rays, sections of circles like the phases of the moon. ...

"What are you looking at?" said Rensa.

"These symbols." Nemain pointed. "I know where I've seen them before. Those standing stones in the Middle Cantrefs."

Rensa looked at Nemain's gloved hand, and a subtle change came over her face. "Come with me."

Gavin started to follow, but she shook her head. "Just the lass. Danu, keep him company."

"All right," said Danu cheerfully.

Rensa took Nemain out to the dye-working shed. Despite the heat and the acrid smells from the simmering pots, Nemain liked it. It was not unlike Rhiannon's cottage, full of herbs and potions, where ancient lore met everyday industry.

"What are you?" asked Rensa. "You have Northern bones, but a Lowland voice. You were raised down there, I think?"

"I was, but my mother was an Outlander."

Rensa snorted. "Our people didn't come from outside. We were here from the beginning. It was the Seafarers and the Plainsfolk who tried to squeeze us out, flanking us on north and south, and then called us 'Outlanders' as if we didn't belong. Many were driven out and forgot where they had come from, but my family stood their ground. We've been in this region for a thousand years."

"Then you really are descended from the ones who raised those stones? The Vanished Ones?"

"Who's vanished?" said the old woman tartly.

Nemain was very excited. "And those symbols—what do they mean?"

"What's it to you?"

"I know they have significance." Seeing Rensa's eyes narrow, she added, "I'm a *caillagh*. I care a great deal about such things."

"Humph! Not many *cailleeyn* would humble themselves to seek answers from the likes of me. Well, I'm sorry that I can't tell you, for I think you would respect our mysteries. But I'm sworn to secrecy."

"Oh."

"Now show me your hand. I want to see what was done to you."

Nemain obeyed, caught off guard by this abrupt change of topic. But as Rensa examined her hand, it was apparent that the old woman's thoughts were still running in the same channel.

"The Seafarers robbed us of so much," she mused. "They stole our holy books—at least those that were not written in stone—and claimed many of our traditions as their own. But there was other lore they stole that we were better off without. Lore that no one in any land should ever have access to. ... I knew this curse existed, but I've never seen someone with the mark."

"Have you any idea how to undo it? The only clue I have is a riddle. It's very like the oath we heard from Jory."

"Jory doesn't know what he's saying. He hears these things from drunken scoundrels and repeats them. ... As you know, the flesh of a child comes from the mother; the bones, from the father."

Nemain did not know any such thing, but she kept listening.

"Your mother's flesh is also your mother's family—everything you get from your mother's side—and likewise with your father's bones. Together, they are everything that makes you *you*. To swear by them is a dreaded oath, and to curse someone else's—well ... How does your riddle go?"

Nemain repeated it, and Rensa nodded as if it was just what she would have expected. "Then someone else will have to be cut off."

"*Cut off?*"

"What else can it mean to 'cleave mother's flesh from father's bone'? That's what was done to you. You are an orphan, are you not? Have you any family?"

"Well ..." She thought of her unknown mother and of Tynan, her father, who could not *be* her father. She thought of Rhiannon, who was not her mother, and yet had been, in a sense. Fragments of parents, that was all she had had. "No."

"And with hands like these, you won't marry, nor risk passing them on to your children. You've been cut off. And your only hope is to be grafted in elsewhere, by cutting off someone else."

"No." Nemain pulled her hand free and put her glove back on. "No. Even if I could—even if I knew how it was done—I *couldn't*."

"Good," said Rensa firmly. "I'm sorry for you, lass, but I'm glad you see this in the right light. You have to bear this evil alone. Let the young man go."

"What young man?"

"Yours, in there." She gestured at the house.

"Oh, he's not mine. I'm just—"

"Borrowing him?"

"No!" Nemain choked on a laugh. "Rensa, you're a wise woman. You know I'm a *caillagh* and I was raised a Lowlander. Do you really think I'm capable of that?"

"I think you're a woman whose element is fire, so yes, you're plenty capable. And he clearly likes you. If you don't give him up, I don't know which of you will be worse off in the end."

Nemain tried to argue, but Rensa merely shook her head and headed back into the house. A moment later Gavin came out.

"What did she say?"

"Long story short—there is no cure."

So far she had not cried, but now the sympathy in Gavin's eyes finished her. She wept quietly, not so much from grief as from tired resignation. It was as if she had given up hope long ago, and her conversation with Rensa merely confirmed her hopelessness.

"What will you do?"

"Nothing! The only way to remove this evil is to wish it on someone else, and that I cannot do." She wiped her eyes on the back of her glove. "Anyway, let's get back to the main road. I'm sorry to have wasted so much of your time."

"You haven't at all, jade. It was worth it to find out, even if that's all there is to find out." He shook his head. "There *must* be another way to interpret that riddle. We can't give up hope."

"And those symbols on the loom—the same as on the standing stones—she won't tell me what they mean." A strangled sob, this one of real grief, escaped from her throat. "*Everything* is closed off to me."

"Oh, jade."

He moved to take her in his arms. But at that moment Danu came bounding outside, and Nemain immediately drew back.

"You're staying the night, aren't you?"

"Are we?" Gavin asked Nemain.

She blinked away her last tears and managed the ghost of a smile. "It's up to you, sir."

"Then yes. And while I'm thinking of it"—his eyes ran approvingly over Danu's outfit—"have you another vest and skirt like those that you'd be willing to part with, for my friend here? I'd pay you."

"How much?"

"Five gold staters."

Danu laughed in disbelief. "You could have *me* for five gold staters."

"Just the clothes, thanks."

"Wait here. I'll even throw in a clean smock, if you like."

Gavin smiled. "There," he said under his breath, "you can have the symbols, at least. And you may find out their meaning in time."

Nemain smiled in earnest. "That's really too good of you, sir."

"Not really."

Danu came back out with the clothes bundled under her arm. "How about these? They're a bit too big for me anyway, and I think these colors would suit her."

Gavin nodded as he examined the fabric. It was patterned in red, gold, and a rich, earthy green. "That they would. Here, jade, will you try them on?"

"Later." She folded them carefully into one of her saddlebags. "Thank you, sir."

They passed a surprisingly pleasant evening at Rensa's house. Jory spent the whole time playing with Moddey, and Danu flirted shamelessly with Gavin—or tried to; he would not flirt back, but was as gallant as propriety allowed. Rensa had dropped her earlier animosity, now that she knew what the "Seafarer's" real errand was. But she still gave Nemain one or two knowing looks, as if to say, *You're not fooling anyone.*

That night as they prepared their beds—Rensa, Danu, and Jory in one room, Gavin and Nemain in the other—Gavin said, "Jade, I've got an idea."

"Oh?"

"This may be a shot in the dark. But why don't we go to Senuna?"

"Senuna? What on earth for?"

"They have healing waters there. I know, I know—it may not do any good. But if there's any chance at all, it's worth it, don't you think?"

"I couldn't possibly ask that of you."

"You're not asking. I'm offering."

"But—*how?* Can you even afford it?"

"Not right now, but if the Good Folk are willing ..."

"It would take you far out of your way. You'd lose a lot of time."

"I'll still have plenty left."

"Gavin ..."

This was the second time she had failed to call him "sir," and he wisely refrained from pointing it out. "Jade, let me do this for you. I still feel I should do everything in my power to help you while I'm on this *immram.* The fact that I've always wanted to go there myself is purely irrelevant."

She laughed. "Well, it is your *immram*. If that's the direction you feel you should go ..."

"Excellent."

A little while later, just as she was falling asleep, she heard him laugh softly.

"What is it?"

"Just thinking. I know I said you were nothing like an Outlander, but—well ..." He chuckled again.

"Well, what?"

"If you took away your *caillagh's* dignity and your Lowland reserve—and if you cleaned Rensa's granddaughter up a bit, and took away her deplorable manners—I could easily believe you were related."

"Now you're talking rubbish."

"It's true. Do you know you have a very similar smile? You don't smile half enough, jade. And she has sort of a dark voice like yours, but without your pretty accent. I can't abide an Outland accent. Never could."

"Good night, Gavin."

He sighed happily. "Good night."

Chapter 23

NEMAIN AWOKE TO find herself alone in the room. As she pulled on her gloves, Danu came in with a bowl of frumenty—the same fare as supper the night before. "Oh, good, you're up. Have some breakfast."

"Where is everyone?"

"Gran's in the shed, and Jory's out playing with the dog. Gavin took off bright and early. Had to see a man about a thing, he said."

Nemain's brows knit together at this information. She choked down the frumenty, wishing there was some sugar to go with it.

At the sound of galloping hooves approaching, she hurried outside with Danu close behind. Gavin reined in his horse in front of them, not bothering to dismount. "Jade, can you come with me now?"

"Is anything wrong?"

"Not yet, but there's something I have to do today, and time is of the essence. Leave Moddey for now. We'll come back."

She hesitated, then nodded. "I'll go get Peddyr."

"It'll be faster with just Thevshi. Can you climb up behind me?"

Danu gave her a boost, and she clung to Gavin for stability. "I'm sorry there's no pillion seat," he said, "but I need you with me. Hold on tight."

Thevshi took off at what felt like breakneck speed. Nemain was not used to riding bareback, on a horse as powerful as this, and with someone else controlling him.

"Where are we going?" she cried.

"Drughage. It's the first town on the Senuna road."

"What's at Drughage?"

"A tourney."

She asked no more questions—it was his *immram*, after all—but she directed her thoughts to the Good Folk: *Please, please let him have a good reason for this.*

When they reached the tournament grounds at Drughage—after what seemed like a hard, jolting lifetime—Gavin dismounted and helped her get down. Feeling how shaky she was, he laughed and clasped her in his arms for a moment. "Oh, jade, you weren't scared, were you?"

"No," she lied. "What are we doing here?"

"Signing up for archery. Well, that's what *I'm* doing."

"And I?"

"Staying with me." He met her eyes and smiled apologetically. "I really do need you here. I would have explained, but there wasn't time."

"How about now?"

"Well, you'll see soon enough."

The scribe taking down names for the archery contest dismissed Gavin at a glance. "I'm sorry. An entrance fee is required."

"I have it."

"And a seal."

"I know." Gavin reached into his surcoat pocket and took out a gold signet ring on a silver chain. On it was the finely wrought emblem of a stag.

The scribe gasped. "The house of Airleas! Forgive me, sir, I didn't—"

Gavin put his finger to his lips.

"Of course, of course."

Gavin affixed his seal to the paper, thereby signing away his anonymity, and then handed over the staggering entrance fee. Nemain hoped anew that he had a good reason for this.

He took his place at the end of the line, and she went over to join the spectators. At the cry of "Nock! Draw! Loose!" she held her breath; and as the first contestants loosed their shots with a collective *ping!*, her heart began to sink. Oh, these fellows were very good.

At last Gavin stepped up to take his first shot. He looked so calm, so oblivious to the derisive sniggers around him, that she couldn't help smiling. No one would have guessed from his clothes that he was a nobleman, but he certainly had the demeanor of one.

"Nock! Draw! Loose!"—and in one fluid, unthinking motion, beautiful to witness, he let his arrow fly. It hit the center of its mark, and the sniggering stopped.

As he stepped back to wait his turn in the next round, his eyes sought her in the crowd. He grinned at the expression on her face; it was the first emotion he had shown thus far.

He won the next round, and the next. Eventually it was down to him and one other, a man who had acquitted himself just as well, but had grown increasingly pale and tense as the contest progressed. "I *can't* lose to this lout!" was written all over his face. Nemain could not bear to watch the final shot.

Ping! And it was over. Gavin had won.

"Congratulations, sir!" An official came forward with the prize, a purse full of gold.

"Give it to my lady," said Gavin, beckoning to Nemain. "She can dispose of it as she will."

She went to join him, blushing with shy pride. As she accepted the prize, the crowd cheered.

"How about a kiss for your champion?" someone shouted.

What could she do! Impossible to comply; equally impossible to refuse. Instead, she grinned and sidled up close to Gavin with a confidence that was surprisingly easy to assume. "I'll reward him in private."

They roared with approval at that. She whispered in his ear, "Can we go now?"

"The sooner the better," he said, and put his arm around her. They made a hasty exit amid more cheering.

"I do apologize," she said as they mounted Thevshi once more.

"For what!" he laughed. "That was very well done."

"Likewise. What are you going to do with the money?"

"What are *you* going to do with it?"

"But it's yours. You won it."

"For you," he corrected. "I'm on an *immram*, jade. I can't be trying to make money for myself."

"So you mean this whole thing was—?"

"For you."

She laughed—so touched, bewildered, embarrassed, that she didn't know how to respond. "What can I say? 'Thank you' doesn't seem like enough."

"Oh, it was no great sacrifice." The satisfaction in his voice belied his earlier stoicism. "Now, it really is your money, jade. You do what you like with it. But if I might make a suggestion …"

"I hear Senuna's very nice this time of year."

"So do I!—with the orange trees in bloom, and all that."

"And it seems a shame to go alone."

"That it would be."

"Would you like to come too?"

He laughed. "I would. Thanks so much."

"You're very welcome."

⇥ ⇤

They spent one more night at Rensa's house, then returned to the Senuna road at dawn. "We should get to Gwehara within the week," said Gavin. "Now, that's a place everyone should see. You'll love it."

"Gwehara?" Somehow she had forgotten that Gwehara lay before Senuna.

He looked at her curiously. "Is something wrong?"

"No. I, er … I've never been."

"Well, you should. It's the seat of all things noble and holy—the highest of the high. And beautiful! There are so many kinds of beauty in the world, but Gwehara's is all its own."

Nemain had never troubled herself to learn much about Gwehara, though it was a place dear to the hearts of *cailleeyn*. Its name meant "the place of winds," on account of its high elevation and lack of natural shelter from the elements. The most revered and pious clans of the North had built their strongholds there as a sort of protest against cities like Senuna, which was famous for its dissipations even in ancient times. And while Senuna boasted hot springs and lush scenery, the very austerity of Gwehara became the backdrop for a great flowering of genius: philosophy, architecture, all the arts. But now few of the ancient clans remained, and they guarded their heritage with a jealousy bordering on fanaticism. That was pretty much all Nemain knew about the place—that, and she hated it on principle.

"The thing is"—she stopped, bit her lip, then decided to get it over with—"my father was from Gwehara."

"Really? Didn't you say he was a farrier?"

"He was."

There was a pause. "Well, there's no shortage of farriers in the North," he said slowly. "I've known many a nobleman who cared for his own horses."

"Then you understand … ?"

"I think I do." He sounded ominously excited. "Jade, I could easily find out whose child you are."

"No, you couldn't. I don't even know that the name he used was his own."

"That's a small matter. There aren't many names to choose from among the highest of the high. All *my* claim to nobility rests on my Gweharan blood, and it's a distant strain at that. Why, jade, don't you see what that makes you?"

"Not your relative, surely."

"Oh, no! Any blood tie between us is centuries old; I would never presume on that. But it's said that the ancient clans of Gwehara are descended from one of the Good Folk—you know, Him whose nickname is 'Skilled-in-every-art'—and that His direct descendants share His gifts. Poetry, philosophy, medicine … *music* …"

"Don't."

Her voice was quiet and controlled, but vibrant with anger. It silenced him at once.

"You know my mother was an Outlander, so you can guess why my father left his home. It was not by choice."

His eyes wavered, but he nodded.

"I don't want to know who his people are. They cast him out, and they made him take vows he could not keep. As far as I'm concerned, they caused his death."

"I see."

There was something in his tone she did not like. She asked, still more quietly, "Do you think it was just?"

"I'm sorry. I do understand."

"But … ?"

"You're overlooking one thing." He took a deep breath. "I know the vows you speak of, and he must have taken them willingly. No man can be forced to take a *geis*."

"Oh yes, I'm sure my noble kinfolk didn't 'force' him—didn't bind him or starve him or anything like that. But a fine position they put him in, all the same! I *knew* him, Gavin. I watched him die. He would never have taken those vows if he'd had any real choice in the matter."

Gavin was silent.

"You seem to think he would have. Why?"

"Oh, jade, I didn't know him. I can't judge."

"No, tell me. This I want to know."

"There's no way to say this without hurting you."

"Say it."

Her voice was still controlled, but now there were tears in her eyes. Gavin looked pained.

"If it had been me," he said, "if I had—accidentally started a family, and I did not want to accept that responsibility—I would look on those *geasa* as the only honorable means of escape."

Now Nemain was silenced.

"Who knows how I might feel about it later? I might regret it. I might even blame my family, as if I'd had no choice. But the choice would have been quite simple. If she was not an Outlander—or, the Good Folk forbid, another man's wife—I could marry her and keep my inheritance, or I could take the *geasa* and be disowned. If she was an Outlander, I'd be disowned anyway, so there'd be nothing preventing me from marrying her if I really wanted to. … Do you understand?"

A little of the righteous anger went out of her, displaced by a chill of disillusionment. She did not want to think of her father in that light, but Gavin's words rang true. "I made a mistake when I was young," Tynan had said. Oh, she knew he had loved *her*, in spite of himself; but what of her mother?—that poor, forsaken girl who had followed him so bravely? Nemain could not bear to think he might not have deserved or even wanted such devotion.

"Perhaps they didn't kill him," she said flatly, "but they still ruined him. They cut him off."

Again Gavin said nothing.

"Well, go on. Defend them."

He sighed. "My family would have done the same. I know it's a harsh law, but it's how I was raised. We're chaste, and we don't intermarry with Outlanders. That's just how it's always been."

Nemain decided to let the matter drop. There was more sorrow in her now than anger, partly because of Gavin's attitude. She had thought he would be more sympathetic. But no, he seemed to think *she* was in the wrong.

"Stop," said Gavin, and Nemain brought Peddyr to a halt alongside Thevshi.

"What is it?"

"Direct me," he said. "We don't have to go this way. Where do you wish to go?"

"It's your *immram*."

"I've lost my sense of it. I think it rests with you."

Nemain doubted that, but did not argue. "Let's keep going."

"You're sure? I don't want to cause you pain."

"*You* haven't. I'm not angry with you."

"No? I saw the Raven in your eyes two minutes since. I thought I was done for."

She managed a wry smile. "You're doing me a great service by going to Senuna. And I know of no other way to get there except through Gwehara. So let's go."

"You forgive me, then?"

"For what?"

"For speaking on the matter at all. As I said, I'm not one to judge. It's just that I can't bear to think of you hating your own blood. You've spoken of loneliness; I can't imagine anything lonelier than that." He paused. "And, you know, a drop of that blood runs in me, too. I would not have you think of me as just one of 'those people.' "

Nemain's smile became genuine. "I never should."

"And you're sure you don't want to know who they are? You spoke of having no family, no lineage …"

She shook her head. "He didn't want anyone to know. I'll honor that."

"Then so will I."

That was the last they spoke of Gwehara until they actually arrived there. It *was* a beautiful region, she had to admit … beautiful and forbidding. Against the stark moorland, in the early morning light that Gavin loved so much, the white towers and battlements of the ancient castles glowed with pure, unadorned loveliness. But they were towers and battlements all the same—built to defend, to conceal, to keep people out—and she felt oppressed in their shadows.

"Want to go inside the walls?"

"We're allowed inside?"

"Oh, yes, in the courtyards. They maintain the grounds well, even for the fortresses that are all but empty. Here, this gate's open."

Nemain followed him inside and suddenly found herself in a vast, well-appointed garden. "Oh!"

Gavin laughed. "It's a bit of a shock, isn't it?"

She nodded, looking around in wonder. Carefully laid-out waterways … fruit trees and shade trees … terraces of flowers that, by rights, shouldn't grow in the North Country at all. It was not clear where the garden ended and the fortress began; the marble stairways and colonnades, the ivy-draped turrets and balconies seemed to have grown up here as naturally as the trees, for all their finely wrought symmetry. She saw a few people quietly coming and going—amazing that the place wasn't more crowded even at this hour!—but they were so unobtrusive and so clearly at home, unlike herself and Gavin, that they seemed like part of the scenery.

"What would we find if we went into those buildings?"

"What wouldn't we find! Paintings, sculptures, all manner of art by the masters of every land. Libraries …"

"Libraries?"

The lust in her voice made him smile. "Aye, with a thousand years of knowledge inside. But they're very protective of these things, as you can imagine. We're not free to wander just anywhere. Well, *you* would be, if you had on your black robe, but I— What are you looking at?"

"These herbs." She laughed. "This plot here is just a medicine garden. I planted this same stuff at the Deep Valley Inn."

"Well, everything here has its uses. It doesn't mean it can't be beautiful. I love that—the emphasis on beauty in every aspect of life." He sighed. "Northwaite is home to me; it'll always come first. But if I could choose anywhere else on earth to spend my days, it would be here."

Nemain thought of her father and the pain he must have felt in his exile. To come down from this to a life of drudgery on another man's estate! To think that in a different life, as his lawful daughter, she could have called this place her home! *Oh, Tynan, no wonder you didn't want me to know.*

"What do you think, jade? Do you want to see more?"

"You mean—inside?"

He nodded. "You can, if you go put on your black robe. I'll wait here."

"Oh!" For a moment she was torn between longing, bitterness, and fear. Finally she shook her head. "No, I don't dare."

"Why not? They don't know who you are, and even if they did, they'd have to honor the robe."

"But what of this?" She lifted a gloved hand, which trembled slightly. "They wouldn't trust me. If they turned me away, on any account, I couldn't bear it."

Gavin took her hand and tucked it into the crook of his arm. That simple, gentlemanly gesture, so foreign to her, was both startling and comforting.

"Where to, then?" he asked.

"Onward. Unless there's anything else you wish me to see."

"Oh, there is, but it'll have to wait until tonight. There'll be a full moon— how lucky is that!—and you'll find that moonrise here is different from anywhere else."

"How so?"

He smiled mysteriously. "You'll see."

That evening, as they were rolling out their bedding in the twilight, Nemain heard a strain of unearthly music carried on the wind. It sounded at first like a distant, lonely voice, then gradually grew in volume and complexity until it became hundreds of voices, both far away and all around her.

"What is that?" She turned around in utter delight and bewilderment, seeking vainly for the music's source. "Where is it coming from?"

Gavin was enjoying her reaction. "It's the *arrane oie.*"

" 'Song of night'?"

He nodded. "They do this for the full moon. They gather on the hilltops and sing."

Each distant choir was singing the same song in the Northern tongue, all in flawless, crystalline harmony; but each had begun at a different point, and the effect was sweet, shimmering, profoundly haunting. Oh, there could be no doubt that these were Nemain's people!—and yet they were not her people. She could never share in this. *This, too, is closed off to me. ...*

Gavin took her hand, and at once the sense of isolation left her. Suddenly it was enough that she was here, now, with someone who wanted her here. In that moment there was no loneliness; there was only communion, and perfect beauty of sight and sound.

The song slowly died away, and he still held her hand. She wondered if he had forgotten he was holding it—if he had even been aware of taking it.

"Well?" he asked.

Unable to speak, she merely looked at him, shining-eyed. He smiled, gave her hand a little squeeze, and then let go. So it had been a conscious move on his part after all. He had not merely been bewitched by the music.

Nemain lay awake that night for a long time. She felt no regret for anything she had experienced thus far; it had been worthwhile to come here, despite her feelings about the place. But she was full of troubling and contradictory emotions, of which Gwehara and its associations were not the only cause.

Chapter 24

IT WAS WELL past dawn when she woke up. Gavin was already awake but seemed in no hurry to get moving. He was half reclined on his bedding, idly gazing at his miniature portrait of Monessa. When he saw Nemain stir, he put it back in his pocket.

"Why didn't you wake me?"

He shrugged. "Didn't feel like it. Shall we eat and get a move on?"

"Actually, I'd like to try and play something first. Do you mind?"

"I command it, if you recall."

"Oh, right." She opened up her fiddle-bag. "Don't look at me."

She played the *arrane oie* from memory, unable to reproduce its harmonies on the fiddle, but following them in her mind. Even without them, the effect of the solitary melody on the morning air was rather lovely. She went over it a few times, then packed up her fiddle and bow. "That'll do."

Gavin stared at her. "How do you do that?"

"It was in my head all night. Now it's in my hands as well, so I won't forget it."

"*How?*" he laughed.

"Oh, let's see." She thought for a moment. She had never had to describe the process before. "You've copied paintings before, haven't you?"

"I used to, when I was younger. How did you guess?"

"I would be surprised if you hadn't. You have a keen eye and a steady hand, as I've seen. And you're always pointing out the quality of light and the colors of things."

Gavin looked flattered.

"When you're doing that, does it change how you view the original?"

"Well, yes. You get very familiar with little details as you go along—things you might never have noticed, no matter how many times you looked at it before—and you can't un-see them afterward."

"You come to know it thoroughly as you re-create it."

"Aye. But it doesn't happen at one immaculate stroke. That's the difference between you and other mortals, jade."

Nemain laughed and bit into an apple. "I should like to see your paintings."

"I doubt any of my efforts have survived. If they weren't destroyed, they ought to have been. And it's long since I even held a brush."

"Why is that?"

"Oh, I don't know. I suppose because my father thought it a waste of time. My mother encouraged it, but"—he hesitated—"my father has a positive genius for making me ashamed."

"Ashamed? You?"

"I'm not beyond shame, jade, though I may give that impression."

"Well, if I had a son, I'd worry about him turning out stupid, or wicked, or incompetent. And if he was very much none of those things, and just liked to draw"—she snorted—"I'd count myself lucky indeed."

"It was not his only or his biggest grievance with me, but I thank you for the compliment. I hope you'll talk me up to Lady Monessa. 'He's very much not stupid, or wicked, or incompetent.' "

"I will, in good conscience."

He laughed and then sighed.

"What's troubling you?" she said.

"I should like to ask you for counsel again."

There was a pause. "*Are* you asking me for counsel again?"

"No, for I don't want to show a lack of faith. I just want to know—now that you know me, and not just from my hand or my face—do you still think I'm good enough for her?"

Nemain looked him in the eye. "No part of my assessment has changed."

"Are you sure?"

"Do you doubt it?"

"It's myself I doubt."

"Why? Why now?"

His eyes fell. It was the water side of him fighting the fire, she guessed—that impulse to flow in a different direction, no matter how auspicious the path ahead.

"Gavin, you must answer this for yourself. *Are* you on the right course? Can you feel it?"

"I feel something."

"If you're feeling unsure about Senuna, I'll understand ..."

"Oh, we're going there. I feel strongly enough about that."

"Then what other course could you possibly be on right now? Don't second-guess yourself. The Good Folk have obviously trusted you with a great deal."

He smiled faintly. "I suppose They have."

"So trust Them. Trust me." She paused. "You do trust me, don't you?"

His smile suddenly turned perverse. "Of course," he said, getting up and preparing to leave.

"You don't?"

"Oh, I do. It's just ... well, you're very young, jade. And not just for a *caillagh*."

Nemain was not sure what he meant by that, but she was indignant. "Why should that make a difference? Three in one, and one in three." That was part of a Dark Saying, reminding him that in each single aspect of Maid, Mother, and Crone, the other two were always inherent.

"You're right," he said, "it shouldn't make a difference. Anyway, let's get going."

⋯⟞ ⟝⋯

Even after the splendor of Gwehara, Nemain was unprepared for Senuna. For one thing, it was vastly more crowded; for another, it was set on a low plain not far from the coast, where the climate was warm and the air was rich. The kinds of plants that had to be so carefully tended and sheltered in Gwehara were in natural profusion here. Even from a distance, she could smell the orange groves in bloom.

Whereas the greatest riches of Gwehara were hidden from public view, in Senuna everything was on display. There was much that was beautiful—fine old palaces, statues, gardens—but much that was gaudy and cheap. Anything you could possibly want, of any quantity or quality, you could find in Senuna.

"It's kind of awful," said Gavin, "but splendid too." Which matched Nemain's feeling exactly.

"Shouldn't we be going to the waters?"

"You really are all business, aren't you," he teased. "There's no rush. Let's get ourselves settled for the night first."

"You want to stay the night, then?"

"I want to stay several nights. I'm tired, jade. I want a rest before we get to the mountains. Don't you?"

"Oh, yes!" she cried joyfully. "But I didn't think it was an option."

"Why on earth not?"

"It's your *immram*. And you've done so much for me already." Her face grew warm. "We're only here because of me. You'd be at Briarvale by now, easily, if it weren't for—"

"Jade." He put his hand on her shoulder. His smile was both annoyed and amused. "Don't question it. Just take it."

Get whatever you can from him, I say, said Henry's voice in her mind. She stifled a laugh.

Once they had paid up at an inn and their animals were safely stabled (including the unhappy Moddey), they went down to the bath houses. There were recreational baths of varying temperatures and medicinal baths for various complaints. "Take as long as you need," said Gavin, "and then meet me back at the dining hall for supper."

Nemain was skeptical about the curative virtues of the baths; her main concern was privacy. The rooms were divided by sex, but still distressingly public. She whispered her concern to a female attendant, who directed her to what looked like a little shed behind the main houses. "In there, and down the steps."

She went down and found herself in a large cavern, illuminated by many candles and echoing with the sound of bubbling waters. In a niche on the far wall, she saw a small statue of a woman, and she stopped short, realizing she was in a shrine.

So this was not only a healing spring, but a holy one! She bowed her head, her pulse quickening with solemn excitement, and advanced very slowly.

"Welcome, sister." The attendant, an old woman in a *caillagh*'s robe, rose from her stool and hobbled forward with the aid of a stick. Her eyes were pale and opaque. She reached out and touched Nemain's arm with a clawlike hand. "Are you bleeding?"

"No."

"Good. Wash yourself in the stall before you enter the spring. You'll find a bucket of water, soap, and a sheet on the shelf."

"Thank you." Nemain headed for the stall, then stopped. "How do you know to call me 'sister'?"

"By your tread," the *caillagh* replied. "Not many who enter here know what manner of place it is."

Nemain washed, leaving the sheet to dry off with later, and descended another series of steps that spiraled sun-wise down into the spring. The water was surprisingly hot, but not painfully so, and had an odd, earthy smell. Her skin liked it; even the fragile and much-cracked skin of her hands did not sting, as it usually did in water, but tingled pleasantly.

She waded in shoulder-deep, then tipped her head back to see the statue in the wall. In its indistinct features she recognized the Great High Queen, who wore as many aspects as the moon. With a heart full of thanks for the privilege of being there, whether she was healed or not, she bowed completely beneath the water.

⇥⇥ ⇤⇤

The transition between the outer walls of a Gwehara fortress and its interior garden had been one kind of shock; the transition between a sacred spring and the dining hall of a Senuna inn was another. The Raven and Stag was as noisy and bustling as the Deep Valley Inn, but on a larger scale, and there were as many Lowland voices as Northern ones raised in song and laughter. Nemain did not see Gavin inside, and she loitered by the doorway, afraid to traverse the crowd.

"You look nervous," said his voice in her ear, making her jump.

"Oh! I didn't see you."

"I only just got back." His hair was wet, she noticed. "Took the hot plunge, and then the cold. It was marvelous. How are you feeling?"

"Good, overall," she said absently, not sure how to describe her experience in this setting. That, and Gavin had just taken her hand, which momentarily distracted her. "I mean … well, anyway, it was nice. I think it may have been a good omen."

"An omen?"

"I'll tell you about it later."

"Oh, tell me now! Here, we'll order our supper and have it brought outside. It'll be easier for you to eat out there anyway, won't it?"

"Yes," she said, surprised at this thoughtfulness. It *was* hard for her to remove her gloves and eat in a crowded room. Then she blushed a little as she realized that was probably why he was holding her hand and keeping her close to him—so that fewer people would notice her gloves, and those who did would leave her alone rather than reckon with him.

How nice it was to be protected thus! And how funny that she should feel that way. With a name of power, surely she didn't need protecting. But then again, who could say what form the Good Folk's protection might take? Why not a big, red-headed Northman who seemed to have a knack for the task?

Don't question it. Just take it. She smiled.

"What'll you have?" he asked, pointing at the menu on the wall. She gaped a little at the vast array of dishes—roast lamb with mint, pork with mustard and sage, fish with lemons and parsley sauce—and the rich smells coming from the kitchens made her dizzy with hunger. They settled on roast chicken and junket with strawberries. "Have you ever had heather mead?"

Her eyes widened. Heather mead was rare and expensive stuff. "No."

"Then you'll have it now. Careful, though. A little goes a long way."

They took their drinks outside to a little table near a privet hedge. "Try it," said Gavin, and Nemain took a hesitant sip. It had a sweet, smoky aroma, but it burned like fire down her throat.

He laughed out loud at her expression. "Oh, jade! You may not be a real Lowlander, but you drink like one. Now tell me about that omen."

"Did you know one of the springs here is a holy one? A shrine?"

"What was it like?"

Nemain described what she had seen in the underground chamber, including the blind attendant in the *caillagh*'s robe. As she spoke, Gavin leaned forward intently.

"There *were* shrines here, when the city was young. They probably looked very much like that a thousand years ago. But it can't have really been like that today. And they wouldn't have just let you walk into such a place unless you wore a *caillagh*'s robe yourself."

"What did I see, then? An *ashlins?*"

"Must have been." He took her hand, his eyes shining. "Jade, this is wonderful. If this isn't cause for hope, I don't know what is."

She smiled diffidently, not wanting to get her hopes up, and thinking at the same time how weirdly comfortable he was with holding her hand. "I don't know what may come of it, but I think it's safe to say that it's—*Their* will—that we're here. And for that alone, I can't thank you enough."

Feeling suddenly near to tears, she reached for her cup and took another swallow, much more stoically than she had taken the first. "Actually that's not bad."

That supper was the best she had had in many years. At the Deep Valley Inn and at Rhiannon's house before that, the food had been basic and none too plentiful. Her brush with starvation during her *immram* had made her grateful for whatever she got, but she still keenly missed the good food at Briarvale. How novel it was to really enjoy what she was eating and to take as much of it as she wanted, exactly as Lady Bronwyn used to scold her for doing!

"What's in this sauce? Oranges?"

"I believe so. Ginger, too."

"That is amazing! … Why are you laughing?"

"I've just never seen anyone react that strongly to oranges before."

She started to make a retort, then stopped herself. He couldn't appreciate what such things meant to her. Heather mead and roast chicken and oranges were not miracles to him. Why, at Northwaite he probably ate like this every day.

"Do you know how adorable you are just now?"

She nearly choked. "I'm sorry?"

"The way your face lights up when you're just being happy, enjoying yourself. You're intense in your pleasures, aren't you?—such as they are. Oranges … libraries …"

"Sugared almonds."

"Sugared almonds?"

She hesitated, then added—feeling an unusual sense of daring—"There was a boy at Briarvale who used to bring me sugared almonds."

"A boy?"

Her eyes faltered under his suddenly piercing gaze. "Oh, it was nothing."

"Really?"

"Really. Less than nothing."

She reached again for her cup and was surprised to find it empty. "You know, this is awfully good."

"I think you've taken to it a little too well. Let's stop there."

"Oh, do let's have more. Unless you don't want to. Sorry, that was rude."

His mouth twitched. "A little more, but that's all."

He went to get their cups refilled, and she leaned back comfortably in her chair. The evening air was warm and scented faintly with orange blossoms, and someone in the dining hall was playing a fiddle. Not as *she* could play, of course, but for once it was nice just to sit and listen and drink the heather mead. She suspected Gavin had watered hers down, but she was quite willing to drink it anyway.

"His name was Swayne," she said, twirling her twice-emptied goblet by the stem.

"Who?"

"Swayne. The boy."

"Ah, the boy." Gavin's eyes glittered over the rim of his cup. "Tell me about him."

"He was Lord Winworth's squire. About four years older than me, and very handsome. Dark hair, dark eyes. He played the guitar …"

Gavin rolled his eyes.

"He kissed me once, when I was fifteen."

"Oh? Was it no good?"

"What?"

"You just looked melancholy all of a sudden."

Nemain giggled. "Well, he was drunk at the time, and pulled away very quickly. The only time I ever *was* kissed."

"Oh, jade."

"I can't help thinking he came to his senses and was disgusted."

"Not likely," scoffed Gavin. "I'll warrant he came to his senses and was ashamed. And rightly."

"Why 'rightly'?"

"Because look at you. It was one kiss, years ago, and you're still living on it. You *are* intense. No man should ever kiss you unless he means something by it. ... You've really never been kissed but once?"

"Just the once."

"Not even at a wedding? Everyone kisses at weddings."

"I've never been to a wedding."

"Oh, jade."

"You can stop saying that. I know you pity me."

"I do," he said, "and even more so, I pity the man who has the task of wooing you."

Nemain snorted. "So do I!"

"Indeed. Nine out of ten men won't be good enough for you, and you'll send the tenth packing if he hasn't got dark eyes and a guitar. But why do *you* pity this man, jade?"

"Because if he exists, which I doubt"—she held up a hand—"he'll have to be blind."

For a long moment Gavin looked at her with an expression she did not understand. Then he emptied his cup in one swallow. "Well. If I ever meet Swayne, I'll poke his eyes out for you."

She shook with laughter. It felt giddying to laugh about this after so many years of crying over it in secret.

"So how many have you had?" she asked, propping her chin on her fist.

"How many what?"

"Kisses."

"Ha! I've no idea."

"Well, girls you've kissed, then."

He began to count on his fingers, and she hooted. "And you a betrothed man! You dog!"

"I'll have you know, all but one of those were before my betrothal was final."

"And the last?"

"Oh, well …"

"Come, now, I told you mine. And it was ever so sad."

He laughed. "You're right about that. Well, it was about six years ago. She was a girl on our estate—of good family, though not noble—and I loved her."

He paused for a moment, apparently deep in thought, and went on, "Long story short, I was going to ask her to elope. But before anything was said, my father guessed what was in my mind. He has a way of doing that. He took me aside and told me very plainly what I stood to lose."

"And then what?" Nemain was interested to hear more, but she was having difficulty keeping her eyes open.

"Then, nothing. I broke it off." He stood up. "You're starting to nod off, jade. Let's call it a night."

If she had not been feeling the genial effects of the heather mead, Nemain would have been nervous about the prospect of sharing a bed with Gavin. As it was, she was thrilled just to have a bed to sleep in—about a blink away from collapsing onto it, in fact—and whether Gavin was a few feet or a few inches away mattered little. But as she slipped between the sheets, she saw him unrolling his bedding on the floor.

"What are you doing?"

"What's it look like?"

"Gavin, we didn't come here so you could sleep on the rushes."

"I'll be all right."

"*I'll* take"—she interrupted herself with a profound yawn—"the floor, if you like."

"Absolutely not."

"Are you sure?"

"Just leave it, jade."

Silence. A few minutes later, he gave a rueful chuckle and said softly, "The guitar, jade? Really? *You* were impressed by that?"

But Nemain was already asleep.

Chapter 25

THEY SPENT THREE days in Senuna, days that Nemain would count among her fondest memories. She had absolute freedom to do whatever she liked, as she had during that summer in her youth that Lady Bronwyn had spent abroad (here, as a matter of fact!—though the irony of that was killing). She visited the spring twice more, and while it really was just a little underground chamber—no shrine, no statue, and the blind attendant wore no *caillagh*'s robe—she still felt that glad, humbling consciousness of a sacred presence, as she had at the start of her own *immram*. And now, for the first time since her early childhood with Monessa, she was with a friend whose company satisfied her completely and who never seemed to tire of hers.

Yet there was a slight constraint between them, a certain stubborn innocence on both sides, to the bafflement and amusement of each. Nemain would not touch heather mead again, despite Gavin's teasing; and Gavin still refused to sleep in the bed or to let her sleep on the floor, though she felt honor-bound to keep offering. Actually, she was relieved about that.

On her side the constraint was perfectly straightforward. She refused the heather mead because she feared to embarrass herself again; she still smarted over confiding so much. And she was relieved that Gavin chose to sleep on the floor because, well, there *was* a difference—logical or not—between sleeping next to a man out in the open and sleeping in the same bed with him. But she could not fathom why the chaste and scrupulous Gavin, having seen her horrible deformity, was not in the least reticent about holding her hand in public or private. Nor could she understand why, on occasion, he seemed to want to test the barrier of innocence between them.

On their last night in Senuna, in the dining hall after supper, he called for a fidchell board. "Anyone up for a game? How about you, jade?"

Fidchell was a game anyone could play, but like so much else in the North, it was rich in ancient symbolism. For a *caillagh*, it was part of her education; for other people, it was just amusement. Nemain had learned the game from Rhiannon but had never played it with anyone else. "I'm out of practice, but all right."

They had hardly begun when Gavin remarked, loudly enough for a few people to take notice, "You know what just occurred to me? I'm playing fidchell with Nemain."

Nemain started at the sound of her own name, and then blushed deeply. In old Northern tales, a classic test of a warrior's prowess or a king's right to rule was a game of fidchell with the Raven. If he lost, She would devour him; but if he won, he was guaranteed success in all his endeavors. It went without saying that She would also reward him with Herself, in the form of a maiden (though the favor of the Raven in any form was probably a formidable thing). Hence, Nemain's blush; and she could tell by Gavin's low chuckle that his thought was following the same line.

"What will you give me if I win?" he asked.

She smiled slowly, realizing that they were on the verge of a contest of wits—the kind of quasi-blasphemous conversation that also occurred in the old tales, and that, much like the game of fidchell, frequently determined a man's fate. Nemain could not resist a contest of that sort.

"My favor, of course," she replied, letting her eyes flick up to his—"in proportion to the victory."

Gavin met her look with a knowing grin. "Ah! Well then."

That game went very quickly. Gavin was a better player than she, and he captured her pieces with a zeal that was almost as flattering as it was funny. By now a knot of curious onlookers had formed around their table, having caught the drift of the conversation, and they cheered at the outcome.

"All right, how much of your favor is that worth?" said Gavin.

"A fidchell board's worth?" She stood up and took off her belt, ignoring the laughter and sly hoots from the men, and tossed it to him. "There. Consider yourself lord of that much terrain."

"Of what it encompasses?" He gave her a look that, under other circumstances, might have earned him a slap. "Gladly!"

"Right now it encompasses empty space," she retorted, "so I guess you're learning wisdom."

He laughed heartily, and the others applauded, apart from one or two Lowlanders who merely looked confused. "Well done! Here, I concede."

He handed her her belt, and she primly refastened it. "Now, do have a drink with me," he said. "You liked it well enough when you tried it."

"A little too well, as you remarked. I also talked a lot of nonsense."

"And what were we doing just now? Nonsense can be fun."

"Actually, I think I'll just go to bed. Unless you want the bed tonight."

"We've been over this, jade."

She shook her head. "You know, you puzzle me sometimes."

"I? I'm an open book."

"But in a script I can't always read."

"Maybe that's a good thing." He smiled, not looking at her. "Sleep as long as you like in the morning. We'll leave when you're ready."

·⟶▬◎ ◎▬◀·

Three days in Senuna was a good length of time: long enough to rest and enjoy themselves thoroughly, and short enough that they did not become addicted to it. It was hard to be on the road again after three days of blissful ease, but at the same time it helped her morale greatly to be setting out well rested, with fresh supplies, clean clothes, and a full stomach. If only her own *immram* had been so well provided for! To be sure, she sometimes wondered if Gavin interpreted the rules of *immrama* a little too freely; but by those rules, she could not interfere with his direction. And she certainly had no cause for complaint.

Her only regret about the whole business was the necessity of leaving Moddey penned up. When he was finally freed, he bounded into her arms with a bark that might have been a sob. "Oh, my love, what did you think? That I'd left you for good?" she laughed, stroking him. "Well, never again. I promise."

Moddey calmed down readily enough, but as Nemain released him, he growled at Gavin with unmistakable malevolence. "I see he knows whom to blame," Gavin remarked.

"I'm sorry. He doesn't like people at all, really, but he gets used to them if he sees them often enough. I don't know why he still has a problem with you."

"Must be a good judge of character."

Apart from Moddey, who showed no sign of forgiving or forgetting, the travelers were in good spirits. "That was the best time I've ever had," Nemain reflected as they rode along. "Thank you again."

Gavin shrugged. " 'Twas your money, jade."

"Let's not quibble. It was all you."

"It was the Good Folk."

"Really?" She smiled skeptically.

"Really! It was I who won that tourney, but it was the Good Folk who gave me the victory. I could have injured my hand, or a sudden strong wind could have come up, or one of those fellows could have been a better shot than I"— he interrupted himself with a laugh—"well, let's stick to probabilities. And I wouldn't have even known about the tourney if that helpful information had not come my way."

"How did that come about? I wondered."

"Well, my father has men stationed at certain checkpoints from Northwaite to Briarvale. That was his condition for allowing me to make this *immram*." He rolled his eyes. "One of them was camped in a mountain pass near the main road. That morning, I had ridden out early to tell him I was changing course, and why."

"You told him? About me?"

"Of course. I had to so that he could inform the others further south. Don't worry; they're only out to report on my progress, not to interfere with it. Anyway, he asked me how I was going to afford a trip to Senuna, and I said I didn't know. Then he said, 'You didn't hear this from me, but …' You laugh, but it's entirely within bounds."

"Oh, I suppose. It just seems—"

"Too easy? Jade, on an *immram* you've got to leave behind unnecessary baggage, make do with what you have, and take whatever comes your way. Have I got that right?"

"Yes, but—"

"That's what I've done. And so far, everything that's come my way has been lovely and unexpected."

Nemain smiled, recognizing the compliment but not willing to acknowledge it. "Well, my *immram* was a different experience … though, to be fair, that was largely my own fault. I got on a wrong road."

"A wrong road?"

"Against my direction."

"Oh." His face turned grave. "I'm sorry."

"So was I. It could have been worse, but—well, let's just say it made me grateful for my name. Anyway, seeing as I'd chosen to go north from the start, I was expecting hardship."

"Why? Was it late in the year?"

"That too," she replied, thinking of the old magical text that had helped her choose her direction. *In the west, learning; in the east, treasure; in the south, music; and in the north, battle.* Or *ancient lore,* depending on your point of view. Either way, it meant a hard struggle.

When they had stopped to rest and eat, Gavin asked her, "So what did you take with you on your *immram* that you couldn't bear to part with?"

"My fiddle and the Book of Dark Sayings."

"*The* Book of Dark Sayings? That's exceedingly rare."

"Heavy, too. I had come to hate the thing long before I committed to dragging it up North. But it was stolen from me, along with my horse. What about you?"

"Lady Monessa's portrait. And also this."

From one of his saddlebags he took out a small book with elegant tooled-leather covers, much like one of Tynan's books. Unlike Tynan's books, however, the text was not laid out in straight lines, but blossomed on the pages like a living thing, illuminated in gold and green. She could not read it, but its beauty took her breath away.

"What is it?"

"You haven't seen one of these? It's the book of my clan."

"Oh." No wonder Tynan hadn't had one.

"The whole house of Airleas is in here." He turned to the last written page and pointed at a flourish of script. "This is me. Gavin Alroy mac Airleas."

She liked the way it rolled off his tongue. "Your middle name is Alroy?"

"Aye, and let's never speak of it again."

Alroy meant "the Red." She laughed.

"This is my mother, Isleen, and my sister, Nairne." He smiled. "You know, when I first met you, you reminded me of Nairne a bit."

"Oh?"

"Not so much now; you don't remind me of anyone but yourself. But she was dark like you, and funny, and strong-minded. She used to joke about running away to train as a *caillagh,* to tease our father. He disapproves of young *cailleeyn.*"

"Dear me."

"Aye, I've no idea what he'd make of you. But my mother and Nairne would have liked you a lot."

"May I look at that book some more?"

"Sure."

Nemain flipped back several pages, studying the closely written names. She was not very familiar with the archaic Northern script, but she would recognize the word "Gwehara" if she found it … ah, there it was. Gavin's seventeenth great-grandfather, if she was counting these entries correctly, had been a man of Gwehara; and he, too, had been an "Alroy." She smiled.

Here in her hands was a crossroads of sorts: Gwehara and Northwaite, bound in one—both roads she had rejected long ago. Obviously that had been a mistake, but until now she had thought only in terms of its immediate consequences. What else had that decision cost her in the long run? If she had gone to Northwaite, she might have met Gavin and his family long ere this; she might have been friends with Nairne, as she had always felt she should be. If she had gone to Gwehara, who knew what she would have learned or whom she would have met?

It made no difference, she told herself sternly. Condemned as she was to loneliness, *something* would have defeated her happiness every time. One small act of rebellion in youth could not have had that much impact either way.

"Can you even read it?" Gavin's voice broke into her thoughts.

"No, but it's informative all the same." She handed it back to him. "Why this for an *immram?*"

"To remind me of my *immram*'s purpose."

"Are you in danger of forgetting it?"

"I came close to it once, years ago."

"When you fell in love, you mean?"

He nodded. "I was young and stupid."

"Was it so stupid to fall in love?"

"In my case, yes. See here?—my parents, side by side. Theirs was an arranged marriage, of course, and you wouldn't have thought them well matched if you'd met them. But their love was great; no man ever loved a woman more than my father loved my mother. I haven't always found it easy being his son, but he did give me that. He showed me how it *can* work—how it should work—when two people are carefully chosen for each other and carefully abide by that choice. That's the tale of many of these marriages, as far back as the book goes. And that's what I want. That's what my inheritance means to me, more than my fortune or my estate. I want Monessa's name written next to mine, and our children listed with us, in the book of my fathers." He stopped abruptly. "I'm sorry. You probably don't care to hear this."

"I asked. Go on."

"So yes, I was young and stupid. I can't say I've left stupidity behind me, but that was the year I ceased to be young. It ages you, falling in love. You may think you know now, but you don't. I was 'in love' several times as a boy, but only once have I loved as a man. Afterwards, even after it ceased to hurt, I wasn't the same. And then I had six years of just *nothing.* Waiting for a little girl in the Lowland to grow up. You're smiling. Well, I understand loneliness, jade—not as well as you do, but I get it. And you may think you know love as *I* do, but you don't."

Nemain was smiling because she did know. She well remembered how it had felt to pour Rhiannon's potion onto the cobblestones—to hold such power in her hands and then watch it trickle away. And then years of *nothing!*—nothing but dreams, regrets, stifled longings—in her case, nothing even to wait for. Yes, all these things made her smile, and she felt not a particle of pity for this man, at the venerable age of twenty-eight, speaking with such grave authority on the pain of love.

"Now, even though I *know* this marriage is what I want more than anything else, and I *know* my father was right to bring me to my senses—ask me if I'm still angry about it."

Nemain's smile broadened. Oh yes, she understood quite well.

"So that's why I carry the book. I do need reminding. That, too, is why I tend to doubt myself from time to time." He put the book back in his saddlebag. "But I don't doubt that my stars are guiding me aright. Lady Monessa is the one. . . . You're coming to the wedding, aren't you, jade? Then you can say you've been to one."

"What will it be like?"

He thought about it. "I actually don't know. If a Lowland wedding is anything like a Northern one, it'll be quite simple. A vow, a handclasp, and a kiss before witnesses."

"That's it?"

"That's it. Well, the public part of it."

"Ah."

"The private part is much the same in every land."

"Yes, I gather."

"But in between, there's a party. Lots of dancing and kissing and mead."

"Sounds like fun," she said indifferently.

"You don't sound convinced."

"Well, mead can be fun, though it and I should probably not mix. Dancing can be fun, as I recall; I haven't done it since I took lessons as a girl. As for kissing, if I saw that as incentive, it would just be sad."

Gavin stifled a laugh. "Granted. But if you don't come for the experience, come because I want you there."

"Of course I'll come."

They rode onward, talking of other things, but the thought of Gavin's wedding left her slightly depressed. Once he was married—actually, once they reached Briarvale—they couldn't go on as they were, so free and easy in each other's company. She would have him to herself only for a short while longer, and then no more. What would she do then?

At least she wasn't in love with him, she thought, trying to console herself. That would have been infinitely worse. But she had grown so accustomed to his presence beside her day and night, and so comfortable in their conversation and their silence alike, that the thought of being parted from him was painful. Even her old beloved solitude would not satisfy her then. She would miss him—oh, how she would miss him! She could feel it already.

But as she looked at him, so handsome on horseback (she thought with affectionate pride—nothing warmer), laughing at something she'd said, she pushed away all thoughts of parting. There would be time enough for loneliness—all the rest of her life, in fact; it need not rob her of happiness now. She would enjoy what remained of this journey, this strange and delightful interlude, as the gift from the Good Folk that it was. This was her time with him, no one else's, and nothing could mar it or take it from her.

Chapter 26

THE MOUNTAINS WERE as lovely at the height of spring as they were in autumn, but in a different way: cloaked in green and carpeted with wildflowers, resonant with birdsongs and haunted by butterflies. Nemain enjoyed Gavin's reactions to the scenery as much as the scenery itself. "Oh, look at that!"—as the pale golden dawn poured into a misted valley, or as shadows of rain drifted over a distant slope. The trails were still steep, the terrain as wild and rugged as ever; but Gavin's constant delight in their surroundings replaced some of Nemain's fear with a pleasant sense of adventure.

"Of all the landscapes you've seen," she asked him once, "which is your favorite?"

He laughed at the thought of trying to pick a favorite. "There are so many kinds of beauty in the world, in the North alone, I don't know that I could choose. But if I had to … probably Northwaite. The sea."

"What's it like? The closest I've ever been to the sea is Senuna."

"Not at all like Senuna. Different sea, for one thing, and it's not as warm—though it doesn't get as cold as the moors in winter. The castle is on a cliff over-looking the sea … I don't know just how to describe it. It's wild and immense and constantly changing. The light is purer there than anywhere. In storm or in calm, in any season, at any hour, I never tire of it."

"Earth, sky, and sea," she murmured. "The Three Worlds converge on your doorstep."

"That's not a bad way to put it. What about you?"

"The moors."

He laughed again. "Somehow that doesn't surprise me. But most people, I think, have an affinity for wherever they grew up."

"Oh, the Lowland is nice. It's very sunny, and its colors are very bright."

"Hmm. Charming, but it doesn't sound like you at all—and, as you say, the stars are just stars there. No wonder you fled to the mountains and the moors."

They camped one night in a valley where, to Nemain's delight, every sound cascaded into a series of echoes. Of course she immediately got out her fiddle and played to her heart's content: first the *arrane oie,* very nearly achieving the magical effect of the original, and then whatever else she could think of, until the moon was high and it occurred to her that Gavin probably wanted to sleep.

As she turned to pack up her fiddle and bow, she saw with chagrin that he was watching her. Heretofore she had always said, "Don't look at me," before playing; she had thought that was understood.

"Were you looking at me?"

"I was."

"Why?"

"You play beautifully, jade," he said quietly, "and not just to listen to."

How could she respond to that! It would be inappropriate, she felt, to take offense; but wasn't it wrong of him? He didn't seem a bit sorry for it, either. Nor was she as indignant as she confusedly felt she ought to be. After a moment of stillness, blushing furiously, she put aside her fiddle-bag and lay down for the night.

"There really are all kinds, you know," said Gavin.

"All kinds of what?"

"Beauty."

She didn't know how to respond to that, either. She lay awake for a long time, half fearing and half hoping that he would follow up that thought, but he did not.

⋯⟫⟺⟪⋯

"Jade, are you awake? ... Oh, *hysht, mac-imshee!*"—sharply to Moddey, who was snapping at him as usual. "I've just been up on that rise. Come look."

Reluctantly she got up and followed him. It was just after dawn, and the sunlight fell slantwise over the foothills, illuminating a vast scattering of standing stones: rings, cairns, and solitary monoliths. She caught her breath at the sight.

"Those are the ones you saw, aren't they?"

"Yes, but not from up here. I didn't realize there were so many." She looked for the ones she recognized: the carved stone circle on the hilltop, the Peepstone, the Faery Pillars ... "Wait. Some of them are missing."

"Missing?"

"There were seven Faery Pillars, just there. Now there are six. And I do believe there's a boulder missing from the Giants' Hearth. See that gap in the circle?"

"Are you sure those are the same ones?"

She nodded, her brow furrowing. "Who would knock them down?"

"I don't know. How about the ones with the symbols you saw? Are they still standing?"

"Yes—and now that I see all these at once, I wonder if there's a sort of pattern to them, how they're arranged. Maybe the symbols are the key to understanding it. But how will we ever know?"

A horrible thought occurred to her. Even if there was a pattern, and even if someday the symbols could be read, how many more stones might disappear in the meantime? How many of them might have already been lost—dragged away to build houses or pave streets, perhaps—since the time of the Vanished Ones? Suddenly the stones themselves, so massive and so timeless in their mystery, seemed very fragile and transient indeed.

At the first farmhouse they came to, Gavin asked about the stones. "Oh, yes," said the young Lowland farmer, "now and again somebody carts one off. It's not as if there aren't plenty."

"It's bad luck," muttered his elderly father from the rocking-chair in the corner.

The young man smiled. "It's progress, Da. This region's filling up. People have got to have houses."

"And it's a long time since those stone circles were of use to anyone," his young wife put in.

Nemain was quiet, but inwardly she was screaming.

"Stay to dinner?" the wife asked.

"Thank you, no," said Gavin, looking at Nemain. "We'd better press on."

They rode in silence for a long time. Nemain, in the throes of a passionate grief, could not speak or even cry. She remembered the feel of the carved stone beneath her hand, the sense of communion with ancient, unseen forces. Whatever they were—the Good Folk, or perhaps her own ancestral spirits— they were real, and they *wanted* to speak. To desecrate those holy places was to silence those voices, to sever their connection to the living; and it was their grief that Nemain could feel. The grief of being cut off. ...

"I can talk to my father and to Lord Winworth about it," Gavin offered.

"What could they do? The Middle Cantrefs are free."

"But the lords are not without influence here. They could talk to others, put some protective measures in place."

"Yes," said Nemain. "Do that."

"I'll do whatever I can."

When they had stopped to camp for the night, he touched her arm. "Jade, look at me."

She raised her eyes unwillingly, afraid she might start to cry.

"Remember the spring in Senuna?"

She nodded.

"There will always be such places for those with eyes to see," he said. "Take heart."

⊷⊷⊷ ⊶⊶⊶

Traveling through the Middle Cantrefs with Gavin, and without the black robe, was a radically different experience from her first journey. The Lowlanders were unfailingly hospitable, and the Northerners, if they expressed any unease about Nemain's gloves, were quickly persuaded by Gavin's signet ring. They slept in proper beds almost every night (at least Nemain did; if there was only one to spare, Gavin slept on the floor). They shared a farmer's humble supper of bread, butter, and radishes with salt, which Nemain found as delicious as the fare in Senuna. They went to a village festival and danced like any boy and girl, instead of a nobleman and a witch, and no one was the least bit suspicious or disapproving.

"Are you and your lady heading down to the Kell's Crossing fair?" an old herdsman asked them one evening.

"We'll be passing through," said Gavin.

"I'll be heading that way myself. I've never missed it but once, five years ago, when I was laid up with a broken leg. I sent my son down with the herd. Ah, of all years to miss it! That was the year of the fiddler."

Gavin blinked. "The year of the what, now?"

"The fiddler at the Speckled Ox. A witch with a withered hand, who played like you've never heard before. The herders have talked about it every year since. We keep hoping she'll come back."

"Extraordinary."

Gavin was trying hard not to laugh. Nemain could have kicked him.

"Say, lass, you've been rather quiet. You carry a fiddle, don't you?"

"M-hm."

"And you wear gloves. Isn't it a bit warm for that?"

"My hands are cold."

"You're not a witch, are you?" He guffawed. "Fancy a witch with a *lhiannan!* That'd be quite a thing."

Lhiannan meant "lover," and she did not bother correcting him, just as Gavin never objected to the phrase "you and your lady." "That would," she replied.

As soon as the old man left them alone, Gavin turned to her with twinkling eyes. "What else happened on your *immram,* jade?"

"I was treated very shabbily by an innkeeper."

"And chose an interesting method of revenge?"

"I wish! On the contrary, I served him well." She told the story briefly and bitterly.

"You're still angry about it?"

"Wouldn't you be?"

"Well, you heard the old man. You must go back there and play again."

Nemain gave a long-drawn-out sigh.

"Please?" He gave her an impish grin. "For me?"

"If you ask it, Gavin, I won't refuse. But just for one night. And if I'm not recognized, I won't volunteer."

"Fair enough."

When they arrived at Kell's Crossing, the fair was just getting underway. "Think we'll hear the fiddler this year?" Gavin asked a peddler on the road.

"We'll hear plenty of 'em," he replied, "but the witch-fiddler? I wouldn't bet my last stater on it."

"Oi! You should hear the one up at Defena," a Northern voice shouted. "He's better."

Nemain laughed.

At the Speckled Ox, the innkeeper very nearly shut the door in their faces. "Sorry. We're full up."

Gavin stopped the door with his foot. "Are you quite sure?"—inclining his head toward Nemain, who gave a tiny wave of her gloved fingers.

The innkeeper's mouth fell open, and his eyes bulged. "*Yes!* I mean no, I'm sure we can scrape something together. Come in, lass, come in. Shall I take your dog to the stable?"

"The dog stays with me."

"And so do I," said Gavin, slipping in behind her as the door closed.

The innkeeper bowed. "Forgive me, sir, I didn't recognize you."

"From where?"

"Are you not the gentleman who paid her way before?"

Gavin turned to her with a look of consternation. "What gentleman was that?"

"No one you need be jealous of, my dear," she said smoothly. "So, the same procedure as last time?"

"Right, yes," said the innkeeper, red and flustered at his own indiscretion. "Come this way, and start whenever you're ready."

While he sped into action—closing the windows, posting a guard at the door, and spreading the announcement "The witch-fiddler's back!"—Nemain pulled off her gloves and took out her fiddle, ignoring the sudden eruption of cheering. Remembering the last time she had been here, as a friendless child fighting for shelter, she could not repress a grim smile. It *was* satisfying, in a way, to return and find all these people eager to submit themselves to her power.

"I could do with a drink," she said to the innkeeper.

"What'll you have? Mead, ale ... ?"

"Tea," she said, "and keep it coming."

⊷⊷⊷ ⊷⊷⊷

"You were brilliant up there."

It was well after dark. Gavin and Nemain sat outside the inn, sharing a late supper of bread, meat, cheese, and fruit. "Now, tell me you didn't enjoy that just a little."

"More than a little," she confessed, "but it's a strain. It was better at the Deep Valley Inn, where people came just for the music. Here there's an additional novelty." She stretched out her ungloved fingers. "I'm the witch with the withered hand. The monster by the door."

"The what?"

She shook her head. "Nothing."

"Shall I tell you what *I* thought?"

"About what?"

"When you took your gloves off tonight. It surprised me; I know how shy you are, especially with crowds. But when you just let them drop and you took up your fiddle, not caring what anyone thought, it was ..." He chuckled.

"What?"

"Don't take this the wrong way."

"Well, what was it?"

"Tremendously attractive."

Nemain threw back her head and laughed. "You're kidding!"

"I wish I were."

"Should I do that more often? I'd love to see Lady Bronwyn's reaction to that."

"Remind me. Who's Lady Bronwyn?"

"Monessa's aunt." A dark edge crept into her voice along with the laughter. "You'll meet her soon enough."

"And who was the gentleman who paid your way here before?"

"Oh, that? Lord Winworth sent a man ahead to look out for me. He couldn't spare him beyond Kell's Crossing, though."

Gavin nodded thoughtfully. "How far are we from Briarvale?"

"About three days."

"Only that?"

"It's quite a bit later than you were originally planning," she reminded him.

He shook his head. "It's an *immram*, jade. It takes as long as it does."

"Well, I can't thank you enough. Say what you will, this *immram* has taken so long only because of your kindness to me."

"Jade, I'm really not that kind. I've never done a thing for you, at any time, that it didn't please me to do."

"Is that not kindness?"

He looked into her eyes. For a moment he seemed about to say something, but then he merely shrugged and looked away.

Chapter 27

THEY MADE GOOD progress over the next two days, but then they were halted by a sudden heavy rain. It was a most inconvenient spot to be stranded: on the drovers' road, with no shelter at hand and with evening approaching.

"Could we make it to the village near Briarvale if we ride fast?"

Nemain shrank from the prospect of seeking lodgings in the village. "I know a house that's closer."

"Whose house?"

"It was my mistress's. It's in the woods."

Gavin looked dubious, but then he cringed at an especially loud peal of thunder. "Oh, all right. Let's hurry."

It was almost dark when they reached Rhiannon's cottage, so overgrown with moss and ivy that it appeared to be sinking into the earth. The door was unlocked, and Nemain saw with mingled relief and apprehension that the place was abandoned. It had probably not been occupied since Rhiannon's burial.

"Go in," said Gavin. "I'll take care of the horses."

"In a minute. Moddey!"

She waited for the dog to come bounding up, as he always did when she called, but this time he did not. She shouted his name into the wind again, as loudly as she could.

In the distance she heard his bark, followed by another crash of thunder alarmingly close by. Then she heard nothing but rain and wind.

"Jade, be careful!"

Ignoring Gavin, she ran, still calling Moddey's name. On some level she already knew what had happened, but that did not lessen the horror of the sight when she came upon him.

Moddey lay pinned under a fallen tree. When he saw her coming, he strained weakly to free himself, then stopped. She struggled to lift the tree trunk off him.

"Jade," said Gavin behind her.

"Help me!"

Instead of helping her, he pulled her aside. "He's done for. I'm sorry."

A shriek of anguished denial caught in her throat. She knew Gavin was right; there was so much blood, and Moddey wasn't even trying to move anymore. He merely twitched, glassy-eyed.

"Let me ease him," said Gavin. "Turn away."

At first she shook her head uncomprehendingly. Then she saw him reach for his knife, and she shut her eyes tight. There was the hiss of a blade being unsheathed—a few quiet words of encouragement to the dog—and Nemain screamed once. Then there was silence.

"It's done," she heard him say. "He feels no pain."

She clung to Gavin all the way back to the cottage. She was hardly aware of walking; her body, like her mind, had gone numb, and only Gavin's strong arm supporting her felt real. Dear Gavin, who had been kind and brave enough to do what she could not.

While he lit a fire and rolled out their bedding, she went into the other room and mechanically changed into dry clothes in the dark. She knew she ought to help him set up for the night, but this basic task was as much as she could handle just now.

She was glad of the dark—she wanted to blot out sight and sound for a long, long time—but she could not banish the images from her mind's eye. Over here, she had spent many happy hours studying by candlelight; over there had been the basket where Rhiannon kept Béira's puppies. *No, don't think of that.* ... There had been heaps of books everywhere, books she had devoured and wrestled with and loved and hated—books that now lay forgotten in the Briarvale library, unless Lord Winworth had gotten rid of them. She must see about that when they reached the castle. … There was no trace left of her life here, or Rhiannon's—of course there wouldn't be—and yet the place seemed full of ghosts. Oh, what had possessed her to come back here! Moreover, if she had not, Moddey would not have been under that tree. …

"Jade, are you all right?" Gavin called.

She came out, blinking at the firelight, and curled up on her bedding. She was profoundly weary and numb, yet wholly awake and in pain. Her eyes were dry and hot, and every breath she took stabbed at her heart. If only she could cry!

Gavin placed his hand on her back. At his touch, something loosened up inside her and she found that she could breathe normally again. Within minutes she was asleep.

⊷═◉ ◉═◞

In the middle of the night a thunderclap made her cry out. She sat bolt upright, panicking. It was dark and raining—she was cold, scared, hurt—her gloves— *where were her gloves?*

"Jade—ow! *Cre ta janoo ort?*"

"My gloves! I can't find them!"

"We'll find them in the morning."

"I need them now! I can't go back without them!"

"Back where?"

"Home!"

She was crying now, scrabbling blindly across the floor. Where was the Raven, her great protector? Why had She appeared to her tormentors, the village boys, but not to *her?* Why had She left her alone?

And then she was not alone. Someone was gripping her by the shoulders and saying, "Nemain, wake up."

The sound of her name brought her fully back to consciousness. She blinked and shook her head. In the faint light from the dying embers, the anxious face peering into hers was a friend's face, yet somehow not the one she had expected to see.

"I'm sorry," she sobbed through chattering teeth.

"It's all right. Come here."

He put his arms around her and pulled her down with him, drawing a blanket up over them both. The sudden transition from freezing despair to warmth and security was a bit of a shock, but a blessed relief. And how good it was to cry at last! Her composure was utterly broken, but for once it did not seem to matter.

"Was it Moddey that brought this on?"

At the mention of his name, she broke into fresh sobs. "He was all I had. And it's all my fault. If I hadn't insisted on coming here—"

"It was *not* your fault. Don't you dare blame yourself for this."

"I shouldn't have brought him with me at all. He would have been safe in Defena—and Henry warned me he was getting old—"

"If you'd left him behind, he'd have pined for you. You know he would have. And he didn't fear danger; he was no coward. Don't you think he would rather have been with you no matter what?"

She was quiet for a few minutes, sniffling occasionally.

"He was the only creature who loved me."

"That's not true."

"It is and it isn't. Tynan loved me, but couldn't show it. Rhiannon loved me, but also hated me."

"Who?"

"Sorry, I didn't mean to say her name. My mistress, who also cursed me."

"Oh!"

His voice was eloquent; in that "oh" she heard sudden understanding, dismay, and pity.

"She did the best she could for me, but—ha! Do you know who else said that? Lady Bronwyn. 'No one will ever say I didn't do the best I could for you.' *She* hated me, no question of that. ... Monessa loved me, but Monessa loves everyone."

Gavin had to stifle a laugh. "Sorry. Go on."

"Rois and Henry, I think ... at least they pitied me, like a stray animal. That's what I was to them. Lord Winworth ... I doubt it, though he was always good to me. That's it, I think."

"Aren't you leaving someone out?"

"Am I?"

"Think very hard."

She thought. "Swayne? No, he didn't. … Master Ives, possibly, but I rather hope he didn't."

"Keep thinking."

There was a pause, and then Nemain said quietly, "You'll forget me."

"I'll what?"

"When you're married, if not before. That's all right. It's as it should be."

"Jade, I won't cease to be your friend."

"Things will have to change when we reach Briarvale. We can't be so much together." Mentally she added, *Certainly not like this.*

"We'll make it work. I promise you, I'll never forget you. You can lay a *geis* on me if you like."

"I wouldn't do that to you."

"Then I'll take it on myself."

"Oh, please don't! What if some evil befalls you for it?"

"Where's your faith?" He took her hand, and she could not bring herself to pull it away. "What harm could come to me for it, in this world or any other? Did you see anything but joy in my future?"

"No, but—"

"Has any part of your assessment changed?"

"No."

"Then hear me, and witness." He took a deep breath. "As long as I live, Nemain, you'll never want for friend or kin. And thrice death to me, if I ever cease to be such."

In the solemn silence that followed, Nemain thought of everyone she had ever loved, who had either died or drifted away from her for one reason or another. How could Gavin be so fearless of death, so confident that he would not drift away, that he would willingly bind himself between a *geis* and a curse? To be sure, she had seen no calamity in his future, but *cailleeyn* couldn't see everything. Especially when someone took such a drastic step as this.

"You're not afraid?"

His fingers tightened around hers. "I'll take my chances."

Perhaps it was the curse working in her. Or perhaps it was the inevitable result of such a gesture. Either way, Nemain suddenly saw things clearly. There would be no calamity for *him;* but she found herself on the edge of an abyss, a loneliness darker and deeper than she could ever have imagined.

She loved him. Not as she had thought she loved him—as a grateful friend, a would-be sister—and not even as she had loved Swayne. Swayne! Had *that* been love? It paled into nothing beside this. Gavin had been right; she had not known the meaning of it until now.

No, she loved him passionately and completely, with a depth of tenderness and desire she had not known herself capable of—the love of a woman whose element was fire. "You *are* intense," he had said to her once. He had no idea.

"Even if," he went on, "as you say, something in you prevents you from feeling anything for me …"

"Oh, that's not the case."

She sensed he was smiling. "Well, regardless, you have my love. As a friend and kinsman."

Her head was resting against his chest. She listened to the steady rhythm of his heart. How grieved he would be if he knew what was in *her* heart!—and worse, repulsed, though he'd be too much of a gentleman to show it. She must take great care that he never suspected what she felt. She must lie very, very still in his arms now, and tomorrow—and for the rest of her life—be as proper and passionless as any man could wish his actual sister to be.

Well done, Nemain, she thought. *You've finally gained a friend you can love, and his friendship will be the keenest torture you've ever known.*

She wept again, quietly now. He stroked her hair and began to speak softly in the Northern tongue. The words, or perhaps just the sound of his voice, had a lulling effect; she stopped crying and relaxed in his arms in spite of herself. It did not still the grief or the terrible longing in her, but it gave her a certain peace. No matter what tomorrow held, no one else could have this night, this moment, in his arms. It did not even really matter what he was saying; she loved his voice and his language as well as his touch, and for now these were enough.

At length he fell silent, and she realized he had just asked, "*Vel oo toiggal?*"— Do you understand?

"No." She nestled closer to him. "Go on."

He laughed softly and obeyed. She fell asleep to the sound of his voice and the rain on the roof, and for the time being, at least, the little cottage held no more ghosts.

Chapter 28

NEMAIN WOKE UP alone, very warm—Gavin had covered her with the blankets— but with a terrible headache. For a while she just lay there, pressing her fingers against her temples, fighting the tears that were welling in her eyes again. When she felt composed enough, she forced herself to get up, though every movement caused her head to throb.

Gavin had found her gloves, too, and placed them near her. Good man.

She went outside and saw him lounging against a tree, reading the book of his clan. He looked tired; there were shadows under his eyes.

"You didn't wake me."

"No," he said, not looking up. "I didn't."

"I'm sorry."

"For what?"

"For keeping you up."

"It's not likely I could have slept anyway."

That was probably true, Nemain thought. He was meeting his bride-to-be for the first time today. "Well. Shall we get a move on, then?"

Now he looked up. "Are you feeling up to it?"

"Yes," she lied.

"If you need to take some time …"

"Gavin, you've already delayed so long for me, and we're so close to Briarvale now. It would be unforgivable of me to hold you back."

He looked as if he wanted to speak, but she went on, "Anyway, I want to thank you. Again. For everything."

"Well, *mollaght*, jade." He gave a hollow laugh. "It's not goodbye."

It is and it isn't, she thought. "I know. But still."

Feeling tears pricking at her eyes yet again, she hastily turned away to go pack up the bedding or do something else useful. But before she could, Gavin turned her around and caught her up in a tight hug. It was startling to have the breath squeezed out of her like that, but because it was Gavin, it was rather a lovely feeling.

When he released her, his eyes were both merry and sad. "I won't be able to do that at Briarvale, will I?"

"No," she smiled. "And I shall have to call you 'sir.' "

"Don't you dare."

⋅→▸═◉ ◉═◂←⋅

As they rode toward the castle, they met a horseman coming the other way. Nemain recognized the horse before she recognized the man; it was Lord Winworth's gray hunter, the one Tynan had cured of being "withy-cragged" long ago. But the man in the saddle was not Lord Winworth, though he, too, was slender of build and elegantly dressed.

When she realized it was Swayne, her heart gave a painful bound. And yet there was no real emotion in it. It was just that she had been obsessing for so long about seeing him again that the moment her mind said, "Oh, that's Swayne," her heart thrummed briefly, as a reflex—and that was all. It was both a relief and a curious letdown.

"Good day," he said, stopping in their path. "Heading to the castle?"

"Aye." Gavin raised his hand in a salute. "Gavin mac Airleas of Northwaite."

"Ah, yes." Swayne's eyes lingered on Gavin's patched, dirty garb, but he was too polite to betray any surprise or disdain. "We've been expecting you for some time. Your retainers have all arrived, and oh my stars," he interrupted himself seamlessly, noticing her for the first time. "*Nemain?*"

"Hello, Swayne."

He grinned. "How long has it been?"

"Awhile."

"Well, come on! Lord Winworth will be glad to know you're both here. I'll see that you get settled in directly."

"Don't you have an errand?" she asked.

"It can wait."

"Thanks, son," said Gavin.

They rode up to the castle together, Swayne and Nemain doing most of the talking—or rather, Swayne talked and Nemain made the minimal replies that courtesy demanded. After the initial non-emotion at seeing him again, other feelings had succeeded: strong, troubling, contradictory. She found she was not indifferent to him; she still liked him, still found him a beautiful man. But that was all. And yet it wasn't.

If that were really all, it wouldn't matter that he clearly had no memory of their last encounter, their kiss. She should have been relieved at that, and was. But far more so, irrationally, she was *angry*. How dared he not remember it! Oh, she knew it was quite natural that he should forget it. He had been just a lonely, frustrated boy, and it had meant nothing. Really, she ought to feel sorry for him. But she had no compassion for anyone else's loneliness or frustration just then.

She swallowed her futile rage, smiled, chuckled, said the correct things, and for once in her life felt a real gratitude to Lady Bronwyn for teaching her to hide her feelings.

It was Lady Bronwyn who showed her to her room—the same room she'd had before, away from the ladies' wing. "When will your maid be arriving?"

"I don't have one."

Lady Bronwyn's lip curled, but she refrained from saying whatever she was thinking. "I'll send Amala up with water for your bath."

"Thank you," Nemain said with a curtsy, and grinned to herself as Lady Bronwyn stalked off.

Amala was a new servant of about twelve. She was strong for her age, accustomed to hauling water and kindling, but she had the look of a frightened rabbit. Nemain pitied her on sight, as she pitied anyone who had to take orders from Lady Bronwyn all day. But she was already out of humor, and it didn't help to have a child freeze with fear in her presence, the same way Ita used to do.

"That'll be all," Nemain said as the girl set down the brimming water pails. "You can go."

Amala paused at the door. "Is it true what they say about you?"

"Which part?"

"That you're a witch."

"Do you really want to find out?"

That sent her scurrying.

As Nemain was drying off after her bath, she realized in dismay that the Outland clothes were the cleanest ones she had. She unfolded them and looked them over critically: a plain linen smock and a vest and skirt of Rensa's wonderful design, trimmed with spangles. As glad as she was to have the ancient symbols in any form, she had not really intended wearing the clothes. There was nothing objectionable about the ensemble itself—it would fit her, it was modest enough, and the colored weave was undeniably beautiful—but her Lowland sensibilities objected all the same. It was so obviously Outlander's garb.

She laid the fabric against her arm and saw how its colors brought out the warm tints of her skin. The skirt was unhemmed and had a rakish asymmetry that she liked. She had no mirror, but she could tell the overall effect was quite different from that of the plain, dark, shapeless kirtles she usually wore ... and she wasn't sure how she felt about that.

Well, why not wear her Outland heritage? Why not own her connection to the people who made such beautiful things, who wove into cloth the mysteries their ancestors had carved into stone? Even if she was debarred from ever learning their meaning, they were *hers* as much as anyone's.

So she put them on, braided her wet hair, and went to the presence chamber. The door was open, and Lord Winworth was conversing with a strikingly handsome red-headed man she actually didn't recognize for an instant.

Was this *her* Gavin? Clean-shaven, with his hair trimmed, in a green silk tunic with Northern designs embroidered on it in gold? Oh, surely not! This was a nobleman indeed, Lord Winworth's equal if not superior—miles above her in station. Hard to believe she had grown used to calling him by his first name, or that just the night before, she had slept in his arms. No, she must not think of that!

"Nemain!" Lord Winworth came forward, clearly pleased to see her but unsure how to greet her. A hug was not quite the thing, but a kiss on the hand was out of the question. Instead he clapped her on the shoulder, man-to-man fashion. "You haven't seen Monessa yet, have you? Good, good. I haven't told her you were coming. She's arranging the flowers in the great hall. Wait here a moment."

He left the room, and Nemain, ill at ease to be alone with Gavin, stood with her hands folded and her eyes downcast, as she would in the presence of any strange gentleman. She listened to him take several deep breaths.

"I hate being shaven," he muttered, rubbing his jaw. "I look like I'm twelve."

"No, you don't."

"*You* look well." He eyed her outfit and gave a judicial nod. "That was a good investment."

Before she could respond, Monessa entered the room, carrying a basket of roses. She was twenty-one now—so changed, was Nemain's first thought—and yet, at second glance, hardly changed at all. Still as slender, as graceful, as heart-rendingly lovely as ever. She wore a tunic and skirt of some fluttery silver-blue material, and her hair was coiled in a pearl-studded net, with a few ringlets escaping around her face. But her eyes—what was different about her eyes? … Just then she saw Nemain, and she gasped and ran towards her, letting her basket crash to the floor.

"Nemain!" She threw her arms around her. "I didn't know you were here! When did you arrive? My goodness, what on earth are you wearing? I love it. Oh, it's good to see you!"

Nemain patted her awkwardly, startled by the force and enthusiasm of the embrace. Over Monessa's shoulder she caught Gavin's eye, and he put up his hand to smother a laugh.

"Come, daughter, where are your manners?" Lord Winworth scolded gently, smiling. "We have another guest."

She released Nemain, somewhat to the latter's relief, and her pale face flushed beautifully at the sight of Gavin. "How do you do," she said with a nervous curtsy. "I … we weren't sure when to expect you."

"It's a pleasure to meet you, my lady." Gavin took her hand and kissed it. He clearly thought no less of her for her girlish show of affection; on the contrary, it set him at his ease. Had she made a more dignified entrance, she could hardly have made a better impression.

"We'll dine in my privy chamber," Lord Winworth announced. "Just the family—us four and my sister. The ladies and gentlemen can have the great hall. I'm sorry Swayne can't join us tonight; he has business in the village."

Nemain was sorry for that too. She wanted to observe Swayne and Monessa together and discern just what feeling, if any, still lay between them. And she wanted to know this not for her own sake, but for Gavin's.

Supper that evening was roast lamb with cameline sauce, Monessa's favorite. Watching her, Nemain again thought there was something different about her eyes, but she couldn't look in them for long enough to be sure. At any rate, Monessa smiled and sparkled throughout the meal, and there was a good deal of laughter. Nemain said little, preferring to watch and listen to the betrothed couple.

Gavin was evidently charmed with her. How could he not be, with his eye for beauty, his sense of humor, and the tender, generous, protective nature Nemain had both read in his palm and come to know? He was made to love a woman, and Monessa was immanently lovable.

But what Monessa thought of him, Nemain could not tell. Monessa was *always* sparkling, smiling, charming; it was no indication of her frame of mind. The disquieting thought occurred to Nemain that she had never been able to tell what Monessa was really thinking.

"Nemain, do eat," Lord Winworth's voice interrupted her thoughts. "None of us will mind your hands."

She smiled apologetically and obeyed, though she wasn't hungry.

"You all right, jade?" Gavin asked softly. She nodded.

Monessa turned to her. "So tell us, what have you been doing up North?"

"Oh, nothing much. Fiddling. Plying my trade."

"Fortune-telling?" said Lady Bronwyn.

Gavin almost choked on a mouthful of food.

"Something like that," Nemain said evenly.

"She's made quite a career with her fiddle," Gavin put in. "She's a legend in Kell's Crossing, though she's only performed there twice. And in Defena …"

"Pfft. No one's ever seen *that* fiddler. You couldn't prove that was me."

Monessa giggled.

"She's quite mad, you know," said Lord Winworth to Gavin.

"How so?"

"You should have seen the way she left. Fifteen years old. Tried to head up to the North Country on foot, with nothing but a book and a fiddle."

"I think that's splendid," Gavin smiled.

"So do I," said Monessa, "though at the time, it scared me dreadfully. I couldn't just let you do it."

"I'd have expected something of the sort from her," Lady Bronwyn said acidly.

"Meaning what, madam?" said Gavin.

There was a moment of tense silence, which Monessa promptly broke. "Well, it turned out all right anyway. And I'm glad you're back."

"How's the lamb?" Lord Winworth asked Gavin.

"Oh, very good. You know, I haven't tried many Lowland dishes, but there's one that I've heard of—what's its name? Mawmeny?"

Monessa, who had been taking a drink of wine, suddenly snorted and had to put her cup down. She clapped a hand over her mouth, shaking with laughter. Gavin caught Nemain's eye, and they both broke down laughing as well.

"Monessa, what ails you?" Lady Bronwyn snapped.

She shook her head and finally managed to swallow. "I'd forgotten all about that! Oh, it was so funny! *Why* was that word so funny?"

"I don't remember," Nemain gasped.

"I think you had to be there," said Lord Winworth, rolling his eyes. But he couldn't help smiling.

After supper, Lord Winworth asked to talk to Nemain alone. Gavin patted her arm as he left. "See you later, jade."

She nodded demurely, and the door closed.

"How are you really?" Lord Winworth asked.

"Well, my dog died yesterday."

"The same one you used to have? I'm sorry, I remember how fond you were of him. I can get you another if you'd like."

"Perhaps, in time." She managed a wan smile.

"You're looking well, at any rate." He gestured vaguely at her outfit. "I can't approve of that getup, but I won't deny it suits you."

"Thank you, my lord."

"So tell me. You know Sir Gavin pretty well by now; what do you make of him?"

She took a deep breath. "He's a thoroughly good man. I suppose you know why we arrived so late in the season?"

"Yes, that was a grand thing he did for you, taking you to Senuna. Did it—er—have any effect?"

"Not as I can tell. But he still thought it worth a try."

Lord Winworth nodded thoughtfully. "He's generous, well-bred, well-spoken. He's Northern and noble, so I know he's virtuous. And when I was talking to him earlier, it was clear he thinks the world of *you*."

Nemain bowed her head.

"His hair's awfully red though," he went on with a slight frown. "Think he's got a temper to match? The way he brought Bronwyn up short—not that she didn't deserve it—"

"I would say he's patient and good-humored generally. I've never seen him angry."

"I suspect he can be, though, in defense of his friends."

"I don't need my battles fought for me. But yes, Gavin's the sort who will do it."

Lord Winworth was silent, and Nemain blushed, realizing she had left the "Sir" off Gavin's name.

"Will that be all, my lord?"

He nodded. "Thank you, Nemain. The fact that you think well of him is greatly in his favor."

She curtsied.

"And thank you for coming," he added. "It will do Monessa good to have you here. I haven't heard her laugh like that in a very long time."

Chapter 29

BRIARVALE WAS ALIVE this summer, and especially tonight, as it had never been before in Nemain's time. Music and laughter rang through the halls and the open windows, and torchlight cast a flickering glow over the stone walls. The castle was the luminous beating heart of the warm, fragrant night; and Nemain, though she could not bear to stay inside, could not bear to leave the grounds either. The castle was where Gavin was, and while she might as well be far away—Monessa had far greater claim on his attention than she had—she still wanted to be near him.

There was an additional factor making it difficult to be near Gavin: the recent arrival of his father. Lord Airleas had not been expected until autumn, but he had made the trip early, accompanied by his two *cailleeyn*. Nemain was both intrigued and intimidated by this tall, dark, spare man, who lacked his son's good looks and charm, but had his strong chin and shrewd gray-green eyes. His voice was similar too, but in a lower key, and with a constant dour, jaded note. Nemain could tell at sight that he was an air character, and a very dry one at that. No wonder he and Gavin had had their clashes.

And yet Gavin had been touchingly glad to see him. "Da!" he'd cried like a boy, his eyes lighting up, as his father strode unexpectedly into the great hall. "I thought we wouldn't see you till the hunter's moon!"

Lord Airleas could not repress a smile. "I didn't want to wait to see how you were getting on," he said, "and of course meet the young lady."

He bowed to kiss Monessa's hand, and as he straightened, his eye caught Nemain's. He frowned slightly. "And you are?"

For a moment Nemain was actually not sure how to introduce herself. How *could* she explain to him her connection to the Winworths or to Gavin? For that matter, could she even say her name?

Lord Winworth unwittingly came to her rescue. "This is Nemain," he said, "formerly my ward."

"Aye. Of course."

Nemain swept him a deep curtsy, both to spare him the option of hand-kissing and to atone for her rudeness in staring at him. As she rose, she saw him looking askance at her Outland attire. (She had been measured for new gowns, at Monessa's insistence, but none of them were ready yet.)

He turned to Lord Winworth with some question, and only then did Nemain notice the two elderly women standing behind him. These, then, were the *cailleeyn* who had been counseling Gavin all his life. They looked benign and grandmotherly, but the sight of them filled her with terror. They would read her in an instant—her love for Gavin was so strong, so poorly concealed, it wouldn't have taken a *caillagh* to see it—and they would inform Lord Airleas of whatever they saw. They might also condemn her for the mark of black magic on her hands, as the Elmwold *caillagh* had done. No, she must not cross their path!

She hastily excused herself, and since then she had successfully avoided them. She kept to the shadows, as she had done as a child, and hovered on the edge of the crowd, always ready to slip away. (There was a constant crowd at Briarvale these days, with Gavin's gentlemen as well as Monessa's ladies in residence.) But she could not avoid Gavin's friends and family without avoiding Gavin himself. She saw him only occasionally in company, never in private, and had no relief from the dreadful heart-hunger that had been with her ever since Moddey's death.

Tonight, as she sat on the stone bench out in the courtyard, gazing up at the illuminated castle against a starry purple sky—hardly noticing its beauty—she wondered how much more of this she could take. The wedding was five months away, and she had promised to stay for it. Five months of this torture! … But then however long after that, when the winter snows had melted and the new-lyweds had gone home to Northwaite, it would be worse. For then he would be gone, and she would have nothing. She would be right back where she had started before her *immram*.

As she contemplated this, trying desperately to hold back tears, she saw him walking towards her. Immediately the phantom of the future vanished like a bad dream. She smiled up at him, then quickly lowered her eyes to hide the joy in them.

"There you are!" He sat down beside her. "I've been looking for you."

"What for?"

"Why, just to see you. What have you been doing with yourself?"

"Very little."

"I haven't even heard you play in a long time." He looked at her in concern. "Are you well?"

She nodded. "Just tired."

He put his arm around her, and she let her head rest against his shoulder. She felt vaguely guilty—knew she ought not to lean on him in *any* sense—but she couldn't help it.

"How are you liking it here?" she asked.

"Oh, very much. It's a charming place, and the people are nice, on the whole." He paused for a moment. "It jars me, though, to hear them call you by name. Don't they *know*?"

Nemain grinned. Gavin did not know that Monessa had whispered to her earlier, "Why does he call you 'jade'? That's a bit rude, isn't it?"

"I don't mind," she said. "I rather like hearing my own name again."

They were silent for a while. Nemain thought of asking "What do you think of Monessa?" but could not bring herself to. She knew perfectly well what he thought of Monessa. And it seemed wrong, somehow, to talk of Monessa just now, with Gavin's arm around her and her head on his shoulder.

"Have you given any thought to the future?" he asked.

She winced. "What do you mean?"

"After the wedding. What will you do? Where will you go?"

"Oh. No, I haven't thought about it. I suppose I'll go back to Defena eventually."

"Would you like to come to Northwaite with us?"

"To visit?"

"No, to live."

"Oh!" She caught her breath. "That's too … I couldn't ask that of you."

"Once again, jade, you're not asking. I'm offering."

"But—"

"I'll talk it over with Monessa, of course, but I'm sure she'll be glad to have you."

"And your father?"

There was the slightest hesitation in his reply. "Oh, I'll discuss it with him too. I don't see why he should object. You could either live in the castle with us, or have a little place of your own on the estate. You'd prefer that over the Deep Valley Inn, wouldn't you?"

"Oh, undoubtedly I would. But I—I don't know what to say."

"Well, think it over." He sighed and stretched. "I'd better get back. You're sure you don't want to come inside?"

She nodded. "I'll stay out here."

When he was gone, she slumped down on the bench, trembling with happiness and relief—and something else. Something dark and disquieting that she did not want to acknowledge, but that had kept her from saying yes.

⋯⊷⊶⋯

As bad as the days were, the nights were worse. In her solitary little room—mercifully far from the noise of the ladies' wing and the great hall—loneliness kept her awake like a physical pain. Her tea habit didn't help matters, but there was absolutely no way she was giving *that* up.

One night she could not stay in bed any longer. Throwing a cloak on over her night shift, she took her candle to the library. She picked up a volume of poetry that had once belonged to Master Ives, made herself comfortable in Lord Winworth's big padded chair, and read until her eyes closed and the book slipped from her hand.

She was awakened by a breeze, as fresh and gentle as the air of spring. She sniffed deeply—thinking herself out in the open again, with Gavin—and opened her eyes.

He was there, in the chair opposite hers, next to the open window. There was a book on his lap, but instead of reading, he was watching her in apparent amusement.

"Do you always sleep in here?"

"Not generally." She wiped some spittle from the side of her mouth and struggled to sit up straight. "How long have you been here?"

"Awhile. Are you ill?"

"No." She self-consciously drew her cloak a little closer around her and hid her hands in the sleeves. "I'd better go dress."

"Oh, stay! I hardly ever see you anymore."

"Suppose someone comes in and sees me like this?"

"So what?"

Her face reddened as she got up. "I'll be back."

"Ten minutes, jade. No more."

She went to her room, keeping an eye out for *cailleeyn*, gossiping servants, or Lady Bronwyn; but the corridors were deserted. She dressed, braided her hair, and returned as quickly as she could.

"Where is everyone?"

"Hunting."

"Even your father and your men?"

"My father's conferring with the *cailleeyn* in his chamber, and I don't know what our men are up to. Monessa offered to stay here with me, but I told her to go."

"Why? You know she hates it."

"I know, but she won't have many more chances to go with her father. She ought to spend time with him while she can." He turned to the flyleaf of his book—the book that she had been reading the night before. "What's this? 'To'—you, actually—'from Ives.' My, he writes a pretty hand. Who is he?"

"Don't be horrid. He was my tutor."

"Humph. Did he address soppy poetry to all his students, or just you?"

"Give it back. I'll put it away."

Chuckling, he handed it over and followed her to the shelves where all of her old books were stacked. "Where in the world did you get this?" he exclaimed, picking up one of Tynan's books.

"It was my father's. Have you read it?"

"I've only heard of it. Were all these his?"

"On that shelf, yes."

He turned over a few pages, then carefully put the book back. "Your father was quite a scholar."

Nemain glowed with pride. She had always suspected as much, but it was nice to have it confirmed.

"I can't believe you left all these behind. This is really *your* library, isn't it?—more than Lord Winworth's. Most of these volumes are yours."

"I couldn't very well take them on an *immram*," she sighed, "but I've missed them terribly."

"Tell you what, jade. Wherever you decide to end up, I'll see that you're not separated from them again."

She smiled and bowed her head—grateful, a little embarrassed, and glad that he wasn't pressing the matter of taking her to Northwaite. She still hadn't made up her mind about that.

"What else did you leave behind?"

"Not much. Some clothes. My little fortune."

"You have a fortune?"

"A very little one, I assure you. Four hundred and fifty staters in gold, which Lord Winworth is holding in trust for me. I don't want it."

"Why not?"

Nemain told him how Tynan had set aside his wages for her. As she spoke, Gavin's eyes widened.

"Oh, jade, you must take it."

"How can I? What would I use it for? What would be worth it?"

"How can you not! That money represents all the earthly good he could do for you. Did he mean for it to sit forever in Lord Winworth's coffers?"

She flinched as from a slap in the face.

"I'm sorry, jade. I'm too plain-spoken."

"No, you're right. You're right. I don't know why I didn't see it that way before."

"Sometimes I wonder—" He abruptly bit off whatever he was going to say.

"What?"

"Nothing."

"Tell me."

He sighed. "Sometimes I wonder," he said very gently, choosing his words with care, "if your curse partly consists in your inability to believe that you deserve anything."

Nemain did not reply. She understood each part of that sentence, but put together, it made no sense to her.

"And for that," he went on, with a harder edge to his voice, "I think I owe a grudge to Lady Bronwyn."

She gave a startled laugh. "Poor old Lady Bronwyn? Why on earth?"

"You've told me a little, and Monessa has told me a little more; and Lord Winworth won't speak against his sister, but he apologizes for her out the side of his mouth, Lowlander-fashion. She really does hate you—always has, just for being you. I don't think much of a woman who wreaks her spite on a little girl."

Nemain dismissed Lady Bronwyn with a gesture. "I'm not a little girl now. Besides, no one takes her seriously. She's just sad, bitter, and useless."

As she spoke, she suddenly remembered a long-ago conversation with Rhiannon about names of power and the vengeance of the Good Folk. "I've been crossed plenty of times, and nothing ever happened," she had said. Perhaps in Lady Bronwyn's case, that *was* the vengeance of the Good Folk: nothing at all. Lady Bronwyn had simply been left to herself to grow sad, bitter, and useless.

"She deserves pity more than anything," Nemain realized aloud.

"Well, she's wronged you nonetheless. By the way, jade, it might interest you to know—since you expressed doubt about this awhile ago—Lord Winworth does love you."

She stared at him, taken aback and a little amused. "Er—all right. How did that come up?"

"It's obvious. He has quite a fatherly regard for you, although he's a bit intimidated by you as well."

That made her laugh outright. "Oh, rubbish."

"It shouldn't surprise you. *I* find you intimidating. But he also respects you greatly. If you'd been a boy, I think he'd have made you his heir—Outland blood and all—instead of Swayne."

She gasped. "*Swayne?* When did that happen?"

"You didn't know?"

"No, I've hardly talked to him since we arrived. How splendid for him!"

"Indeed."

In that dour tone, he sounded just like his father. Nemain's mouth twitched. "Are you actually jealous of him?"

"No," said Gavin darkly. "I just don't like him."

"Why not?"

"Because you're in love with him, and he's not worthy of you."

"I'm not in love with him. And what do you know of his worth?"

"That's just a given." His eyes met hers briefly. "But I'm glad to hear it."

Nemain turned away in some annoyance. She did not want Gavin connecting her with Swayne, with her foolish fifteen-year-old self, or with the notion of love in general. The less said on that subject, the better.

"Anyway, why would I be jealous?"

"Oh, you know. Because of Monessa."

"No, I don't. What do you mean?"

At once she knew she had said too much. "Nothing. Forget it."

"No, what?"

She sighed. "All I know is that he fancied her a long time ago. I don't know if he still does."

"Oh, is that all!" He laughed softly. "I must say, that explains a lot."

"Please forget it. I just thought you knew."

"Humph! What do you think I'm going to do, challenge him to a duel?" Gavin yawned, as if the subject of Swayne suddenly bored him. "Come on, jade. Let's get something to eat, and then you must play for me. It's been ages."

⋄⟫⊜⟪⋄

That evening, after the first comparatively happy day Nemain had spent at Briarvale in a long, long time, there was a knock at her door. "Come in," she said, thinking it was Monessa or Amala.

"I have a message," said a male Northern voice she didn't recognize.

She opened the door to find a young page in Airleas livery, green and gold, with the emblem of a stag embroidered on his baldric. He made a stiff little bow. "Lord Airleas wishes to speak with you, my lady, in his chamber, first tomorrow morning."

Nemain was not used to being my-lady'ed. "Are you quite sure he meant me?" she asked, knowing Lord Airleas would not have used her name.

The boy's eyes wavered slightly. "With respect, my lady, he said, 'Go find the yellow-eyed Outlander and tell her I wish to speak to her in my chamber, first thing tomorrow morning.'"

"That does sound like me. All right."

He bowed again and departed.

Nemain had a sinking feeling in the pit of her stomach, much like in childhood whenever she had been summoned before Lady Bronwyn. Was she "in trouble"? Or worse, was Gavin in trouble because of her? She could think of no other reason why Lord Airleas would want to speak to her in private. Judging from his look and his tone when they had first met, it could be no friendly message.

Suppose the *cailleeyn* wanted to meet with her as well? At that thought, she broke out in a cold sweat. Oh, yes, undoubtedly that was it. There was no hope for her, then; it was known—or as good as known—that there was something amiss in her relationship with Gavin. For Lord Airleas, all that remained was to determine who was at fault and then act accordingly.

She gritted her teeth. Whatever they said or did to her, they would not find Gavin at fault; she would make certain of that. Gavin, who had sworn his friendship and loyalty to her on pain of death, asking nothing in return, must not suffer on her account. If he was brave enough to do that for her, couldn't she be brave enough to stand up to his father? Surely that was a less terrible prospect!

Still, she did not sleep that night.

Chapter 30

WELL BEFORE DAWN Nemain rose, lit a candle, and tried to decide what to wear for the interview. She had had four new gowns made: three of them dark and plain, but the fourth—again, at Monessa's insistence—of golden brocade, with amber velvet paneling in the bodice and long flared sleeves that helped conceal her hands. It was the prettiest thing she had ever owned, but as yet she had not dared to wear it. There was nothing wrong with it; it was modest, and it was no more extravagant than what the other ladies wore. It was just ... well, so very yellow. Not to mention impractical. You couldn't do any real work wearing material and sleeves like those.

Rois would have advised her to look pretty. She eyed the yellow gown doubtfully for a moment, then chose the dark brown one instead. For this interview, "sober and dignified" would probably stand her in better stead than "pretty." Besides, with no mirror, no lady's maid, and no sleep the night before, "pretty" was beyond her reach no matter what she wore.

She laughed at herself a trifle bitterly. To think that a day had come when she even cared.

At first light, she knocked at the door of Lord Airleas's chamber. "Enter," he said. "Have a seat."

There were no *cailleeyn* in the room. Breathing a little easier, she sat down in the chair opposite his. He folded his hands together and for a minute or two said nothing at all—just watched her. It was a tactic she recognized; she often used it herself, as a *caillagh*, to analyze people before they spoke. Not to be disadvantaged by him, she used it now.

First his hands. His fingers were quite long, even longer than Gavin's; he was a thorough thinker, a careful planner, not easily swayed by emotion. No diplomacy in *his* thumb, either. She wished she could see his palm, but she knew it would be useless to ask.

Then his face. It was deeply lined, and not just from age. He was prone to melancholy and, probably for that reason, accustomed to keeping his feelings to himself. His was not a particularly warm or affectionate nature, but he had loved well and suffered much; it had nearly killed him to lose his wife and then his daughter. And his love for and pride in his son were immense. He worried about him constantly.

Nemain had been ready for a fight, but instinct told her to remain cool and calm no matter what was said. A confrontation between an intense fire character and a dry, rigid air one could be disastrous. Besides, if she couldn't have this man's liking, she thought she would like to have his respect. Once again she felt grateful to Lady Bronwyn for the long years of training in self-control.

"What's this business about the stones of the Middle Cantrefs?" he asked abruptly.

"Oh!" Hope and relief surged through her. Was *that* what this was about? And was he actually willing to hear her out on the subject?

Keeping her hopes firmly in check, she told him what was happening to the monuments of the Vanished Ones. "Gavin suggested that you might use your influence to help—"

His eyes narrowed ever so slightly, and she stopped, realizing in horror that she had just used Gavin's name, without "Sir," in front of his father. But he let it pass.

"Why do those stones matter to you? You're not even from there."

"I believe it was my ancestors who raised them."

"Ah," he said in a condescending, that-explains-it tone. "Well, no one really knows anything about the Vanished Ones, *nee shen myr t'eh?* Anyone could claim them as ancestors. They left no trace of their existence but those stones, and no writings but some carvings that no one can read."

"I met an Outland woman who could. She even weaves the designs into fabric. But she was sworn to secrecy about their meaning."

"Aye, I'm sure the Outlanders have their own meanings for things—their own narrative of the past. I just doubt its authenticity. Remember, in the earliest records of *our* people, the Outlanders are described as a corrupt and benighted race, workers of black magic. If they ever had any ownership of those stones, they had abandoned them by the time our ancestors came ashore. But of course you know all this."

Nemain was stunned by his bluntness. She wondered if he meant that she knew all this because of her descent from that benighted race (!), or because she ought to have studied those particular records during her apprenticeship. But she had not studied them. Rhiannon had avoided all mention of Outlanders, past and present, as Nemain's parentage was a sore subject for them both.

"I know who and what you are," he went on. "You're not so soft, nor so simple, that you must be sheltered from history. Now then, if there's no clear evidence linking those stones to your people, why should you care about them?"

Cool and calm, she reminded herself, but she could not keep a little heat out of her reply. "I care on principle. A sacred place is a link between worlds, and the severance of that link is a loss to all worlds. I've spent my life seeking knowledge; I can't look the other way when ancient lore is devalued and destroyed. Even if that lore is never available to me—even if those stones have nothing whatever to do with my people—I'll still care."

Lord Airleas was silent for a minute. "I'll think about it, but I make no promises. Middle Cantref folk can be stubborn, and I haven't a great deal of time or resources to spare."

"I understand." She bowed her head. "Thank you, my lord. Will that be all?"

"No. There's another little matter I wish to discuss with you."

She looked up bravely, but she could feel the color draining from her face.

"I came down early from Northwaite because my advisors told me there'd been a hitch in the progress of the wedding."

"Oh?"

"I have reason to think it's you."

She took a deep breath and tried to keep her voice steady. "My lord, I know of no hitch. I've neither spoken nor acted against this marriage. It's a good match."

"And one I've taken great pains to secure. I won't have it jeopardized by anyone, even the bastard daughter of a Gweharan prince."

A muscle in her jaw twitched. "How do you know that?"

"Lord Winworth told me, but I guessed it when I first saw you. Eyes like yours are rare even among those close-knit clans, and scandals like your father's are even rarer. I remember it well. Yellow eyes, Northern bones, Outland dress—I put two and two together."

"Then you realize it's not a connection I'm likely to presume upon."

He almost smiled. Or rather, he smiled as Henry sometimes did—with eyes, not lips. "Good. And speaking of presumption, you can drop your *caillagh*'s airs. It's nonsense for a lass of twenty to wear the black robe."

"Are not the Mother and Crone inherent in the Maid?"

The almost-smile became a sneer. "Aye, that's the sophistry used to justify it. But it's life experience that makes a *caillagh*, not the mere possession of a womb. It cheapens the holy calling to view it as a fallback for an unmarriageable girl. ... Do you think I speak in jest?"

"No, I agree with you. That's what makes it funny."

"Moreover," he went on sternly, "it's dangerous for anyone to have access to that kind of learning and power before reaching maturity. Without life experience, *and* great intelligence, *and* a strong moral center, a young apprentice can easily become unstable, a danger to herself and others. ... You're no longer smiling. Do you still agree?"

I was young, Rhiannon had said. *I didn't know my own power.* "I do."

"You think yourself the exception, do you?"

"I do."

Again, that almost-smile. Nemain couldn't tell if he was approving of her or sadistically relishing her unease. For that matter, her own feelings were quite a muddle. She liked him; she was irritated by him; she was afraid of him; she was sorry for him.

"Answer me not as a *caillagh*, but as an honest girl, which Lord Winworth assures me you are. What exactly is between you and my son?"

"Friendship."

"Why did you travel here with him?"

"I felt like seeing the Briarvale folks again."

"Why did my seal end up on a tournament list in Drughage?"

Nemain could not repress a grin. "Because your son is a generous man and a bit of a show-off."

"Explain."

She explained.

"And did it work? Did the Senuna waters cure you?"

"No."

"What happened there?"

"I had a remarkable *ashlins*. I'd tell you about it, but I wouldn't want to start sounding like a *caillagh*."

Lord Airleas cleared his throat.

"Did he offer you anything—make any promises—above and beyond the trip to Senuna?"

That caught her off guard. Did he have any notion of the *geis*, or of Gavin's offer to let her live at Northwaite?

"Ah, so he did. What did he promise you?"

"Nothing," she said quickly. "Nothing that wasn't out of kindness alone. And nothing that would offend honor in any way."

His eyebrows went up. "Thrice nothing? I reckon that's something."

Nemain suddenly recalled the Dark Saying that began with *Thrice nothing is everything*, and could have kicked herself. She merely bowed her head.

"I never should have consented to the *immram*," he sighed. "I was afraid he'd abuse it in just such a fashion. He's far from home, he meets a girl he likes, and in the absence of normal rules ... You shake your head, but you must admit that's how it looks. Did you never wonder at his interest in you? Never think for a moment that it might be more than brotherly?"

"No. Never."

He looked at her incredulously, then scoffed. "You're not much of a *caillagh*, then. Barely even a woman."

"Oh, I'm both. I'm just an exception to many things."

As she spoke, she stripped off her gloves. Lord Airleas recoiled, but controlled his revulsion manfully; he set his teeth and did not look away.

"You tell me, my lord. Would *any* man look on me that way?"

When he answered, the dourness was gone from his voice. "Regardless, I don't want you near my son."

Nemain slowly put her gloves back on. Showing her hands had been her last resort, and she had lost. It didn't matter that she was honest, that she was innocent, that she loved Gavin too well to interfere with his marriage. Nothing she could do or say would clear her own name or his. She wondered why Lord Airleas had bothered speaking to her at all, if he had been set against her from the start.

"How can I avoid meeting him in company?"

"Avoid him as far as possible. And you are not to meet him in private at all."

"May I not at least say goodbye?" A lump rose in her throat. "I owe him that."

"You don't owe him anything," he said firmly. "I'll talk to him."

He waved her away, and she curtsied low before leaving. Strangely, she felt no anger or bitterness toward him—only sorrow that they had met under such circumstances. She felt sure that in another life he, like Nairne, would have been her friend.

Stranger still, underneath that feeling was *relief*. It broke her heart to be parted from Gavin like this, all at once, without even a goodbye; but at the same time she was a little glad not to have to say it. She would not have to tell him that no, she couldn't live at Northwaite—because now it had finally dawned on her why she could not.

She could not love a married man. And as long as she was near Gavin, connected to him by any tie, she would not be able to stop loving him. Either she had to be part of him, or she had to be a world away.

Really, Lord Airleas was doing her a favor, though he might think he was just protecting his son's interests. He was sparing them an awkward, painful final scene together. She and Gavin would remember each other as friends, and he would never have reason to suspect her true feelings. Surely there was some comfort in that.

Chapter 31

TALK TO GAVIN Lord Airleas did, and wasted no time in doing so. That very afternoon Nemain was with Monessa when the ladies-in-waiting burst in upon them, breathless with fright and glee.

"My lady, Sir Gavin is having a terrible row with his father! You must come!"

They gathered outside Lord Airleas's closed door, where they could hear the men shouting at each other in the Northern tongue. Nemain felt sick, but forced herself to stand her ground. If she fled, they would all know she had some part in this.

Monessa listened, white and trembling. Lowland gentlemen never settled their differences like this, and no one, including her father, had ever yelled at *her* in her entire life. The sound of men's voices raised in anger was clearly distressing to her, and Nemain hated her ladies for dragging her here to listen.

"What are they saying?" one of them whispered.

Monessa shook her head. "I can't tell. Come away. We shouldn't eavesdrop."

As the ladies dispersed in obvious disappointment, Nemain touched Monessa's arm. "Can you really not tell?"

"They're arguing about a girl, but I didn't hear a name."

Nemain hid her face in her gloved hands, wondering how she could have been so stupid as not to foresee this. Of course Gavin would fight back. Of course he wouldn't just give in, as a Lowland gentleman would—as *she* had—because his *geis* would outweigh the proprieties. She wouldn't have considered it breaking his *geis* to submit to his father in this instance, but he undoubtedly would.

"Oh, Nemain, you've nothing to worry about. Anyone who knows you would know you'd never ... I'll talk to Lord Airleas."

"I have talked to him," Nemain said drearily, "and so has your father. He's determined to think the worst. He's forbidden me to go near Gavin." Her voice broke as she started to cry, and Monessa put an arm around her.

"I should just go away."

"What, now? You've only just come back!"

"I should. I never meant to cause all this. He doesn't deserve it. *You* certainly don't."

"I want you here," said Monessa firmly, "and I want you at my wedding. Lord Airleas won't gainsay that. If he tries, I *will* have words with him."

Nemain looked at her, and in spite of her grief, her mouth quivered on the verge of a smile. Sweet, gentle Monessa, who looked as if a strong wind might blow her away, was not afraid of Lord Airleas in the least. And why should she be, with the potent weapons of sweetness, beauty, and charm at her disposal? No man with a heart would come off well in a confrontation with her.

"Let's hope it doesn't come to that," said Nemain.

⊷⊷◉ ◉⊷⊷

One morning she went down to the stables to saddle up Peddyr for a ride. It was getting harder to avoid certain people at the castle. She dared not go to the library in case Gavin looked for her there. She dared not join the ladies and gentlemen when they gathered for dancing or entertainment. And she seemed to encounter one or the other of Lord Airleas's *cailleeyn* in the corridors almost daily. Today the old woman had waved as if she wanted to speak to her, but Nemain had hurried past, pretending not to notice.

What could the *cailleeyn* want of her now, anyway? Ever since her chat with Lord Airleas, her behavior had been impeccable. Not once had she seen or attempted to see Gavin, in company or in private. Must she also bear the humiliation of having strangers look into her heart?

To her surprise, Swayne was at the stables as well, getting ready to head out on the gray hunter. "Where are you off to?" he asked.

"Just out."

"Me too. Want some company?"

She didn't, but she said, "Sure."

They rode out together, not saying much—unusually for Swayne. It was a relief to Nemain, who had no talent or love for small talk. Friendly silence was infinitely preferable, although friendly silence with Swayne was different than it was with Gavin or had been, long ago, with Tynan. It was not the silence of being comfortable in each other's company, but of being too preoccupied, respectively, to care about potential discomfort.

"Did you know they've moved the wedding up?" said Swayne suddenly.

She stared at him, feeling as if she'd been punched in the stomach. "Moved it up?"

He nodded, looking straight ahead. "It'll be at the harvest moon."

"Why?"

"Lord Airleas's advisors think it best, and Lord Winworth gave his consent." He paused for a moment and then added in an oddly flat tone, "Lady Monessa consented, too."

"And Sir Gavin?"

Swayne shrugged as if it hardly mattered. "Apparently."

"But the harvest moon is only—"

"Less than a fortnight away. There'll be a great deal to do."

Nemain pondered this. To her it could not make much difference. It might even be a good thing; the sooner the wedding was over, the sooner she could leave Briarvale. Why then this sense of foreboding, of things spinning out of control? And why did the thought of Gavin's wedding cause her fresh agony every time? Why could she not get used to it, as she had always gotten used to loneliness before?

She glanced at Swayne, who still looked moodily straight ahead, and realized he was feeling the same way. Worse, perhaps, because he couldn't leave Briarvale after the wedding. As Lord Winworth's heir, he must remain at Briarvale year in and year out, like Lady Bronwyn ... well, not quite like Lady Bronwyn. As a handsome young man with excellent prospects, he could have his pick of any girl in the village and beyond. *He* wouldn't remain alone unless he wanted to. Nemain looked him over and decided she need not pity him overmuch.

He chuckled.

"What is it?"

"I was just thinking of when we were young. Monessa and I used to ride down this path together. And I'd go over to see you now and then, when you were an apprentice, and bring you sugared almonds." He smiled. "Do you remember that?"

"Oh yes," said Nemain, as if she were only just remembering it.

"You still play the fiddle, don't you?"

"Yes. Do you still play the guitar?"

"Not much. I have so little time for that sort of thing now."

They were silent again for a while.

"You all right?" she asked.

The question seemed to surprise him. He thought about it and then smiled. "No," he said, "but thanks for asking."

⊷⊕ ⊕⊶

There were two days left before the wedding.

"Nemain, do come out and be with us," Monessa coaxed. "You spend far too much time moping alone."

"I'm not much for moping in company," she said with a feeble smile.

"But I've missed you! And I'm certainly not the only one."

"Who else?"

"Gavin, of course."

Nemain sighed. "You know what Lord Airleas said. I'm not to see Gavin at all."

"Oh, forget what Lord Airleas said! What harm will it do, in a room full of people, to remind Gavin that you still exist? Besides"—she hesitated—"he's changed, these past weeks, ever since that fight with his father."

"Changed? How?"

"Not so much in how he behaves. He's still civil to me, and to others for the most part. But he's restless, distracted. I really think it will do him good to see you."

"Or it'll make things worse."

"At this point I think it's worth the risk." Monessa spread her hands in a helpless gesture. "You're not the one who has to marry him in two days."

"I'm aware." Privately she added, *I'm also not the one who consented to have the wedding moved up.*

"So please try to make things right, even if you have to speak to him in private. If you get caught, I'll answer for you."

Nemain swallowed hard. "All right. Just give me a few minutes."

Alone in her room, she took a few deep breaths to compose herself. Then, yielding to an impulse she did not understand, she took off her plain, dark gown and put on the yellow one.

Gavin was sitting near the entrance of the great hall. At the sight of her, he immediately sat up straighter. She dared not acknowledge him with anything more than a slight bow, but she felt his gaze following her as she walked past. Swayne was there, too; he smiled at her, and she gave him a brief smile in return.

One of Monessa's ladies was playing the lute and singing in a plaintive voice, shrill on the high notes. Nemain took a seat beside Monessa, wishing she had some needlework or something to keep her busy, as the other ladies did; but she could hardly do much with gloves on.

"Very nice," said Monessa as the song ended. "Shall we have a dance?"

"What style of dance?" one of the gentlemen asked. "Northern or Lowland?"

"Honestly, I prefer the Northern style," Gavin remarked. "Lowland dancing is so slow, and there's so little contact. One wonders what the point is."

His men agreed, and some of the ladies blushed and smiled.

"The point is to appreciate distance," said Nemain, causing a few people to turn around in surprise. Most of them had never heard her speak before. "It's the space between you that makes even a little contact significant."

"Hmm." Gavin looked at her thoughtfully. "Will you show me what you mean?"

She stood up and turned to Swayne. "Would you mind?"

"Not at all."

He bowed and she curtsied. As Monessa clapped a rhythm, the two of them began a sedate Lowland dance with almost no contact—Nemain's gloved fingertips just resting on Swayne's hand—except for that of eyes. She neither blushed nor trembled at his nearness; she met his eyes with equanimity, and went through the motions as smoothly and unthinkingly as she played songs from memory.

"Prettily done," said Gavin. "Appreciating empty space … I suppose there's wisdom in that."

Nemain smiled as she sat down.

"Why don't you play your fiddle for us?" Swayne asked her. "I don't believe this lot have ever heard you."

"Oh, yes, let's have some more music," one of the ladies chimed in. " 'The Lily and the Woodbine'—does she know that one?"

"You couldn't name a song that Nemain doesn't know," smiled Monessa. "Will you play, dear?"

Nemain nodded, and Monessa turned to Amala, who was seated on her other side. "Fetch her fiddle and the latticed screen, please."

"She shouldn't have to hide," said Gavin. There was a brief, uncomfortable silence as those who knew about Nemain's deformity were unsure how to respond, and those who didn't know about it were afraid to ask.

"Then don't bring the screen," Nemain said as Amala hesitated. "Take my fiddle up to the gallery. I'll play up there. But I will ask that you all look away."

She looked at Gavin as she said this, and he looked steadily back at her. Again she felt his eyes on her as she went out, heading for the passageway up to the minstrels' gallery.

As it happened, "The Lily and the Woodbine," a lovely old Lowland ballad, had the same melody as an extremely bawdy Northern song that Rois used to sing. Nemain smiled to herself as she hitched up her sleeves and began to play. After the first few notes, she heard a stifled laugh among the gentlemen.

For a moment she wondered which song she was actually playing and which one the people gathered below were hearing. Down there was a Lowland gentleman she had once loved, who would be hearing one tune; there was also the Northman she loved now, who might, possibly, be hearing both. But whichever song it was, there was no question she was playing it for *him*. How could she ever have preferred Swayne! No; for Nemain—part Northerner, part Outlander, and all mystic—there could only be one kind of man: a man of two elements, who spoke two languages, who had ears to hear multiple meanings, and who had eyes to see that the stars were more than just stars.

She was shaking as she put down her fiddle and bow. He was watching her, just as she had told him not to, and the look in his eyes made her terrified that he really had heard and understood.

Mentally apologizing to Monessa for her cowardice, she fled to the garden. She made her way to a shadowy, neglected corner, overgrown with honeysuckle and climbing roses, and sat down on the edge of a mossy stone heap that had once been a fountain. The sun was just setting, and in the shade of the garden wall it was already rose-hued twilight. Soon the castle would be noisy with revelry, but for now there was no sound but the music of crickets. She closed her eyes, drinking in the warm sweet air like wine, searching for the peace that she usually found here.

She did not see his shadow or hear his footsteps, but she sensed his presence even before he sat down beside her.

"Monessa told me about this thing you do," he said, "and I saw you doing it tonight. When someone's singing off-key, your expression doesn't change, but your hand twitches—so. It's quite funny."

Nemain laughed. "I didn't know that."

"M-hm."

He was quiet for a few moments, during which Nemain cast about desperately for something to say. Friendly silence didn't seem possible between them now.

"Where'd you get that gown, jade?"

"Monessa chose it."

"I would almost say *it* had chosen *you*. Red and gold ... those are your colors. You should always have one or the other about you."

Her face grew warm, and she still failed to think of something to say. At least he was being nice, as usual, and didn't seem upset. But she trembled to think how Lord Airleas would react if they were found here together.

"I'd better ..." She stood up, but Gavin stopped her with a touch on her arm.

"Don't go," he said. "There are no spies here. And I don't care if there are."

Warily she sat back down.

"What did my father say to make you avoid me?"

She wasn't sure how to answer that. "He told me to," she said finally.

"Just that?"

She nodded.

"And you gave in?"

She looked at him questioningly and was shocked to see the pain in his face.

"I didn't believe him," he muttered.

"I thought it best," she cried. "I didn't want to cause any trouble for you."

"You don't think I'd bear a little trouble for you?" He gave her the same incredulous look his father had, and then laughed bitterly. "Oh, but this—you've hurt me, jade. Do you not know the power you have to hurt me? Or are you unable to care?"

She flinched. "You know that's not the case."

"I really don't. I've no idea what's in your mind."

Cool and calm, she told herself again.

"It's important to me that people think well of you," she said. "Especially the people who love you. Your father loves you greatly."

He looked away. "If my father doesn't think well of me, that's no fault of yours."

"Isn't it?"

"No, he made that clear. He quite likes you."

"What!"

"I know." Gavin smiled somewhat grimly. "He can be hard to read sometimes. But I gathered he found you very pleasant to talk to."

Nemain laughed helplessly. "How does he talk to people he doesn't like?"

"Well, you've a bit of an idea how he talks to his son."

"What did he say to you?"

Gavin scowled. "Long story short—I've been trifling with a fine girl I can have no intention of marrying, and if I had any sense of honor or decency, I'd have left you alone from the start."

She shook her head. "You've been just what you promised to be. No friend or kinsman could have been truer." Her voice quavered. "And it seems I've repaid you very ill."

"I don't want to be repaid. I want you to be happy, and I want you in my life. That's all."

Oh, is that all! she thought.

"I can't be in your life, Gavin. It's nothing you've done. It's nothing, even, that your father has said. It's just not possible."

"Why not?"

She tried to think of an answer that wouldn't give her away.

"Since when do you care what people think?" His voice took on a warm, teasing note. "I've always cherished that in you. The girl who went on an *immram* at age fifteen … the girl who wears Outland garb, and wears it well, in front of lords and ladies … the 'witch-fiddler' of Kell's Crossing, not a bit afraid to show her hands then! …"

"Are you saying I should stop wearing gloves? Because I won't."

"I wouldn't mind if you did."

"Liar."

He took her hand in both his own. She quickly looked around to make sure they weren't being watched, then looked down at her hand in his. He was very gently pulling her glove off.

"Gavin—"

He glanced up. "I'm sorry. May I?"

"What for?"

"I just want to show you I'm not a liar."

She hesitated, then looked straight ahead, and with an effort relaxed her fingers.

He removed her glove and brought her hand to his lips. It was not the perfunctory hand-kiss a gentleman gave a lady; it was deliberate, and it did not stop there. He turned her hand over and kissed her palm, then the underside of her wrist. His unshaven cheek felt prickly against her palm.

She knew there was nothing in it—he was only doing it to make a point— but that did not stop her pulse from quickening or her breath from catching in her throat. At the slight involuntary sound she made, almost a sob, he looked up and saw her face.

"Oh." His voice was not quite steady. "Oh, I see."

He knew. He could see it—anyone could have seen it just then. And to think she had been afraid of the *cailleeyn* finding out!

She could not bear to look in his eyes and see the dismay and regret she knew would be there. She snatched her hand away, caught up her glove, and ran.

Chapter 32

NEMAIN CRIED HERSELF to sleep that night, not only from humiliation, but for the ruin of the dearest friendship she'd ever had. This spoiled everything; she would never be able to look back on her time with Gavin without also remembering *this*. It would certainly ruin things for him, too. At least now he recognized the necessity of being parted from her—she had gathered as much from the tone of his "Oh, I see"—but she had not wanted him to come to it this way!

She hoped no misguided consideration of his *geis* would induce him to seek her out one last time. At this point, the kindest option for the friend and kinsman would be to let her go without another word. He must understand that. His father had understood that all along. …

In the morning she lay awake for a long time, fretting. Where could she go where she wouldn't have to see anyone? She could not face Gavin, Lord Airleas, or the *cailleeyn;* she had no desire to see Swayne, Lord Winworth, or anyone else. She thought of taking Peddyr and riding out over the hills, just to be alone, as she used to do over the moors. But with the wedding tomorrow, she couldn't get as far away as she wanted to.

The wedding. Briarvale would be in chaos with the preparations today. At that thought, she decided to seek refuge in the one area of the castle where she could be idle and ignored, if not alone. She stopped in the library just long enough to get a book—on second thought, several books—and then went to claim an out-of-the-way corner for herself in the ladies' wing.

Monessa was there, of course, but far too busy to pay her much attention. Lady Bronwyn, mercifully, was directing wedding business elsewhere in the castle. The other ladies were a little discomfited by Nemain's presence at first, but soon forgot her in the excitement of trying on gowns and jewels. She read steadfastly all the morning, ignoring the chatter.

The word *witch,* followed by some smothered giggling, caught her attention at one point. "Hush, you fool!" someone hissed. "She's right there."

There was a pause. Nemain did not look up.

"She's not listening," said another. "Anyway, she *does* look it. With her eyes, and the way she dresses—well, not last night, but usually—all she needs is a rook on her shoulder."

Nemain laughed outright, and the ladies subsided in guilty silence.

"Carry on," she said, still not looking up, and the various conversations resumed in muted tones. The girl who had made the quip about the rook stayed silent.

There was one bad moment in the afternoon. A page in Airleas livery came to the door and announced that he had a message for the lady fiddler; was she there? Nemain hurriedly ducked behind a curtain and heard Monessa say in puzzled tones, "Oh, I thought she was here. She must have just left."

The page was dismissed, and Monessa came over to her. "Nemain, what on earth!"

"I'm sorry. I can't go to him. I just can't."

Monessa looked at her thoughtfully for a moment. Oh, *mollaght,* could Monessa see it in her, too? She hung her head in shame and fear.

"All right," said Monessa, and left her alone.

In the evening the ladies prepared to join the gentlemen in the great hall for supper. "Go on without me," Monessa said to them. "I need a rest. Amala, will you have supper brought up for me and Nemain?"

Nemain glanced up in surprise and a little apprehension, but did not demur.

As the ladies filed out, Monessa sighed in relief. "Thank goodness," she said quietly. "We haven't had a real talk in ages, you and I. I haven't had a real talk with anyone in ages."

Nemain looked at Monessa and realized for the first time how tired she was, physically and emotionally. It was not just the strain of the wedding. There was a chronic weariness in her eyes.

"What do you want to talk about?" Nemain asked, pushing her own sorrows to the back of her mind.

"Gavin tells me you're a—an advisor of sorts? Like those two old women who travel with his father."

She nodded.

"And that you can't refuse advice to anyone who asks it."

"That's right."

"Even me?"

"Why would I refuse you?"

"Oh, you know. Because I don't believe in faeries and such."

"That doesn't matter. Show me your hand."

Monessa obeyed, giggling a little. "What do you see? Happiness?"

"Oh, yes."

"Love?"

"Yes." The corner of her mouth turned down. "And children."

Monessa smiled. "That's good, isn't it? You sound so sad."

"Do I? I don't mean to."

"So what advice would you give me, based on what you see?"

Nemain studied Monessa's face. She saw a great deal she had never seen before—things Monessa had kept hidden from everyone. Fear. Insecurity. Months, perhaps years, of melancholy. How had she missed all this?

She took a deep breath and gave the first counsel that came to her mind. "Don't fear the future."

"Don't fear the future?"

"Your future's bright. It'll require some courage of you. It does right now, in fact. But if you go forward to meet it—"

Monessa was still smiling, but her mouth was quivering now.

"—you'll be all right." Nemain returned her smile as bravely as she could. "Better than all right."

Monessa slumped down in her chair. There were tears in her eyes.

"Go forward," she mused. "That's interesting. Do you know, I don't think I've ever gone forward in my life—not really. I've just sort of passively done this, said that …"

"Flowed?"

"Exactly!" By now she was crying, but she spoke with great animation. "Like a stream, with no control over its course. And now I'm up against a dam of things I should and shouldn't do, and things I have no choice in, and there's no way round it. I'm afraid of—what's the word—"

At that point Amala came in with a tray of food and a jug of wine. When she saw Monessa weeping like a melting ice-maiden, she nearly dropped it all. Nemain hastened to her aid.

"Thank you, Amala," Monessa sniffled. "Run along. I shan't need you again tonight."

"Thanks for that," Nemain said wryly, shutting the door behind Amala. "She already thinks I'm a monster. Now she'll be wondering what on earth I did to you."

Monessa laughed. "Oh, Amala's a good sort. I've told her not to be afraid of you, but you know how the other servants talk."

"Unfortunately I do. Now then, stagnation?"

"What?"

"The word you were looking for."

"Oh, yes, yes. That's how I feel. It's absurd, isn't it? But you're saying if I stop being afraid—if I just go forward and *do* what frightens me—I'll be all right?"

"Yes."

Monessa wiped her eyes. "It sounds so simple."

"It often does. There's a very fine line between good counsel and rubbish."

Monessa laughed again.

"I assume it's the wedding that frightens you?"

She nodded. "That's why I agreed to have it sooner. I wanted to get it over with."

It seemed incredible to Nemain that any woman could feel that way about marrying Gavin, but she tried not to show it.

"But that's not courage—not the kind you were talking about. I feel the lack of that. What can I do about it?"

Nemain shrugged. "Take another look at the dam, perhaps. If there's no way round it, there might be an opportunity *in* it."

"What does that mean?"

"I don't know. It's probably rubbish."

Monessa grinned. "Do people pay you for this?"

"Not for counsel. They pay me for medicine, mostly. Say, if you'd like, I can make you a tea that would help you sleep tonight."

"Would you? That would be nice. I haven't slept well in ages, either. But— oh! I almost forgot. Before you do, I have something for you."

"What?"

Monessa clasped her hands gleefully. "Close your eyes."

With a sigh, Nemain humored her.

"I knew that yellow gown would suit you. I also knew you wouldn't be per-suaded to get more than one really nice gown. So I didn't try to persuade you."

"Oh, Monessa, you didn't ..."

"You can look now."

She opened her eyes, and the sight took her breath away. It was a red gown— wonderful, deep, vivid, shimmering red—tailored in the same style as the yellow one, but richly embroidered with gold thread and trimmed with seed pearls. Nemain had never seen anything like it. It would rival what Monessa herself was wearing tomorrow.

And not only a gown, but embroidered gloves and slippers to match. She saw them through a blur of tears.

"This is too much," she murmured. "Far too good for the likes of me."

Monessa put an arm around her. "It's not too good for the sister of the bride."

⋅→▬ ▬←⋅

It was dark and raining when Nemain retired to her room. She knew she wouldn't sleep tonight, but rather than take any of the sedative tea, she had decided to meditate. Just as Monessa felt her lack of courage, Nemain felt a need for all the help, strength, and peace she could get.

By candlelight she loosened her hair (it was best to undo all braids and knots prior to meditation, except for the *caillagh*'s plaited belt), changed into her night shift, and put the black robe on over that. Then she lit a stick of incense, opened the window, and held out her bowl of pebbles to catch the rain.

She knelt down before the gathered elements and tried to clear her mind, but her mind clung stubbornly to the one thought that filled it. She wanted Gavin—oh, she wanted him terribly. She could not deny it, could not suppress it, could not even reproach herself for it. It made no difference that she had just given Monessa counsel, sincerely and compassionately, promising that she would have love, children, and happiness in her marriage. It made no difference that she had nothing to say to Gavin and he could not possibly have anything to say that she wished to hear. She wanted him anyway, hopelessly and against all reason.

A noise at the window made her look up. Was it hailing? No—still just raining—but it had sounded like a stone glancing off the windowsill.

There it was again. A few moments later she heard a grunt, followed by a muffled Northern oath, as Gavin hoisted himself up over the sill and into her room. She stifled a cry, both aghast and overjoyed to see him. Had she *wished* him here?

"Jade—"

"Shh." She closed the window lest he be seen or heard, then set aside the candle, bowl, and incense. "What are you doing here? How did you even know—"

"I've been looking for you all day. I've been reduced to wandering outside, hoping for a light in a window. And here you are."

Evidently he had been out in the rain for quite a while. He was in his shirt-sleeves, wet to the skin, and he looked pale and haggard. The word *fey* rose to her mind, and she began to tremble. But before she could ask him what was wrong, he spoke again.

"Marry me."

For a second she stared at him, not comprehending, and then her heart did a strange, quick, painful thing. She put her hand over it as if she could still it manually.

"Gavin, if this is about the *geis*—"

"It isn't," he said quietly, "though this would be the best way to keep it."

"—I will witness that you've kept it," she went on talking over him. "You've done nothing wrong, and you owe me nothing. You need not—"

"Nemain, I'm in love with you."

That silenced her. Her name, combined with those words, from his lips … no, this could not be real. She had to be dreaming. Hadn't she had this dream before?

"I never meant for you to know," he continued, coming closer. "I didn't think that was what you needed from me. I would have buried it forever to serve you. But last night, the way you played that song, and then ran off, you had me so confused—and then in the garden, that look you had …" He caught his breath. "I realized you must feel as I do. *Nee shen myr t'eh?*"

He had taken her hand, and now he kissed it. Her eyelids fluttered closed for a moment, but she dared not surrender to the dream. Not yet.

"What do you have in mind?"

He smiled at the question, but he answered it seriously. "I mean to leave tonight. Now. If you'll come with me."

"What about Monessa?"

"She'll get over it. Her heart is elsewhere."

Nemain had not thought anyone else knew that. He sounded as if he had known it for a long time and it bothered him not at all. How extraordinary that a man like Gavin and a woman like Monessa could fail to love each other!

"Would you risk your children inheriting this?" she demanded, pulling her hand away and holding it up.

He didn't hesitate. "Aye. I would love and defend them—teach them to be strong and good, like their mother—and I don't doubt others would love them too."

He put his hands on her waist, drawing her close to him. "Come with me. We'll go anywhere you like—be married at the first place we stop—and never be parted again. Upon my life, Nemain, I can't go another day without you."

The desire in his voice both alarmed and thrilled her. The sound of her name, spoken by him in that tone, was the sweetest sound in the world. No dream, this! He meant what he said—no Northerner would utter a name of power in a lie—and she could see, with her *caillagh*'s eyes, what her future would be if she gave in to him. An end to loneliness. Love, children, every joy she had assumed could never be hers. She had only to say yes. …

But she could see the past just as clearly. She saw a book of generations, illuminated in gold and green: a long, long history of noble blood and sanctioned marriage. She saw other beautiful books, stacked on a table in a bare, shabby room. She saw a man who could not hold up his head, so that for years she had not noticed the color of his eyes.

"Have you thought this through?" she asked.

"I have."

He met her gaze, but behind the passion in his eyes, she saw a tiny flicker of fear. Oh yes, he had thought this through very carefully. He knew exactly what he stood to lose, and it scared him. Already he was mourning the loss of it all—his family, his home, his rank, the only life he had ever known—in a corner of his heart that he would never willingly let her see. But she would always know.

"I can't let you do this."

His hands fell to his sides. "So you won't?"

"I can't."

The light died out of his eyes. He stepped back, turned to the window, then hesitated.

"Gavin—"

"Don't." He held up his hand, and she realized in horror that she—*she*, not her music!—had just made a man cry. "Just give me a minute."

Nemain sat down on the edge of her bed, her hands clenched against her knees. She had no doubt that she had done the right thing, but that was no comfort at all. As yet she was not thinking of her own pain; to witness Gavin's mute suffering was torment enough.

When he spoke again, his voice was sad but calm. "Did I read you wrong, jade?"

"No."

"Then why?"

"Because this isn't what you want. You want Northwaite. You want a name written next to yours in the book of your fathers, and your children listed with you. You want a marriage where the two of you were carefully chosen for each other ..."

Gavin winced.

"You could have all that with her," Nemain concluded.

"You can say this, loving me?"

"If I loved you less, I could not say it."

"But Monessa doesn't care for me."

"She'll learn in time. So will you."

He bit his lip.

"Jade, you once told me I would come to a crossroads someday, and that whichever way I chose, it would turn out all right. What if this is it? What if *this* is what I choose?"

"It isn't. I'm not allowing you this choice."

There was a pause.

"And what of the stars?" he asked.

"What of them?"

"Can I truly have the life I want with a woman who doesn't see them as I do? As *we* do?"

"The stars govern her destiny as well as ours, and they themselves say she's a good match for you. I'd trust them."

"And is there only one good match—one right match—for every person?"

"I doubt it. Some of us aren't lucky enough to have one."

"Oh, jade." He passed his hand over his eyes in a weary, despairing gesture. "This again! You don't think you deserve any happiness, and so you won't take it when it's offered. I think you *give* the curse all the power it has over you."

"If you'd known my father, you'd understand. When I saw Gwehara, I realized what he'd come down to, everything he'd lost because of me."

"He lost it all because of *him*," said Gavin harshly. "He made his choices before you were even born. You can't blame yourself."

"I have a choice in this, though. I won't see *you* ruined."

"Jade—"

"No, hear me. Everything you've always wanted is within your reach. If you throw it all away now, you'll be sorry. You're sorry even now, and fearful; I can see it. You can't do this with a whole heart, and you can't keep a *geis* with anything less."

Gavin stared at the floor. The passion and the misery alike seemed to have gone out of him.

"You're right," he said at last. "If I'm holding back at all, I shouldn't do this. I'm sorry."

She sighed in mingled relief and despair. *Well done, Gavin.* Giving in, changing course—very sensible, very water-like. No pure fire nature could have done that quite so readily.

"Well, what then?" he asked. "What will *you* do?"

"I'll figure something out."

"Will you let me know?"

"I'd better not."

He closed his eyes briefly.

"Promise me that if you ever need anything—any service from a friend and kinsman—you'll come to me. Allow me to do what I *can* do with a whole heart."

"All right."

"Promise."

Reluctantly she placed her hand in his. He held it for a good deal longer than was necessary to seal a promise, but when he finally let go, she felt cold and empty.

"Now then, before I go"—he stepped back a few paces and sat down cross-legged among the rushes—"let's talk. If this is to be our last talk, I want nothing left unsaid."

There followed one of the saddest, strangest, sweetest hours Nemain had ever spent. It was hard to sit at this distance from Gavin, with body and soul aching for his nearness, and talk of love. Indeed, being Nemain and having been raised a Lowlander, she found it hard to talk of love at all. But it was a relief, too. She need have no more secrets from him—no more cause for shame or fear—and no regrets, later, when he was married and gone.

"When did you first know you loved me?" he asked. "Actually, *do* you love me? You haven't yet said."

"Haven't I?"

"Not quite. Say it, jade. Give me something to comfort myself with when I'm doing the honorable thing tomorrow."

She chuckled. Odd that he could joke and she could laugh at a time like this. But it was preferable to weeping.

She told him, hesitantly but candidly, everything that had been in her heart since the night he had held her in his arms and sworn his *geis*. "What about you? When did you know that you … ?"

"Well, for me it was a good deal simpler than that." He wiped his eyes with the back of his hand. "And less depressing."

She laughed. "Oh?"

"It was when you read my hand."

"What? You mean when we first met?"

He nodded, grinning at the memory. "I was noticing your gloves, and you asked if I was afraid. I said, 'Why would I be?' And then you smiled at me. I felt as if I'd passed a test, like in one of the old tales. I knew then that you would be *something* to me—that I couldn't just leave you there. Even though I really didn't have any designs on you at first—even though I knew I'd be fighting myself the whole journey, and probably long afterward—I felt it would be worth it to have you near me."

"And was it?"

"Oh yes. I regret no part of it. Do you?"

"No." And she did not, even though she knew she'd be lonelier than ever when he had gone. Her memories of their time together were pure and unspoiled again; the bitterness had left them from this hour. It would still hurt to invoke them—perhaps forever—but she would not exchange them for anything. "No, I don't."

"Even this. I'm glad we had this talk. I know you'll probably punish yourself later for telling me so much—"

Nemain's mouth twitched. She knew she would.

"—but please don't. You've given me courage for tomorrow, and goodness knows I could use it."

He got up, opened the window, and looked up at the sky. The rain had stopped, and the nearly-full moon shed a soft, silvery radiance over everything.

"It's past midnight." He turned to her and smiled wanly. "Kiss me, jade, before I go. It's my wedding day."

Nemain rose, intending to kiss him on the cheek. Instead he turned her face up to his and kissed her mouth—a kiss that quite erased the memory of Swayne's. He held her tightly, and she clung to him, wondering how such delight was possible amid such sorrow.

"Are you sure?" he whispered in her ear.

Nemain, at the moment, was hardly sure of her own name. But she forced herself to step back, folding her arms tightly to keep from shaking. "I'm sure."

He sighed. "Well, at least now you don't have to say you've only been kissed once."

"It's truer now than it was before."

He smiled, a smile that was equal parts pleasure and pain. "*Slaynt-lhiat,*" he said, and climbed out the window.

Chapter 33

IN THE EARLY morning she fell into a fitful sleep. She dreamed she was back at the stone circle on the hilltop, at twilight, with Moddey and her horse waiting for her below. But instead of going down to them, this time she stayed in the circle. Three lovely women appeared—one fair, one red-headed, one dark—and spoke to her.

"My husband was alone and grieving, with a child of his own," said the fair one, whose eyes were arrestingly blue. "He could have placed you in a poorhouse. I put it into his heart to keep you."

"And *I* put it into my brother's heart to seek you out," said the dark one. She quickly added, "I'm sorry we didn't meet, for we would have been friends. But so we are, and shall be, in all worlds."

"You already know what I did for you," said the red-headed one. She spoke with an Outland accent, and her smile was the mirror of Nemain's own.

"We are not without influence, even here," they said in one voice.

There was a knock at the door. Nemain stirred and moaned in her sleep, but, refusing to wake, grabbed the fading edges of the *ashlins* and pulled herself back in.

"Do you understand now, *inneen?*" Tynan was in his work clothes, leaning against a fortress wall. "What I was sorry for? And what I wasn't sorry for?"

The knock came again, louder this time, and Nemain lost the vision. She was back in her room, and it was the morning of Gavin's wedding day. "What!" she snapped.

"Lady Monessa sent me," said Amala's piping voice. "To dress you."

"Go attend your lady. I can dress myself."

"She's gone on an errand. She told me to attend you in the meantime."

Sighing heavily, Nemain dragged herself out of bed and opened the door. Amala entered, carrying a basket of flowers, ribbons, and jewels. "What's all this for?"

Amala opened her mouth to reply, but was dumbstruck at the sight of Nemain's hands. Rolling her eyes in exasperation, Nemain quickly put her gloves on. "There. Now, then?"

"These are to help you make ready," she managed to say. "Lady Monessa said to use my best judgment."

Nemain shrugged. "Fine."

She submitted to being dressed and combed like a child, though it seemed a grim farce to her. It wasn't *her* wedding day, and that gown was really too good for her, whatever the occasion. Who would care what she wore or how she looked today?

"There," said Amala at length, positioning two hand mirrors so Nemain could see what had been done. "How's that?"

Nemain looked, and then stared. The child's best judgment was astonishingly good. Her hair was plaited—the style she was most comfortable with—but more elegantly than she could have done it herself, with a golden ribbon woven through it and a few little yellow roses tucked into it. She was wearing a necklace with amber pendants that matched her eyes and set off the red gown well.

"I'm a beauty!" she realized aloud in consternation. "When did that happen?"

Amala giggled.

"You're a first-rate lady's maid. You're wasted carrying wood and water for Lady Bronwyn."

"Would you be wanting a lady's maid?" Amala asked shyly. "Lady Monessa has her own—she's been training me some—but she's going up to Northwaite."

"No. Your skills would be wasted on me." She nodded toward the door. "Thank you."

Amala curtsied and left. In the corridor Lady Bronwyn was barking orders at the servants, and Amala was quickly caught and weighted down with chores. Poor child! No wonder she wanted to work for someone else.

Deborah Bradford

Nemain sat down on her bed to steal a few more minutes of solitude before she must go out and be seen. She *would* be seen—and stared at—looking like this. Yet for once that prospect did not fill her with unmixed terror.

⇥⊜ ⊝⇤

It was a perfect day for a wedding, fresh-scented and sparkling from the night's rain, summer-warm but with the slightest hint of autumn in the air. As Lord Airleas's *cailleeyn* had advised, the wedding would take place at the potent hour of twilight, under the rising harvest moon. Nemain both admired the *cailleeyn's* timing and resented it. It was lovely, romantic, auspicious, and it would make for a wretchedly long day.

A few people stared at her and whispered, but she kept to the shadows as much as possible and was generally left alone. Now and then she glimpsed Gavin and Monessa among the crowd: Gavin in a nicely tailored doublet of cloth of gold, and Monessa in silver-white samite, her hair crowned with flowers. Looking at them, Nemain thought of the sun and the moon, side by side. The whole scene was a wealth of good omens ... well, except for the two black-robed *cailleeyn* watching the festivities like a pair of crows. It was customary for *cailleeyn* up North to wear their robes to a wedding, but Nemain wished they hadn't.

Late in the afternoon, in the courtyard, she felt a tap on her shoulder and turned. "Here," said Lord Airleas, handing her a cup. "You look as if you need it."

It was heather mead. She drank it with reckless haste. "Thanks."

He half smiled.

"I've been thinking," he said, "you have a point about those stones in the Middle Cantrefs. I'm willing to look into the matter, on one condition."

"What's that?"

"That you bear me no ill will." He held out his hand. "I don't wish to be your enemy—and not just because of whose name you carry."

"I don't wish to be yours," she said, "and not just because of whose name you share."

240

She gave him her hand, and he clasped it very briefly and gingerly—rudely, she thought, for someone seeking assurance of goodwill. Then she wondered if he merely feared to hurt her, as Gavin had when he first saw her deformity.

"Actually, it's already begun," he confessed. "I've sent some men up there to record the current number and positions of the stones and to discuss other building options with the locals."

"You have?" Her face lit up. "Why didn't you tell me? I could have used some good news!"

"You've been rather hard to find lately."

She smiled and bowed her head.

"What are your plans when this is over?" he asked. "Will you be staying at Briarvale?"

"No. I mean to take my bit of money and my books, and go … I'm not sure where yet. I just want to be gone."

Lord Airleas nodded slowly. "If it comes to it, I can help you find a situation. Gavin need not know."

"Would you? That would be—" She stopped, puzzled. "What do you mean by 'if it comes to it'?"

Instead of answering, he looked past her at someone approaching. "Look out," he said under his breath, and walked away.

"Nemain!" Monessa was running towards her, holding up her voluminous skirt in one hand and pulling Gavin along with the other. Nemain noticed detachedly that the wreath on Monessa's hair was made of rosemary and hawthorn blossoms, though it was well past the time for hawthorn to bloom. Yet another good omen? "Gavin, have a dance with my sister. I'll be back."

Monessa kissed Nemain's cheek and then pushed her towards Gavin. She glanced nervously in Lord Airleas's direction, but he was deep in a discussion with Lord Winworth about something.

Gavin kissed her cheek, too, causing her to blush, and then led her out in a Lowland dance. She tried to keep her head up and look him in the eye, as she had done with Swayne; but she was finding it difficult to meet his gaze, remembering the night before. What he was thinking of, she could not guess. He led the dance well, and the hand that held her gloved one was quite steady.

"Monessa tells me you gave her some counsel last night."

"I did."

"You can be proud. She seems to have taken it to heart."

"Good. I want her to be happy."

"So do I."

The dance ended, and Gavin kept hold of her hand as the next one began. "What's she doing?" asked Nemain, beginning to feel rather anxious for Monessa's return.

"She's gone to find Swayne."

"Oh!" Come to think of it, it was curious that she had not seen Swayne all day. Shouldn't Lord Winworth's heir be attending the wedding of his daughter? Of course she was well aware of why Swayne might not want to, but she was a little vexed that he had evidently found an excuse not to. If *she* had mustered the courage to show up, why couldn't he?

A dreadful suspicion began to dawn on her. "What's going on? She's not— she wouldn't—"

"Elope?" He sounded amused. "I think not. She said she'd be back."

"You seem very calm."

"Under the circumstances, I can hardly be jealous."

Nemain blushed again. "She ought to leave poor Swayne alone."

"But they're dear old friends, you know. She so wants him to be here tonight. And so do I."

"I thought you didn't like him."

"I didn't at first, but he's not a bad sort. ... Where the devil is he?" Gavin muttered darkly. "I'll be severely annoyed if he doesn't turn up. —Ah!"

Nemain followed his gaze. Monessa had returned with Swayne, and as the crowd parted to let them through, the minstrels stopped playing in confusion.

Was *this* Monessa ... the same girl who had been so weary, depressed, and afraid the night before? Her head was held high, her eyes shining, her face a little pale but full of determination. She led Swayne by the hand, and he was gazing at her as if he could not quite believe what was happening.

"Father"—she curtsied before Lord Winworth—"I have some explaining to do."

"Let me," said Swayne, wary of Lord Winworth's darkening expression.

"No, I will. Father, Sir Gavin and I have agreed not to marry."

A gasp and a murmur rippled through the crowd. Half of those assembled turned to look at Gavin, who merely smiled.

"I should have said something long ago," Monessa went on, "but—well, I was afraid of disappointing you. I know you only wanted what was best for me. But it's Swayne that I want to marry. It's always been Swayne. And I don't want to leave you and go up North. I want to stay here at Briarvale." She began to tremble. "Is that all right?"

Lord Winworth did not respond to her. He was looking hard at Swayne. "You bastard."

Monessa gave a strangled little cry, and Nemain winced. She had not seen Lord Winworth this angry since the start of her *immram*.

"You never said a word!" he thundered. "Why did you not tell me this was what you wanted?"

"I would have, years ago," Swayne cried, "but she didn't want me to say anything then. And later—after you had raised me up and provided for my family—how could I ask for more than that?"

"You were just going to let her go? *My* daughter?"

"Yes." Swayne lowered his head. "To serve her, and to serve you, my lord, I wasn't going to stand in the way."

Lord Winworth turned to his daughter. "Why this change of heart? Why now?"

"It was Nemain, actually. She gave me some advice."

Now everyone turned to stare at Nemain. She shut her eyes, wishing the ground would swallow her up.

"She told me to go forward and be brave," Monessa continued. "Of course, she didn't know what I had in mind when she said it. But she was right. And she's the bravest person I know."

"What does Sir Gavin have to say about all this?"

"I think it's brilliant," Gavin spoke up. "Your daughter and your foster-daughter both do you great credit."

Lord Winworth looked from Gavin to Lord Airleas in confusion and concern. "But the terms of the alliance, the dowry ..."

"Aye, we'll have to address all that. But first there's something *I* must say. Da?"

Lord Airleas stepped forward. He looked calm, as if nothing so far had surprised him, but also expectant. There was a certain keenness in his eyes.

"Father," said Gavin with a bow, "you were right. About everything. And for the grief I've caused you, and am about to cause you, I am sorry." He swallowed hard. "But I can no longer be called your son."

Nemain pressed her fist against her mouth to stifle a horrified cry. Everyone else's reaction was complete silence. It was as if they had had all the shocks they could take for one evening.

Lord Airleas began to speak in the Northern tongue, but Gavin cut him off. "No, let them hear. This must be done in the light."

There was something significant about that phrase, but Nemain couldn't remember just what. As she tried to think of it, she was aware that the *cailleeyn* had suddenly turned their heads, both at once, to look at her.

"Why can you not be called my son?" said Lord Airleas.

"Because I love a girl I can't have any other way. An Outland girl."

Over the appalled exclamations of the wedding guests, who had regained the power of speech under this fresh scandal, Gavin went on in a strong, clear voice, "I asked her to elope, and she refused. She didn't want to be the ruin of me."

"She has sense," Lord Airleas remarked.

"She also said that I couldn't leave behind my home and rank with a whole heart. And she was right, at the time. I wanted to run away in secret. I was afraid to face you and do this openly." He looked his father in the eye. "But not now."

Lord Airleas considered this coolly. Nemain stared at him in growing shock. Could *nothing* surprise or move him?

Then it struck her that the *cailleeyn*, too, were very calm. It was as if they had anticipated all of this, as if they were enacting a ritual, and only for Gavin was it real. She had a sudden wild hope that he might be able to take it all back if he could discover what the riddle was, but at present it was dark to her as well.

"So I'm asking you to disown me, before another word is said. She must know—all of you must know—that I do this willingly, and that she is not at fault."

"Very well." Lord Airleas's face remained impassive, but his voice broke slightly. "From this hour, you are no longer my son."

Gavin took a deep, uneven breath and turned to Nemain, who was weeping silently into her gloved hands. "Jade?"

He gently pried her hands away from her face. "Look at me. Do you see any conflict in me now?"

She did not. He was smiling, and there was peace in his eyes. Even the fire and water in his nature were no longer at war.

"Did you not tell me I was destined for happiness?"

"But I never meant for this—"

"I know. Will you have me, jade, though I have little to offer you? Not mac Airleas, not Northwaite—just me?"

"Just you."

He took her hand so that all could see. "Nemain, do you marry me?"

"Yes."

"Give me my name."

"Yes. Gavin. Yes."

He kissed her, and at that moment the sun set completely, leaving the court-yard in blue twilight. He put his arm around her and looked up, half triumphant, half defiant. "You're all witnesses."

Nemain hid her face against his shoulder, overwhelmed with joy and grief. Gavin began to lead her away.

"I don't excuse you," said Lord Airleas sharply. "Now that I am left without an heir of my own blood, I must elect one. What say my advisors?"

On cue, the *cailleeyn* came forward. "You may elect one or more to inherit jointly," said one.

"Provided their stars are auspicious," the other added.

"Hmm," said Lord Airleas. "And if one of them has—say—Outland blood?"

Nemain looked up, startled.

"That's an obstacle," the first *caillagh* admitted. "Northwaite has never had an Outland heir. But in a case as rare as this—where they are rightly wedded, and the Outlander's character is well established for good—we would consult the signs. The Good Folk would have to make their approval very clear, though."

"But my stars have never been read," said Nemain, her voice hoarse with emotion. "And they can't be auspicious. The curse that I'm under renders things unreadable."

"Not so. *We've* read them."

Her mouth fell open. "How? When?"

"We talked to members of your household, Lady Bronwyn among others—"

"Got quite the tenacious memory, that one," the second *caillagh* said dryly.

"—and they gave us the date and time of your birth, as well as a pretty full account of your childhood." She grinned. " 'Twasn't hard to guess your element, little sister, or that you were marked by high favor as well as dark magic."

"As for that," said the second *caillagh*, "your stars were in place before the curse was. They can be read, and they're quite good. You're about as compatible with our dear, wee Alroy"—Gavin snorted at the nickname—"as Lady Monessa would have been. More so, I'd warrant. I always thought the fire in him was stronger than the water."

The first *caillagh* rolled her eyes. Clearly this was an argument of long standing.

"So," said Lord Airleas, "if we receive a sign that the Good Folk approve, what's to prevent my naming Gavin and his wife as my heirs, jointly, in their own right?"

Gavin and Nemain stared at each other, then at Lord Airleas, as the meaning of this fully dawned upon them. "Was this a test?" Gavin cried. "Da, I swear, if this was all a test—"

"Don't swear. Anyway, what does it matter? You passed."

Gavin had been serene and stoic all day, but now his mouth crumpled like a child's and his eyes filled with tears. He could say no more.

"We still need to obtain a sign," one of the *cailleeyn* reminded them.

"Wait," Lord Winworth spoke up. "I ... er ... this is rather a lot to take in, on top of all else. But Lord Airleas, I must advise against this."

"Why?" said Lord Airleas.

Lord Winworth hesitated, looking at Nemain. "I'm sorry, my girl. I know this is indelicate. But they have a right to know."

"Know what?" said Lord Airleas.

"Oh," said Nemain, pulling away from Gavin. "He means my hands."

"What about your hands?"

She looked at Lord Airleas quizzically—he knew full well!—and then he did a strange thing, which neither Gavin nor Lord Winworth saw. He winked at her.

"Well ..." She tried to play along and be grave, but it was hard not to smile. "My hands are defective, my lord. I'm not considered marriageable."

"Hmm. If it's as bad as all that, you'd better show me."

Gavin found his voice again. "Oh, Da, leave it! Jade, you don't have to."

"Quiet, Gavin. Child, come here."

Nemain obeyed. She wasn't sure what he had in mind, but she was not at all afraid. She felt as if she would never be afraid of anything again.

"So that you can all see," Lord Airleas addressed the crowd, "and know that I am not deceived, and that my response, whatever it will be, is honest—child, show us your hands."

Nemain pulled off one glove and was about to pull off the other. Then she stopped. She stared at her hand, turned it over, and removed her other glove with shaking fingers. A collective gasp arose from those in the crowd who had been bracing themselves for horror.

These were her hands, and yet not hers. The joints were in their proper formation, the skin whole and smooth. They still *felt* like hers. She could still hold a fiddle in the same way. All these things flashed through her mind in one wondrous instant.

She nearly fell over with the shock of it. Gavin caught her in his arms. "Look," she whispered in rapture, showing him her palm. "Look. I can read it!"

It was as if she had never seen a mirror before and was beholding her reflection for the first time. These lines were utterly new, and yet utterly familiar; they were hers because they couldn't be anyone else's. Hunger and hardship had etched their record there, but so had the joy she found in magic and in music. She saw children, long life, and strong friendships. She saw a powerful mind, a passionate heart, and the path of a very great love.

"*Inneen*," said a voice nearby.

Blinking in confusion, she steadied herself against Gavin and looked around for the speaker. Who would be calling her that now?

"*Inneen,* I think we have our sign," said Lord Airleas, holding out his hands to her and Gavin. He was smiling—really smiling, not halfway or only with his eyes. "Welcome."

Epilogue

FIVE YEARS HAD passed since the double wedding at Briarvale. Lowlanders and Northerners alike were still talking of it—that shocking announcement of Lady Monessa's, and that even more shocking (and, to Lowlanders, confusing) business of Sir Gavin: disowned, married, and reinstated all in the same evening. Most people, however, felt that things had turned out for the best. The folks at and around Briarvale had always loved Lady Monessa and were glad she was there to stay. And Sir Gavin's new wife, though an Outlander and something of a cipher at first, had somehow won the esteem and welcome of Lord Airleas and his *cailleeyn*—not the easiest people to please. When it was whispered that she also came of noble Gweharan stock, people said, "Ah, that explains it," and were content to leave the matter at that.

But one event of that wedding was rarely spoken of, and that was the "sign" that had been given. To the Lowlanders who knew what Nemain's hands had been like before, it was a frightening and inexplicable event, best not spoken of. To the Northerners who knew, it was a miracle and therefore, also, best not spoken of. And there were a great many people on both sides who never knew what all the fuss was about. But the event was carefully recorded in the books of the Airleas clan, and from then on—at least at Northwaite—the ban on intermarrying with Outlanders was lifted.

Over the following years Northwaite began to be called "the Gwehara of the east," attracting the greatest scholars, artists, and musicians of both the North and the Lowland. However, it differed from Gwehara in several respects. The treasures of art and learning that Northwaite accumulated were not hidden away for the eyes of a select few, but were accessible to anyone. And at

Northwaite, Outlanders were beginning to have a visible presence—most strikingly in the gorgeous textiles that Nemain collected from the Kell's Crossing fair each year that she was able to go. Occasionally Outlanders were also seen conferring with the *cailleeyn* or with Nemain herself over magical texts, diagrams of stone monuments, and rubbings of ancient carvings. These people, like Rensa the Weaver, had been sworn to secrecy about this lore; but they were willing to assist in Nemain's study and preservation efforts as far as their vows allowed. They liked young Lady mac Airleas, who was not ashamed of her Outland blood, and who approached them not as a powerful noblewoman but as a humble seeker of knowledge. At Northwaite, those Outlanders who came a-begging were never turned away empty-handed, and those who came looking for work were always given something to do; but it was really those consultations with Nemain that did the most to improve relations between Northerners and Outlanders, both at Northwaite and beyond.

On this occasion—Midwinter Eve, five years later—there was a knock at the door of her study. "*Quoi t'ayn?*"—Who is it?—she said, scribbling down some notes while the *cailleeyn* looked on.

Gavin entered. He carried a little girl in his arms, a three-year-old with red curls and amber eyes, known to most people as "little Ní Airleas" but listed in the book of generations as Rhiannon.

"It's almost time, jade," he said. "What are you doing?"

"Oh, I just had to get this down. I had an idea about the stones ..."

"She's just solved a mystery that's had us stumped for weeks," one of the *cailleeyn* informed him.

"It's like music," said Nemain, tapping the paper with her pen. "This sequence here, followed by this one—and I'll just bet that the original pattern was like this. ... Can you see it?"

The other *caillagh* laughed delightedly. "Aye! Go on. I think we can fill it in from here."

Nemain grinned and followed Gavin down to the great hall, where the remains of the solstice feast were being cleared away. Outside a storm was raging, but in here the noise of wind and sea was no more than a pleasant counterpoint to warmth, firelight, and laughter. Many of their friends were gathered here, some they had not seen in years. Henry had come with Ita and small Henry (now a strapping lad of eleven). Rois had stayed behind to manage the inn and look after the other children, but Nemain had had one or two letters from her, full of loving congratulations and not a little earthy wit. Monessa and Swayne were there, having decided to sail on the Kell and up the coast rather than brave the mountains; she had been frightfully sick on the voyage but was looking well tonight. No longer elfinly slender, she had a new softness in her face, an added note of richness in her laugh, and no sign of melancholy in her eyes.

Amala had already fetched Nemain's fiddle-bag and was waiting by the entrance. After handing little Rhiannon to Lord Airleas, who cradled her tenderly on his lap, Gavin went to the front of the hall and cleared his throat. Gradually everyone fell silent.

"Friends," he said, "tonight we have the rare good fortune of a full moon on the solstice. It's a shame we can't go out and see it, but nonetheless, we have a tradition here at Northwaite when the moon is full." His eye fell on a few guests who were from Gwehara, and he smiled. "Some of you will recognize it."

Nemain came forward and began to play the *arrane oie*. Its melody held something of the winter wind—of her little girl's laugh—of Tynan's voice when he spoke the Northern tongue. It held something of her mother's pain and the feel of ancient stone beneath her hand. In the remembered harmonies that echoed from the hilltops in Gwehara—present, and yet not present, in the sound of her fiddle—she sensed countless benevolent forces, far distant in time and space, but close all around her, in this hour and at this place where the Three Worlds met as one.

About the Author

Deborah Bradford is an editor and an amateur musician. She holds a bachelor's degree in linguistics from Brigham Young University, and her passions include mythology, anthropology, and comparative religion. She currently resides in Kearns, Utah, with her husband Joe.

Made in the USA
San Bernardino, CA
29 July 2015